THE PRINCE AND BETTY
by P. G. WODEHOUSE
[American edition] 1912

CONTENTS

I THE CABLE FROM MERVO
II MERVO AND ITS OWNER
III JOHN
IV VIVE LE ROI
V MR. SCOBELL HAS ANOTHER IDEA
VI YOUNG ADAM CUPID
VII MR. SCOBELL IS FRANK
VIII AN ULTIMATUM FROM THE THRONE
IX MERVO CHANGES ITS CONSTITUTION
X MRS. OAKLEY
XI A LETTER OP INTRODUCTION
XII "PEACEFUL MOMENTS"
XIII BETTY MAKES A FRIEND
XIV A CHANGE OF POLICY
XV THE HONEYED WORD
XVI TWO VISITORS TO THE OFFICE
XVII THE MAN AT THE ASTOR
XVIII THE HIGHFIELD
XIX THE FIRST BATTLE
XX BETTY AT LARGE
XXI CHANGES IN THE STAFF
XXII A GATHERING OF CAT SPECIALISTS
XXIII THE RETIREMENT OF SMITH
XXIV THE CAMPAIGN QUICKENS
XXV CORNERED
XXVI JOURNEY'S END
XXVII A LEMON

CHAPTER I

THE CABLE PROM MERVO

A pretty girl in a blue dress came out of the house, and began to walk slowly across the terrace to where Elsa Keith sat with Marvin Rossiter in the shade of the big sycamore. Elsa and Marvin had become engaged some few days before, and were generally to be found at this time sitting together in some shaded spot in the grounds of the Keith's Long Island home.

"What's troubling Betty, I wonder," said Elsa. "She looks worried."

Marvin turned his head.

"Is that your friend, Miss Silver?"

"That's Betty. We were at college together. I want you to like Betty."

"Then I will. When did she arrive?"

"Last night. She's here for a month. What's the matter, Betty? This is_Marvin. I want you to like Marvin."

Betty Silver smiled. Her face, in repose, was rather wistful, but it lighted up when she smiled, and an unsuspected dimple came into being on her chin.

"Of course I shall," she said.

Her big gray eyes seemed to search Marvin's for an instant and Marvin had, almost subconsciously, a comfortable feeling that he had been tested and found worthy.

"What were you scowling at so ferociously, Betty?" asked Elsa.

"Was I scowling? I hope you didn't think it was at you. Oh, Elsa, I'm miserable! I shall have to leave this heavenly place."

"Betty!"

"At once. And I was meaning to have the most lovely time. See what has come!"

She held out some flimsy sheets of paper.

"A cable!" said Elsa.

"Great Scott! it looks like the scenario of a four-act play," said Marvin. "That's not all one cable, surely? Whoever sent it must be a millionaire."

"He is. It's from my stepfather. Read it out, Elsa. I want Mr. Rossiter to hear it. He may be able to tell me where Mervo is. Did you ever hear of Mervo, Mr. Rossiter?"

"Never. What is it?"

"It's a place where my stepfather is, and where I've got to go. I do call it hard. Go on, Elsa."

Elsa, who had been skimming the document with raised eyebrows, now read it out in its spacious entirety.

On receipt of this come instantly Mervo without moment delay vital importance presence urgently required come wherever you are cancel engagements urgent necessity hustle have advised bank allow you draw any money you need expenses have booked stateroom Mauretania sailing Wednesday don't fail catch arrive Fishguard Monday train London sleep London catch first train Tuesday Dover now mind first train no taking root in London and spending a week shopping mid-day boat Dover Calais arrive Paris Tuesday evening Dine Paris catch train de luxe nine-fifteen Tuesday night for Marseilles have engaged sleeping coupe now mind Tuesday night no cutting loose around Paris stores you can do all that later on just now you want to get here right quick arrive Marseilles Wednesday morning boat Mervo Wednesday night will meet you Mervo now do you follow all that because if not cable at once and say which part of journey you don't understand now mind special points to be remembered firstly come instantly secondly no cutting loose around London Paris stores see.

SCOBELL.

"*Well!*" said Elsa, breathless.

"By George!" said Marvin. "He certainly seems to want you badly enough. He hasn't spared expense. He has put in about everything you could put into a cable."

"Except why he wants me," said Betty.

"Yes," said Elsa. "Why does he want you? And in such a desperate hurry, too!"

Marvin was re-reading the message.

"It isn't a mere invitation," he said. "There's no come-right-along-you'll-like-this-place-it's-fine about it. He seems to look on your company more as a necessity than a luxury. It's a sort of imperious C.Q.D."

"That's what makes it so strange. We have hardly met for years. Why, he didn't even know where I was. The cable was sent to the bank and forwarded on. And I don't know where he is!"

"Which brings us back," said Marvin, "to mysterious Mervo. Let us reason inductively. If you get to the place by taking a boat from Marseilles, it can't be far from the French coast. I should say at a venture that Mervo is an island in the Mediterranean. And a small island for if it had been a big one we should have heard of it."

"Marvin!" cried Elsa, her face beaming with proud affection. "How clever you are!"

"A mere gift," he said modestly. "I have been like that from a boy." He got up from his chair. "Isn't there an encyclopaedia in the library, Elsa?"

"Yes, but it's an old edition."

"It will probably touch on Mervo. I'll go and fetch it."

As he crossed the terrace, Elsa turned quickly to Betty.

"Well?" she said.

Betty smiled at her.

"He's a dear. Are you very happy, Elsa?"

Elsa's eyes danced. She drew in her breath softly. Betty looked at her in silence for a moment. The wistful expression was back on her face.

"Elsa," she said, suddenly. "What is it like? How does it feel, knowing that there's someone who is fonder of you than anything—?"

Elsa closed her eyes.

"It's like eating berries and cream in a new dress by moonlight on a summer night while somebody plays the violin far away in the distance so that you can just hear it," she said.

Her eyes opened again.

"And it's like coming along on a winter evening and seeing the windows lit up and knowing you've reached home."

Betty was clenching her hands, and breathing quickly.

"And it's like—"

"Elsa, don't! I can't bear it!"

"Betty! What's the matter?"

Betty smiled again, but painfully.

"It's stupid of me. I'm just jealous, that's all. I haven't got a_Marvin, you see. You have."

"Well, there are plenty who would like to be your Marvin."

Betty's face grew cold.

"There are plenty who would like to be Benjamin Scobell's son-in-law," she said.

"Betty!" Elsa's voice was serious. "We've been friends for a good long time, so you'll let me say something, won't you? I think you're getting just the least bit hard. Now turn and rend me," she added good-humoredly.

"I'm not going to rend you," said Betty. "You're perfectly right. I am getting hard. How can I help it? Do you know how many men have asked me to marry them since I saw you last? Five."

"Betty!"

"And not one of them cared the slightest bit about me."

"But, Betty, dear, that's just what I mean. Why should you say that?_How can you know?"

"How do I know? Well, I do know. Instinct, I suppose. The instinct of self-preservation which nature gives hunted animals. I can't think of a single man in the world—except your Marvin, of course—who wouldn't do anything for money." She stopped. "Well, yes, one."

Elsa leaned forward eagerly.

"Who, Betty?"

"You don't know him."

"But what's his name?"

Betty hesitated.

"Well, if I am on the witness-stand—Maude."

"Maude? I thought you said a man?"

"It's his name. John Maude."

"But, Betty! Why didn't you tell me before? This is tremendously interesting."

Betty laughed shortly.

"Not so very, really. I only met him two or three times, and I haven't seen him for years, and I don't suppose I shall ever see him again. He was a friend of Alice Beecher's brother, who was at Harvard. Alice took me over to meet her brother, and Mr. Maude was there. That's all."

Elsa was plainly disappointed.

"But how do you know, then—? What makes you think that he—?"

"Instinct, again, I suppose. I do know."

"And you've never met him since?"

Betty shook her head. Elsa relapsed into silence. She had a sense of pathos.

At the further end of the terrace Marvin Rossiter appeared, carrying a large volume.

"Here we are," he said. "Scared it up at the first attempt. Now then."

He sat down, and opened the book.

"You don't want to hear all about how Jason went there in search of the Golden Fleece, and how Ulysses is supposed to have taken it in on his round-trip? You want something more modern. Well, it's an island in the Mediterranean, as I said, and I'm surprised that you've never heard of it, Elsa, because it's celebrated in its way. It's the smallest independent state in the world. Smaller than Monaco, even. Here are some facts. Its population when this encyclopaedia was printed—there may be more now—was eleven thousand and sixteen. It was ruled over up to 1886 by a prince. But in that year the populace appear to have said to themselves, 'When in the course of human events….' Anyway, they fired the prince, and the place is now a republic. So that's where you're going, Miss Silver. I don't know if it's any consolation to you, but the island, according to this gentleman, is celebrated for the unspoilt beauty of its scenery. He also gives a list of the fish that can be caught there. It takes up about three lines."

"But what can my stepfather be doing there? I last heard of him in London. Well, I suppose I shall have to go."

"I suppose you will," said Elsa mournfully. "But, oh, Betty, what a shame!"

CHAPTER II
MERVO AND ITS OWNER

"By heck!" cried Mr. Benjamin Scobell.

He wheeled round from the window, and transferred his gaze from the view to his sister Marion; losing by the action, for the view was a joy to the eye, which his sister Marion was not.

Mervo was looking its best under the hot morning sun. Mr. Scobell's villa stood near the summit of the only hill the island possessed, and from the window of the morning-room, where he had just finished breakfast, he had an uninterrupted view of valley, town, and harbor—a two-mile riot of green, gold and white, and beyond the white the blue satin of the Mediterranean. Mr. Scobell did not read poetry except that which advertised certain breakfast foods in which he was interested, or he might have been reminded of the Island of Flowers in Tennyson's "Voyage of Maeldive." Violets, pinks, crocuses, yellow and purple mesembryanthemum, lavender, myrtle, and rosemary ... his two-mile view contained them all. The hillside below him was all aglow with the yellow fire of the mimosa. But his was not one of those emotional natures to which the meanest flower that blows can give thoughts that do often lie too deep for tears. A primrose by the river's brim a simple primrose was to him—or not so much a simple primrose, perhaps, as a basis for a possible Primrosina, the Soap that Really Cleans You.

He was a nasty little man to hold despotic sway over such a Paradise: a goblin in Fairyland. Somewhat below the middle height, he was lean of body and vulturine of face. He had a greedy mouth, a hooked nose, liquid green eyes and a sallow complexion. He was rarely seen without a half-smoked cigar between his lips. This at intervals he would relight, only to allow it to go out again; and when, after numerous fresh starts, it had dwindled beyond the limits of convenience, he would substitute another from the reserve supply that protruded from his vest-pocket.

* * * * *

How Benjamin Scobell had discovered the existence of Mervo is not known. It lay well outside the sphere of the ordinary financier. But Mr. Scobell took a pride in the versatility of his finance. It distinguished him from the uninspired who were content to concentrate themselves on steel, wheat and such-like things. It was Mr. Scobell's way to consider nothing as lying outside his sphere. In a financial sense he might have taken Terence's *Nihil humanum alienum* as his motto. He was interested in innumerable enterprises, great and small. He was the power behind a company which was endeavoring, without much success, to extract gold from the mountains of North Wales, and another which was trying, without any success at all, to do the same by sea water. He owned a model farm in Indiana, and a weekly paper in New York. He had financed patent medicines, patent foods, patent corks, patent corkscrews, patent devices of all kinds, some profitable, some the reverse.

Also—outside the ordinary gains of finance—he had expectations. He was the only male relative of his aunt, the celebrated Mrs. Jane Oakley, who lived in a cottage on Staten Island, and was reputed to spend five hundred dollars a year—some said less—out of her snug income of eighteen million. She was an unusual old lady in many ways, and, unfortunately, unusually full of deep-rooted prejudices. The fear lest he might inadvertently fall foul of these rarely ceased to haunt Mr. Scobell.

This man of many projects had descended upon Mervo like a stone on the surface of some quiet pool, bubbling over with modern enterprise in general and, in particular, with a scheme. Before his arrival, Mervo had been an island of dreams and slow movement and putting things off till to-morrow. The only really energetic thing it had ever done in its whole history had been to expel his late highness, Prince Charles, and change itself into a republic. And even that had been done with the minimum of fuss. The Prince was away at the time. Indeed, he had been away for nearly three years, the pleasures of Paris, London and Vienna appealing to him more keenly than life among his subjects. Mervo, having thought the matter over during these years, decided that it had no further use for Prince Charles. Quite quietly, with none of that vulgar brawling which its neighbor, France, had found necessary in similar circumstances, it had struck his name off the pay-roll, and declared itself a republic. The royalist party, headed by General Poineau, had been distracted but impotent. The army, one hundred and fifteen strong, had gone solid for the new regime, and that had settled it. Mervo had then gone to sleep again. It was asleep when Mr. Scobell found it.

The financier's scheme was first revealed to M. d'Orby, the President of the Republic, a large, stout statesman with even more than the average Mervian instinct for slumber. He was asleep in a chair on the porch of his villa when Mr. Scobell paid his call, and it was not until the financier's secretary, who attended the seance in the capacity of interpreter, had rocked him vigorously from side to side for quite a minute that he displayed any signs of animation beyond a snore like the growling of distant thunder. When at length he opened his eyes, he perceived the nightmare-like form of Mr. Scobell standing before him, talking. The financier, impatient of delay, had begun to talk some moments before the great awakening.

"Sir," Mr. Scobell was saying, "I gotta proposition to which I'd like you to give your complete attention. Shake him some more, Crump. Sir, there's big money in it for all of us, if you and your crowd'll sit in. Money. *Lar' monnay*. No, that means change. What's money, Crump? *Arjong*? There's *arjong* in it, Squire. Get that? Oh, shucks! Hand it to him in French, Crump."

Mr. Secretary Crump translated. The President blinked, and intimated that he would hear more. Mr. Scobell relighted his cigar-stump, and proceeded.

"Say, you've heard of *Moosieer* Blonk? Ask the old skeesicks if he's ever heard of *Mersyaw* Blonk, Crump, the feller who started the gaming-tables at Monte Carlo."

Filtered through Mr. Crump, the question became intelligible to the President. He said he had heard of M. Blanc. Mr. Crump caught the reply and sent it on to Mr. Scobell, as the man on first base catches the ball and throws it to second.

Mr. Scobell relighted his cigar.

"Well, I'm in that line. I'm going to put this island on the map just like old Doctor Blonk put Monte Carlo. I've been studying up all about the old man, and I know just what he did and how he did it. Monte Carlo was just such another jerkwater little place as this is before he hit it. The government was down to its last bean and wondering where the Heck its next meal-ticket was coming from, when in blows Mr. Man, tucks up his shirt-sleeves, and starts the tables. And after that the place never looked back. You and your crowd gotta get together and pass a vote to give me a gambling concession here, same as they did him. Scobell's my name. Hand him that, Crump."

Mr. Crump obliged once more. A gleam of intelligence came into the_President's dull eye. He nodded once or twice. He talked volubly in_French to Mr. Crump, who responded in the same tongue.

"The idea seems to strike him, sir," said Mr. Crump.

"It ought to, if he isn't a clam," replied Mr. Scobell. He started to relight his cigar, but after scorching the tip of his nose, bowed to the inevitable and threw the relic away.

"See here," he said, having bitten the end off the next in order; "I've thought this thing out from soup to nuts. There's heaps of room for another Monte Carlo. Monte's a dandy place, but it's not perfect by a long way. To start with, it's hilly. You have to take the elevator to get to the Casino, and when you've gotten to the end of your roll and want to soak your pearl pin, where's the hock-shop? Half a mile away up the side of a mountain. It ain't right. In my Casino there's going to be a resident pawnbroker inside the building, just off the main entrance. That's only one of a heap of improvements. Another is that my Casino's scheduled to be a home from home, a place you can be real cosy in. You'll look around you, and the only thing you'll miss will be mother's face. Yes, sir, there's no need for a gambling Casino to look and feel and smell like the reading-room at the British Museum. Comfort, coziness and convenience. That's the ticket I'm running on. Slip that to the old gink, Crump."

A further outburst of the French language from Mr. Crump, supplemented on the part of the "old gink" by gesticulations, interrupted the proceedings.

"What's he saying now?" asked Mr. Scobell.

"He wants to know—"

"Don't tell. Let me guess. He wants to know what sort of a rake-off he and the other somnambulists will get—the darned old pirate! Is that it?"

Mr. Crump said that that was just it.

"That'll be all right," said Mr. Scobell. "Old man Blong's offer to the Prince of Monaco was five hundred thousand francs a year—that's somewhere around a hundred thousand dollars in real money—and half the profits made by the Casino. That's my offer, too. See how that hits him, Crump."

Mr. Crump investigated.

"He says he accepts gladly, on behalf of the Republic, sir," he announced.

M. d'Orby confirmed the statement by rising, dodging the cigar, and kissing Mr. Scobell on both cheeks.

"Cut it out," said the financier austerely, breaking out of the clinch. "We'll take the Apache Dance as read. Good-by, Squire. Glad it's settled. Now I can get busy."

He did. Workmen poured into Mervo, and in a very short time, dominating the town and reducing to insignificance the palace of the late Prince, once a passably imposing mansion, there rose beside the harbor a mammoth Casino of shining stone.

Imposing as was the exterior, it was on the interior that Mr. Scobell more particularly prided himself, and not without reason. Certainly, a man with money to lose could lose it here under the most charming conditions. It had been Mr. Scobell's object to avoid the cheerless grandeur of the rival institution down the coast. Instead of one large hall sprinkled with tables, each table had a room to itself, separated from its neighbor by sound-proof folding-doors. And as the building progressed, Mr. Scobell's active mind had soared above the original idea of domestic coziness to far greater heights of ingenuity. Each of the rooms was furnished and arranged in a different style. The note of individuality extended even to the *croupiers*. Thus, a man with money at his command could wander from the Dutch room, where, in the picturesque surroundings of a Dutch kitchen, *croupiers* in the costume of Holland ministered to his needs, to the Japanese room, where his coin would be raked in by quite passable imitations of the Samurai. If he had any left at this point, he was free to dispose of it under the auspices of near-Hindoos in the Indian room, of merry Swiss peasants in the Swiss room, or in other appropriately furnished apartments of red-shirted, Bret Harte miners, fur-clad Esquimaux, or languorous Spaniards. He could then, if a man of spirit, who did not know when he was beaten, collect the family jewels, and proceed down the main hall, accompanied by the strains of an excellent band, to the office of a gentlemanly pawnbroker, who spoke seven languages like a native and was prepared to advance money on reasonable security in all of them.

It was a colossal venture, but it suffered from the defect from which most big things suffer; it moved slowly. That it also moved steadily was to some extent a consolation to Mr. Scobell. Undoubtedly it would progress quicker and quicker, as time went on, until at length the Casino became a permanent gold mine. But at present it was being conducted at a loss. It was inevitable, but it irked Mr. Scobell. He paced the island and brooded. His mind dwelt incessantly on the problem. Ideas for promoting the prosperity of his nursling came to him at all hours—at meals, in the night watches, when he was shaving, walking, washing, reading, brushing his hair.

And now one had come to him as he stood looking at the view from the window of his morning-room, listening absently to his sister Marion as she read stray items of interest from the columns of the *New York Herald*, and had caused him to utter the exclamation recorded at the beginning of the chapter.

* * * * *

"By Heck!" he said. "Read that again, Marion. I gottan idea."

Miss Scobell, deep in her paper, paid no attention. Few people would have taken her for the sister of the financier. She was his exact opposite in almost every way. He was small, jerky and aggressive; she, tall, deliberate and negative. She was one of those women whom nature seems to have produced with the object of attaching them to some man in a peculiar position of independent dependence, and who defy the imagination to picture them in any other condition whatsoever. One could not see Miss Scobell doing anything but pour out her brother's coffee, darn his socks, and sit placidly by while he talked. Yet it would have been untrue to describe her as dependent upon him. She had a detached mind. Though her whole life had been devoted to his comfort and though she admired him intensely, she never appeared to give his conversation any real attention. She listened to him much as she would have listened to a barking Pomeranian.

"Marion!" cried Mr. Scobell.

"A five-legged rabbit has been born in Carbondale, Southern Illinois," she announced.

Mr. Scobell cursed the five-legged rabbit.

"Never mind about your rabbits. I want to hear that piece you read before. The one about the Prince of Monaco. Will—you—listen, Marion!"

"The Prince of Monaco, dear? Yes. He has caught another fish or something of that sort, I think. Yes. A fish with 'telescope eyes,' the paper says. And very convenient too, I should imagine."

Mr. Scobell thumped the table.

"I've got it. I've found out what's the matter with this darned place._I see why the Casino hasn't struck its gait."

"*I* think it must be the *croupiers*, dear. I'm sure I never heard of *croupiers* in fancy costume before. It doesn't seem right. I'm sure people don't like those nasty Hindoos. I am quite nervous myself when I go into the Indian room. They look at me so oddly."

"Nonsense! That's the whole idea of the place, that it should be different. People are sick and tired of having their money gathered in by seedy-looking Dagoes in second-hand morning coats. We give 'em variety. It's not the Casino that's wrong: it's the darned island. What's the use of a republic to a place like this? I'm not saying that you don't want a republic for a live country that's got its way to make in the world; but for a little runt of a sawn-off, hobo, one-night stand like this you gotta have something picturesque, something that'll advertise the place, something that'll give a jolt to folks' curiosity, and make 'em talk! There's this Monaco gook. He snoops around in his yacht, digging up telescope-eyed fish, and people talk about it. 'Another darned fish,' they say. 'That's the 'steenth bite the Prince of Monaco has had this year.' It's like a soap advertisement. It works by suggestion. They get to thinking about the Prince and his pop-eyed fishes, and, first thing they know, they've packed their grips and come along to Monaco to have a peek at him. And when they're there, it's a safe bet they aren't going back again without trying to get a mess of easy money from the Bank. That's what this place wants. Whoever heard of this blamed Republic doing anything except eat and sleep? They used to have a prince here 'way back in eighty-something. Well, I'm going to have him working at the old stand again, right away."

Miss Scobell looked up from her paper, which she had been reading with absorbed interest throughout tins harangue.

"Dear?" she said enquiringly.

"I say I'm going to have him back again," said Mr. Scobell, a little damped. "I wish you would listen."

"I think you're quite right, dear. Who?"

"The Prince. Do listen, Marion. The Prince of this island, His Highness, the Prince of Mervo. I'm going to send for him and put him on the throne again."

"You can't, dear. He's dead."

"I know he's dead. You can't faze me on the history of this place. He died in ninety-one. But before he died he married an American girl, and there's a son, who's in America now, living with his uncle. It's the son I'm going to send for. I got it all from General Poineau. He's a royalist. He'll be tickled to pieces when Johnny comes marching home again. Old man Poineau told me all about it. The Prince married a girl called Westley, and then he was killed in an automobile accident, and his widow went back to America with the kid, to live with her brother. Poineau says he could lay his hand on him any time he pleased."

"I hope you won't do anything rash, dear," said his sister comfortably. "I'm sure we don't want any horrid revolution here, with people shooting and stabbing each other."

"Revolution?" cried Mr. Scobell. "Revolution! Well, I should say nix! Revolution nothing. I'm the man with the big stick in Mervo. Pretty near every adult on this island is dependent on my Casino for his weekly envelope, and what I say goes—without argument. I want a prince, so I gotta have a prince, and if any gazook makes a noise like a man with a grouch, he'll find himself fired."

Miss Scobell turned to her paper again.

"Very well, dear," she said. "Just as you please. I'm sure you know best."

"Sure!" said her brother. "You're a good guesser. I'll go and beat up old man Poineau right away."

CHAPTER III

JOHN

Ten days after Mr. Scobell's visit to General Poineau, John, Prince of Mervo, ignorant of the greatness so soon to be thrust upon him, was strolling thoughtfully along one of the main thoroughfares of that outpost of civilization, Jersey City. He was a big young man, tall and large of limb. His shoulders especially were of the massive type expressly designed by nature for driving wide gaps in the opposing line on the gridiron. He looked like one of nature's center-rushes, and had, indeed, played in that position for Harvard during two strenuous seasons. His face wore an expression of invincible good-humor. He had a wide, good-natured mouth, and a pair of friendly gray eyes. One felt that he liked his follow men and would be surprised and pained if they did not like him.

As he passed along the street, he looked a little anxious. Sherlock Holmes—and possibly even Doctor Watson—would have deduced that he had something on his conscience.

At the entrance to a large office building, he paused, and seemed to hesitate. Then, as if he had made up his mind to face an ordeal, he went in and pressed the button of the elevator.

Leaving the elevator at the third floor, he went down the passage, and pushed open a door on which was inscribed the legend, "Westley, Martin & Co."

A stout youth, walking across the office with his hands full of papers, stopped in astonishment.

"Hello, John Maude!" he cried.

The young man grinned.

"Say, where have you been? The old man's been as mad as a hornet since he found you had quit without leave. He was asking for you just now."

"I guess I'm up against it," admitted John cheerfully.

"Where did you go yesterday?"

John put the thing to him candidly, as man to man.

"See here, Spiller, suppose you got up one day and found it was a perfectly bully morning, and remembered that the Giants were playing the Athletics, and looked at your mail, and saw that someone had sent you a pass for the game—"

"Were you at the ball-game? You've got the nerve! Didn't you know there would be trouble?"

"Old man," said John frankly, "I could no more have turned down that pass—Oh, well, what's the use? It was just great. I suppose I'd better tackle the boss now. It's got to be done."

It was not a task to which many would have looked forward. Most of those who came into contact with Andrew Westley were afraid of him. He was a capable rather than a lovable man, and too self-controlled to be quite human. There was no recoil in him, no reaction after anger, as there would have been in a hotter-tempered man. He thought before he acted, but, when he acted, never yielded a step.

John, in all the years of their connection, had never been able to make anything of him. At first, he had been prepared to like him, as he liked nearly everybody. But Mr. Westley had discouraged all advances, and, as time went by, his nephew had come to look on him as something apart from the rest of the world, one of those things which no fellow could understand.

On Mr. Westley's side, there was something to be said in extenuation of his attitude. John reminded him of his father, and he had hated the late Prince of Mervo with a cold hatred that had for a time been the ruling passion of his life. He had loved his sister, and her married life had been one long torture to him, a torture rendered keener by the fact that he was powerless to protect either her happiness or her money. Her money was her own, to use as she pleased, and the use which pleased her most was to give it to her husband, who could always find a way of spending it. As to her happiness, that was equally out of his control. It was bound up in her Prince, who, unfortunately, was a bad custodian for it. At last, an automobile accident put an end to His Highness's hectic career (and, incidentally, to that of a blonde lady from the *Folies Bergeres*), and the Princess had returned to her brother's home, where, a year later, she died, leaving him in charge of her infant son.

Mr. Westley's desire from the first had been to eliminate as far as possible all memory of the late Prince. He gave John his sister's name, Maude, and brought him up as an American, in total ignorance of his father's identity. During all the years they had spent together, he had never mentioned the Prince's name.

He disliked John intensely. He fed him, clothed him, sent him to college, and gave him a place in his office, but he never for a moment relaxed his bleakness of front toward him. John was not unlike his father in appearance, though built on a larger scale, and, as time went on, little mannerisms, too, began to show themselves, that reminded Mr. Westley of the dead man, and killed any beginnings of affection.

John, for his part, had the philosophy which goes with perfect health. He fitted his uncle into the scheme of things, or, rather, set him outside them as an irreconcilable element, and went on his way enjoying life in his own good-humored fashion.

It was only lately, since he had joined the firm, that he had been conscious of any great strain. College had given him a glimpse of a larger life, and the office cramped him. He felt vaguely that there were bigger things in the world which he might be doing. His best friends, of whom he now saw little, were all men of adventure and enterprise, who had tried their hand at many things; men like Jimmy Pitt, who had done nearly everything that could be done before coming into an unexpected half-million; men like Rupert Smith, who had been at Harvard with him and was now a reporter on the *News*; men like Baker, Faraday, Williams—he could name half-a-dozen, all men who were *doing* something, who were out on the firing line.

He was not a man who worried. He had not that temperament. But sometimes he would wonder in rather a vague way whether he was not allowing life to slip by him a little too placidly. An occasional yearning for something larger would attack him. There seemed to be something in him that made for inaction. His soul was sleepy.

If he had been told of the identity of his father, it is possible that he might have understood. The Princes of Mervo had never taken readily to action and enterprise. For generations back, if they had varied at all, son from father, it had been in the color of hair or eyes, not in character—a weak, shiftless procession, with nothing to distinguish them from the common run of men except good looks and a talent for wasting money.

John was the first of the line who had in him the seeds of better things. The Westley blood and the bracing nature of his education had done much to counteract the Mervo strain. He did not know it, but the American in him was winning. The desire for action was growing steadily every day.

It had been Mervo that had sent him to the polo grounds on the previous day. That impulse had been purely Mervian. No prince of that island had ever resisted a temptation. But it was America that was sending him now to meet his uncle with a quiet unconcern as to the outcome of the interview. The spirit of adventure was in him. It was more than possible that Mr. Westley would sink the uncle in the employer and dismiss him as summarily as he would have dismissed any other clerk in similar circumstances. If so, he was prepared to welcome dismissal. Other men fought an unsheltered fight with the world, so why not he?

He moved towards the door of the inner office with a certain exhilaration.

As he approached, it flew open, disclosing Mr. Westley himself, a tall, thin man, at the sight of whom Spiller shot into his seat like a rabbit.

John went to meet him.

"Ah," said Mr. Westley; "come in here. I want to speak to you."

John followed him into the room.

"Sit down," said his uncle.

John waited while he dictated a letter. Neither spoke till the stenographer had left the room. John met the girl's eye as she passed. There was a compassionate look in it. John was popular with his fellow employes. His absence had been the cause of discussion and speculation among them, and the general verdict had been that there would be troublous times for him on the morrow.

When the door closed, Mr. Westley leaned back in his chair, and regarded his nephew steadily from under a pair of bushy gray eyebrows which lent a sort of hypnotic keenness to his gaze.

"You were at the ball-game yesterday?" he said.

The unexpectedness of the question startled John into a sharp laugh.

"Yes," he said, recovering himself.

"Without leave."

"It didn't seem worth while asking for leave."

"You mean that you relied so implicitly on our relationship to save you from the consequences?"

"No, I meant—"

"Well, we need not try and discover what you may have meant. What claim do you put forward for special consideration? Why should I treat you differently from any other member of the staff?"

John had a feeling that the interview was being taken at too rapid a pace. He felt confused.

"I don't want you to treat me differently," he said.

Mr. Westley did not reply. John saw that he had taken a check-book from its pigeonhole.

"I think we understand each other," said Mr. Westley. "There is no need for any discussion. I am writing you a check for ten thousand dollars—"

"Ten thousand dollars!"

"It happens to be your own. It was left to me in trust for you by your mother. By a miracle your father did not happen to spend it."

John caught the bitter note which the other could not keep out of his voice, and made one last attempt to probe this mystery. As a boy he had tried more than once before he realized that this was a forbidden topic.

"Who was my father?" he said.

Mr. Westley blotted the check carefully.

"Quite the worst blackguard I ever had the misfortune to know," he replied in an even tone. "Will you kindly give me a receipt for this? Then I need not detain you. You may return to the ball-game without any further delay. Possibly," he went on, "you may wonder why you have not received this money before. I persuaded your mother to let me use my discretion in choosing the time when it should be handed over to you. I decided to wait until, in my opinion, you had sense enough to use it properly. I do not think that time has arrived. I do not think it will ever arrive. But as we are parting company and shall, I hope, never meet again, you had better have it now."

John signed the receipt in silence.

"Thank you," said Mr. Westley. "Good-by."

At the door John hesitated. He had looked forward to this moment as one of excitement and adventure, but now that it had come it had left him in anything but an uplifted mood. He was naturally warm-hearted, and his uncle's cold anger hurt him. It was so different from anything sudden, so essentially not of the moment. He felt instinctively that it had been smoldering for a long time, and realized with a shock that his uncle had not been merely indifferent to him all these years, but had actually hated him. It was as if he had caught a glimpse of something ugly. He felt that this was the last scene of some long drawn-out tragedy.

Something made him turn impulsively back towards the desk.

"Uncle—" he cried.

He stopped. The hopelessness of attempting any step towards a better understanding overwhelmed him. Mr. Westley had begun to write. He must have seen John's movement, but he continued to write as if he were alone in the room.

John turned to the door again.

"Good-by," he said.

Mr. Westley did not look up.

CHAPTER IV

VIVE LE ROI!

When, an hour later, John landed in New York from the ferry, his mood had changed. The sun and the breeze had done their work. He looked on life once more with a cheerful and optimistic eye.

His first act, on landing, was to proceed to the office of the *News* and enquire for Rupert Smith. He felt that he had urgent need of a few minutes' conversation with him. Now that the painter had been definitely cut that bound him to the safe and conventional, and he had set out on his own account to lead the life adventurous, he was conscious of an absurd diffidence. New York looked different to him. It made him feel positively shy. A pressing need for a friendly native in this strange land manifested itself. Smith would have ideas and advice to bestow—he was notoriously prolific of both—and in this crisis both were highly necessary.

Smith, however, was not at the office. He had gone out, John was informed, earlier in the morning to cover a threatened strike somewhere down on the East Side. John did not go in search of him. The chance of finding him in that maze of mean streets was remote. He decided to go uptown, select a hotel, and lunch. To the need for lunch he attributed a certain sinking sensation of which he was becoming more and more aware, and which bore much too close a resemblance to dismay to be pleasant. The poet's statement that "the man who's square, his chances always are best; no circumstance can shoot a scare into the contents of his vest," is only true within limits. The squarest men, deposited suddenly in New York and faced with the prospect of earning his living there, is likely to quail for a moment. New York is not like other cities. London greets the stranger with a sleepy grunt. Paris giggles. New York howls. A gladiator, waiting in the center of the arena while the Colosseum officials fumbled with the bolts of the door behind which paced the noisy tiger he was to fight, must have had some of the emotions which John experienced during his first hour as a masterless man in Gotham.

A surface car carried him up Broadway. At Times Square the Astor Hotel loomed up on the left. It looked a pretty good hotel to John. He dismounted.

Half an hour later he decided that he was acclimated. He had secured a base of operations in the shape of a room on the seventh floor, his check was safely deposited in the hotel bank, and he was half-way through a lunch which had caused him already to look on New York not only as the finest city in the world, but also, on the whole, as the one city of all others in which a young man might make a fortune with the maximum of speed and the minimum of effort.

After lunch, having telegraphed his address to his uncle in case of mail, he took the latter's excellent advice and went to the polo grounds. Returning in time to dress, he dined at the hotel, after which he visited a near-by theater, and completed a pleasant and strenuous day at one of those friendly restaurants where the music is continuous and the waiters are apt to burst into song in the intervals of their other duties.

A second attempt to find Smith next morning failed, as the first had done. The staff of the News were out of bed and at work ridiculously early, and when John called up the office between eleven and twelve o'clock—nature's breakfast-hour—Smith was again down East, observing the movements of those who were about to strike or who had already struck.

It hardly seemed worth while starting to lay the bed plates of his fortune till he had consulted the expert. What would Rockefeller have done? He would, John felt certain, have gone to the ball-game.

He imitated the great financier.

* * * * *

It was while he was smoking a cigar after dinner that night, musing on the fortunes of the day's game and, in particular, on the almost criminal imbecility of the umpire, that he was dreamily aware that he was being "paged." A small boy in uniform was meandering through the room, chanting his name.

"Gent wants five minutes wit' you," announced the boy, intercepted._"Hasn't got no card. Business, he says."

This disposed of the idea that Rupert Smith had discovered his retreat. John was puzzled. He could not think of another person in New York who knew of his presence at the Astor. But it was the unknown that he was in search of, and he decided to see the mysterious stranger.

"Send him along," he said.

The boy disappeared, and presently John observed him threading his way back among the tables, followed by a young man of extraordinary gravity of countenance, who was looking about him with an intent gaze through a pair of gold-rimmed spectacles.

John got up to meet him.

"My name is Maude," he said. "Won't you sit down? Have you had dinner?"

"Thank you, yes," said the spectacled young man.

"You'll have a cigar and coffee, then?"

"Thank you, yes."

The young man remained silent until the waiter had filled his cup.

"My name is Crump," he said. "I am Mr. Benjamin Scobell's private secretary."

"Yes?" said John. "Snug job?"

The other seemed to miss something in his voice.

"You have heard of Mr. Scobell?" he asked.

"Not to my knowledge," said John.

"Ah! you have lost touch very much with Mervo, of course."

John stared.

"Mervo?"

It sounded like some patent medicine.

"I have been instructed," said Mr. Crump solemnly, "to inform Your Highness that the Republic has been dissolved, and that your subjects offer you the throne of your ancestors."

John leaned back in his chair, and looked at the speaker in dumb amazement. The thought flashed across him that Mr. Crump had been perfectly correct in saying that he had dined.

His attitude appeared to astound Mr. Crump. He goggled through his spectacles at John, who was reminded of some rare fish.

"You are John Maude? You said you were."

"I'm John Maude right enough. We're solid on that point."

"And your mother was the only sister of Mr. Andrew Westley?"

"You're right there, too."

"Then there is no mistake. I say the Republic—" He paused, as if struck with an idea. "Don't you know?" he said. "Your father—"

John became suddenly interested.

"If you've got anything to tell me about my father, go right ahead. You'll be the only man I've ever met who has said a word about him. Who the deuce was he, anyway?"

Mr. Crump's face cleared.

"I understand. I had not expected this. You have been kept in ignorance. Your father, Mr. Maude, was the late Prince Charles of Mervo."

It was not easy to astonish John, but this announcement did so. He dropped his cigar in a shower of gray ash on to his trousers, and retrieved it almost mechanically, his wide-open eyes fixed on the other's face.

"What!" he cried.

Mr. Crump nodded gravely.

"You are Prince John of Mervo, and I am here—" he got into his stride as he reached the familiar phrase—"to inform Your Highness that the Republic has been dissolved, and that your subjects offer you the throne of your ancestors."

A horrid doubt seized John.

"You're stringing me. One of those Indians at the *News*, Rupert_Smith, or someone, has put you up to this."

Mr. Crump appeared wounded.

"If Your Highness would glance at these documents— This is a copy of the register of the church in which your mother and father were married."

John glanced at the document. It was perfectly lucid.

"Then—then it's true!" he said.

"Perfectly true, Your Highness. And I am here to inform—"

"But where the deuce is Mervo? I never heard of the place."

"It is an island principality in the Mediterranean, Your High—"

"For goodness' sake, old man, don't keep calling me 'Your Highness.' It may be fun to you, but it makes me feel a perfect ass. Let me get into the thing gradually."

Mr. Crump felt in his pocket.

"Mr. Scobell," he said, producing a roll of bills, "entrusted me with money to defray any expenses—"

More than any words, this spectacle removed any lingering doubt which John might have had as to the possibility of this being some intricate practical joke.

"Are these for me?" he said.

Mr. Crump passed them across to him.

"There are a thousand dollars here," he said. "I am also instructed to say that you are at liberty to draw further against Mr. Scobell's account at the Wall Street office of the European and Asiatic Bank."

The name Scobell had been recurring like a *leit-motif* in Mr._Crump's conversation. This suddenly came home to John.

"Before we go any further," he said, "let's get one thing clear. Who is this Mr. Scobell? How does he get mixed up in this?"

"He is the proprietor of the Casino at Mervo."

"He seems to be one of those generous, open-handed fellows. Nothing of the tight wad about him."

"He is deeply interested in Your High—in your return."

John laid the roll of bills beside his coffee cup, and relighted his cigar.

"That's mighty good of him," he said. "It strikes me, old man, that I am not absolutely up-to-date as regards the internal affairs of this important little kingdom of mine. How would it be if you were to put me next to one or two facts? Start at the beginning and go right on."

When Mr. Crump had finished a condensed history of Mervo and Mervian politics, John smoked in silence for some minutes.

"Life, Crump," he said at last, "is certainly speeding up as far as I am concerned. Up till now nothing in particular has ever happened to me. A couple of days ago I lost my job, was given ten thousand dollars that I didn't know existed, and now you tell me I'm a prince. Well, well! These are stirring times. When do we start for the old homestead?"

"Mr. Scobell was exceedingly anxious that we should return by_Saturday's boat."

"Saturday? What, to-morrow?"

"Perhaps it is too soon. You will not be able to settle your affairs?"

"I guess I can settle my affairs all right. I've only got to pack a grip and tip the bell hops. And as Scobell seems to be financing this show, perhaps it's up to me to step lively if he wants it. But it's a pity. I was just beginning to like this place. There is generally something doing along the White Way after twilight, Crump."

The gravity of Mr. Scobell's secretary broke up unexpectedly into a slow, wide smile. His eyes behind their glasses gleamed with a wistful light.

"Gee!" he murmured.

John looked at him, amazed.

"Crump," he cried. "Crump, I believe you're a sport!"

Mr. Crump seemed completely to have forgotten his responsible position as secretary to a millionaire and special messenger to a prince. He smirked.

"I'd have liked a day or two in the old burg," he said softly. "I haven't been to Rector's since Ponto was a pup."

John reached across the table and seized the secretary's hand.

"Crump," he said, "you *are* a sport. This is no time for delay._If we are to liven up this great city, we must get busy right away._Grab your hat, and come along. One doesn't become a prince every day._The occasion wants celebrating. Are you with me, Crump, old scout?"

"Sure thing," said the envoy ecstatically.

* * * * *

At eight o'clock on the following morning, two young men, hatless and a little rumpled, but obviously cheerful, entered the Astor Hotel, demanding breakfast.

A bell boy who met them was addressed by the larger of the two, and asked his name.

"Desmond Ryan," he replied.

The young man patted him on his shoulder.

"I appoint you, Desmond Ryan," he said, "Grand Hereditary Bell Hop to the Court of Mervo."

Thus did Prince John formally enter into his kingdom.

CHAPTER V

MR. SCOBELL HAS ANOTHER IDEA

Owing to collaboration between Fate and Mr. Scobell, John's state entry into Mervo was an interesting blend between a pageant and a vaudeville sketch. The pageant idea was Mr. Scobell's. Fate supplied the vaudeville.

The reception at the quay, when the little steamer that plied between Marseilles and the island principality gave up its precious freight, was not on quite so impressive a scale as might have been given to the monarch of a more powerful kingdom; but John was not disappointed. During the voyage from New York, in the intervals of seasickness—for he was a poor sailor—Mr. Crump had supplied him with certain facts about Mervo, one of which was that its adult population numbered just under thirteen thousand, and this had prepared him for any shortcomings in the way of popular demonstration.

As a matter of fact, Mr. Scobell was exceedingly pleased with the scale of the reception, which to his mind amounted practically to pomp. The Palace Guard, forty strong, lined the quay. Besides these, there were four officers, a band, and sixteen mounted carbineers. The rest of the army was dotted along the streets. In addition to the military, there was a gathering of a hundred and fifty civilians, mainly drawn from fishing circles. The majority of these remained stolidly silent throughout, but three, more emotional, cheered vigorously as a young man was seen to step on to the gangway, carrying a grip, and make for the shore. General Poineau, a white-haired warrior with a fierce mustache, strode forward and saluted. The Palace Guards presented arms. The band struck up the Mervian national anthem. General Poineau, lowering his hand, put on a pair of *pince-nez* and began to unroll an address of welcome.

It was then seen that the young man was Mr. Crump. General Poineau removed his glasses and gave an impatient twirl to his mustache. Mr. Scobell, who for possibly the first time in his career was not smoking (though, as was afterward made manifest, he had the materials on his person), bustled to the front.

"Where's his nibs, Crump?" he enquired.

The secretary's reply was swept away in a flood of melody. To the band Mr. Crump's face was strange. They had no reason to suppose that he was not Prince John, and they acted accordingly. With a rattle of drums they burst once more into their spirited rendering of the national anthem.

Mr. Scobell sawed the air with his arms, but was powerless to dam the flood.

"His Highness is shaving, sir!" bawled Mr. Crump, depositing his grip on the quay and making a trumpet of his hands.

"Shaving!"

"Yes, sir. I told him he ought to come along, but His Highness said he wasn't going to land looking like a tramp comedian."

By this time General Poineau had explained matters to the band and they checked the national anthem abruptly in the middle of a bar, with the exception of the cornet player, who continued gallantly by himself till a feeling of loneliness brought the truth home to him. An awkward stage wait followed, which lasted until John was seen crossing the deck, when there were more cheers, and General Poineau, resuming his *pince-nez*, brought out the address of welcome again.

At this point Mr. Scobell made his presence felt.

"Glad to meet you, Prince," he said, coming forward. "Scobell's my name. Shake hands with General Poineau. No, that's wrong. I guess he kisses your hand, don't he?"

"I'll swing on him if he does," said John, cheerfully.

Mr. Scobell eyed him doubtfully. His Highness did not appear to him to be treating the inaugural ceremony with that reserved dignity which we like to see in princes on these occasions. Mr. Scobell was a business man. He wanted his money's worth. His idea of a Prince of Mervo was something statuesquely aloof, something—he could not express it exactly—on the lines of the illustrations in the Zenda stories in the magazines—about eight feet high and shinily magnificent, something that would give the place a tone. That was what he had had in his mind when he sent for John. He did not want a cheerful young man in a soft hat and a flannel suit who looked as if at any moment he might burst into a college yell.

General Poineau, meanwhile, had embarked on the address of welcome._John regarded him thoughtfully.

"I can see," he said to Mr. Scobell, "that the gentleman is making a good speech, but what is he saying? That is what gets past me."

"He is welcoming Your Highness," said Mr. Crump, the linguist, "in the name of the people of Mervo."

"Who, I notice, have had the bully good sense to stay in bed. I guess they knew that the Boy Orator would do all that was necessary. He hasn't said anything about a bite of breakfast, has he? Has his address happened to work around to the subject of shredded wheat and shirred eggs yet? That's the part that's going to make a hit with me."

"There'll be breakfast at my villa, Your Highness," said Mr. Scobell._"My automobile is waiting along there."

The General reached his peroration, worked his way through it, and finished with a military clash of heels and a salute. The band rattled off the national anthem once more.

"Now, what?" said John, turning to Mr. Scobell. "Breakfast?"

"I guess you'd better say a few words to them, Your Highness; they'll expect it."

"But I can't speak the language, and they can't understand English. The thing'll be a stand-off."

"Crump will hand it to 'em. Here, Crump."

"Sir?"

"Line up and shoot His Highness's remarks into 'em."

"Yes, sir.

"It's all very well for you, Crump," said John. "You probably enjoy this sort of thing. I don't. I haven't felt such a fool since I sang 'The Maiden's Prayer' on Tremont Street when I was joining the frat. Are you ready? No, it's no good. I don't know what to say."

"Tell 'em you're tickled to death," advised Mr. Scobell anxiously.

John smiled in a friendly manner at the populace. Then he coughed. "Gentlemen," he said—"and more particularly the sport on my left who has just spoken his piece whose name I can't remember—I thank you for the warm welcome you have given me. If it is any satisfaction to you to know that it has made me feel like thirty cents, you may have that satisfaction. Thirty is a liberal estimate."

"'His Highness is overwhelmed by your loyal welcome. He thanks you warmly,'" translated Mr. Crump, tactfully.

"I feel that we shall get along nicely together," continued John. "If you are chumps enough to turn out of your comfortable beds at this time of the morning simply to see me, you can't be very hard to please. We shall hit it off fine."

Mr. Crump: "His Highness hopes and believes that he will always continue to command the affection of his people."

"I—" John paused. "That's the lot," he said. "The flow of inspiration has ceased. The magic fire has gone out. Break it to 'em, Crump. For me, breakfast."

During the early portion of the ride Mr. Scobell was silent and thoughtful. John's speech had impressed him neither as oratory nor as an index to his frame of mind. He had not interrupted him, because he knew that none of those present could understand what was being said, and that Mr. Crump was to be relied on as an editor. But he had not enjoyed it. He did not take the people of Mervo seriously himself, but in the Prince such an attitude struck him as unbecoming. Then he cheered up. After all, John had given evidence of having a certain amount of what he would have called "get-up" in him. For the purposes for which he needed him, a tendency to make light of things was not amiss. It was essentially as a performing prince that he had engaged John. He wanted him to do unusual things, which would make people talk—aeroplaning was one that occurred to him. Perhaps a prince who took a serious view of his position would try to raise the people's minds and start reforms and generally be a nuisance. John could, at any rate, be relied upon not to do that.

His face cleared.

"Have a good cigar, Prince?" he said, cordially, inserting two fingers in his vest-pocket.

"Sure, Mike," said His Highness affably.

Breakfast over, Mr. Scobell replaced the remains of his cigar between his lips, and turned to business.

"Eh, Prince?" he said.

"Yes!"

"I want you, Prince," said Mr. Scobell, "to help boom this place._That's where you come in."

"Sure," said John.

"As to ruling and all that," continued Mr. Scobell, "there isn't any to do. The place runs itself. Some guy gave it a shove a thousand years ago, and it's been rolling along ever since. What I want you to do is the picturesque stunts. Get a yacht and catch rare fishes. Whoop it up. Entertain swell guys when they come here. Have a Court—see what I mean?—same as over in England. Go around in aeroplanes and that style of thing. Don't worry about money. That'll be all right. You draw your steady hundred thousand a year and a good chunk more besides, when we begin to get a move on, so the dough proposition doesn't need to scare you any."

"Do I, by George!" said John. "It seems to me that I've fallen into a pretty soft thing here. There'll be a joker in the deck somewhere, I guess. There always is in these good things. But I don't see it yet. You can count me in all right."

"Good boy," said Mr. Scobell. "And now you'll be wanting to get to the_Palace. I'll have them bring the automobile round."

The council of state broke up.

Having seen John off in the car, the financier proceeded to his sister's sitting-room. Miss Scobell had breakfasted apart that morning, by request, her brother giving her to understand that matters of state, unsuited to the ear of a third party, must be discussed at the meal. She was reading her *New York Herald*.

"Well," said Mr. Scobell, "he's come."

"Yes, dear?"

"And just the sort I want. Saw the idea of the thing right away, and is ready to go the limit. No nonsense about him."

"Is he nice-looking, Bennie?"

"Sure. All these Mervo princes have been good-lookers, I hear, and this one must be near the top of the list. You'll like him, Marion. All the girls will be crazy about him in a week."

Miss Scobell turned a page.

"Is he married?"

Her brother started.

"Married? I never thought of that. But no, I guess he's not. He'd have mentioned it. He's not the sort to hush up a thing like that. I—"

He stopped short. His green eyes gleamed excitedly.

"Marion!" he cried. "*Marion!*"

"Well, dear?"

"Listen. Gee, this thing is going to be the biggest ever. I gotta new idea. It just came to me. Your saying that put it into my head. Do you know what I'm going to do? I'm going to cable over to Betty to come right along here, and I'm going to have her marry this prince guy. Yes, sir!"

For once Miss Scobell showed signs that her brother's conversation really interested her. She laid down her paper, and stared at him.

"Betty!"

"Sure, Betty. Why not? She's a pretty girl. Clever too. The Prince'll be lucky to get such a wife, for all his darned ancestors away back to the flood."

"But suppose Betty does not like him?"

"Like him? She's gotta like him. Say, can't you make your mind soar, or won't you? Can't you see that a thing like this has gotta be fixed different from a marriage between—between a ribbon-counter clerk and the girl who takes the money at a twenty-five-cent hash restaurant in Flatbush? This is a royal alliance. Do you suppose that when a European princess is introduced to the prince she's going to marry, they let her say: 'Nothing doing. I don't like the shape of his nose'?"

He gave a spirited imitation of a European princess objecting to the shape of her selected husband's nose.

"It isn't very romantic, Bennie," sighed Miss Scobell. She was a confirmed reader of the more sentimental class of fiction, and this business-like treatment of love's young dream jarred upon her.

"It's founding a dynasty. Isn't that romantic enough for you? You make me tired, Marion."

Miss Scobell sighed again.

"Very well, dear. I suppose you know best. But perhaps the Prince won't like Betty."

Mr. Scobell gave a snort of disgust.

"Marion," he said, "you've got a mind like a chunk of wet dough. Can't you understand that the Prince is just as much in my employment as the man who scrubs the Casino steps? I'm hiring him to be Prince of Mervo, and his first job as Prince of Mervo will be to marry Betty. I'd like to see him kick!" He began to pace the room. "By Heck, it's going to make this place boom to beat the band. It'll be the biggest kind of advertisement. Restoration of Royalty at Mervo. That'll make them take notice by itself. Then, biff! right on top of that, Royal Romance—Prince Weds American Girl—Love at First Sight—Picturesque Wedding! Gee, we'll wipe Monte Carlo clean off the map. We'll have 'em licked to a splinter. We—It's the greatest scheme on earth."

"I have no doubt you are right, Bennie," said Miss Scobell, "but—" her voice became dreamy again—"it's not very romantic."

"Oh, shucks!" said the schemer impatiently. "Here, where's a cable form?"

CHAPTER VI

YOUNG ADAM CUPID

On a red sandstone rock at the edge of the water, where the island curved sharply out into the sea, Prince John of Mervo sat and brooded on first causes. For nearly an hour and a half he had been engaged in an earnest attempt to trace to its source the acute fit of depression which had come—apparently from nowhere—to poison his existence that morning.

It was his seventh day on the island, and he could remember every incident of his brief reign. The only thing that eluded him was the recollection of the exact point when the shadow of discontent had begun to spread itself over his mind. Looking back, it seemed to him that he had done nothing during that week but enjoy each new aspect of his position as it was introduced to his notice. Yet here he was, sitting on a lonely rock, consumed with an unquenchable restlessness, a kind of trapped sensation. Exactly when and exactly how Fate, that king of gold-brick men, had cheated him he could not say; but he knew, with a certainty that defied argument, that there had been sharp practise, and that in an unguarded moment he had been induced to part with something of infinite value in exchange for a gilded fraud.

The mystery baffled him. He sent his mind back to the first definite entry of Mervo into the foreground of his life. He had come up from his stateroom on to the deck of the little steamer, and there in the pearl-gray of the morning was the island, gradually taking definite shape as the pink mists shredded away before the rays of the rising sun. As the ship rounded the point where the lighthouse still flashed a needless warning from its cluster of jagged rocks, he had had his first view of the town, nestling at the foot of the hill, gleaming white against the green, with the gold-domed Casino towering in its midst. In all Southern Europe there was no view to match it for quiet beauty. For all his thews and sinews there was poetry in John, and the sight had stirred him like wine.

It was not then that depression had begun, nor was it during the reception at the quay.

The days that had followed had been peaceful and amusing. He could not detect in any one of them a sign of the approaching shadow. They had been lazy days. His duties had been much more simple than he had anticipated. He had not known, before he tried it, that it was possible to be a prince with so small an expenditure of mental energy. As Mr. Scobell had hinted, to all intents and purposes he was a mere ornament. His work began at eleven in the morning, and finished as a rule at about a quarter after. At the hour named a report of the happenings of the previous day was brought to him. When he had read it the state asked no more of him until the next morning.

The report was made up of such items as "A fisherman named Lesieur called Carbineer Ferrier a fool in the market-place at eleven minutes after two this afternoon; he has not been arrested, but is being watched," and generally gave John a few minutes of mild enjoyment. Certainly he could not recollect that it had ever depressed him.

No, it had been something else that had worked the mischief and in another moment the thing stood revealed, beyond all question of doubt. What had unsettled him was that unexpected meeting with Betty Silver last night at the Casino.

He had been sitting at the Dutch table. He generally visited the Casino after dinner. The light and movement of the place interested him. As a rule, he merely strolled through the rooms, watching the play; but last night he had slipped into a vacant seat. He had only just settled himself when he was aware of a girl standing beside him. He got up.

"Would you care—?" he had begun, and then he saw her face.

It had all happened in an instant. Some chord in him, numbed till then, had begun to throb. It was as if he had awakened from a dream, or returned to consciousness after being stunned. There was something in the sight of her, standing there so cool and neat and composed, so typically American, a sort of goddess of America, in the heat and stir of the Casino, that struck him like a blow.

How long was it since he had seen her last? Not more than a couple of years. It seemed centuries. It all came back to him. It was during his last winter at Harvard that they had met. A college friend of hers had been the sister of a college friend of his. They had met several times, but he could not recollect having taken any particular notice of her then, beyond recognizing that she was certainly pretty. The world had been full of pretty American girls then. But now—

He looked at her. And, as he looked, he heard America calling to him. Mervo, by the appeal of its novelty, had caused him to forget. But now, quite suddenly, he knew that he was homesick—and it astonished him, the readiness with which he had permitted Mr. Crump to lead him away into bondage. It seemed incredible that he had not foreseen what must happen.

Love comes to some gently, imperceptibly, creeping in as the tide, through unsuspected creeks and inlets, creeps on a sleeping man, until he wakes to find himself surrounded. But to others it comes as a wave, breaking on them, beating them down, whirling them away.

It was so with John. In that instant when their eyes met the miracle must have happened. It seemed to him, as he recalled the scene now, that he had loved her before he had had time to frame his first remark. It amazed him that he could ever have been blind to the fact that he loved her, she was so obviously the only girl in the world.

"You—you don't remember me," he stammered.

She was flushing a little under his stare, but her eyes were shining.

"I remember you very well, Mr. Maude," she said with a smile. "I thought I knew your shoulders before you turned round. What are you doing here?"

"I—"

There was a hush. The *croupier* had set the ball rolling. A wizened little man and two ladies of determined aspect were looking up disapprovingly. John realized that he was the only person in the room not silent. It was impossible to tell her the story of the change in his fortunes in the middle of this crowd. He stopped, and the moment passed.

The ball dropped with a rattle. The tension relaxed.

"Won't you take this seat?" said John.

"No, thank you. I'm not playing. I only just stopped to look on. My aunt is in one of the rooms, and I want to make her come home. I'm tired."

"Have you—?"

He caught the eye of the wizened man, and stopped again.

"Have you been in Mervo long?" he said, as the ball fell.

"I only arrived this morning. It seems lovely. I must explore to-morrow."

She was beginning to move off.

"Er—" John coughed to remove what seemed to him a deposit of sawdust and unshelled nuts in his throat. "Er—may I—will you let me show you—" prolonged struggle with the nuts and sawdust; then rapidly—"some of the places to-morrow?"

He had hardly spoken the words when it was borne in upon him that he was a vulgar, pushing bounder, presuming on a dead and buried acquaintanceship to force his company on a girl who naturally did not want it, and who would now proceed to snub him as he deserved. He quailed. Though he had not had time to collect and examine and label his feelings, he was sufficiently in touch with them to know that a snub from her would be the most terrible thing that could possibly happen to him.

She did not snub him. Indeed, if he had been in a state of mind coherent enough to allow him to observe, he might have detected in her eyes and her voice signs of pleasure.

"I should like it very much," she said.

John made his big effort. He attacked the nuts and sawdust which had come back and settled down again in company with a large lump of some unidentified material, as if he were bucking center. They broke before him as, long ago, the Yale line had done, and his voice rang out as if through a megaphone, to the unconcealed disgust of the neighboring gamesters.

"If you go along the path at the foot of the hill," he bellowed rapidly, "and follow it down to the sea, you get a little bay full of red sandstone rocks—you can't miss it—and there's a fine view of the island from there. I'd like awfully well to show that to you. It's great."

She nodded.

"Then shall we meet there?" she said. "When?"

John was in no mood to postpone the event.

"As early as ever you like," he roared.

"At about ten, then. Good-night, Mr. Maude."

* * * * *

John had reached the bay at half-past eight, and had been on guard there ever since. It was now past ten, but still there were no signs of Betty. His depression increased. He told himself that she had forgotten. Then, that she had remembered, but had changed her mind. Then, that she had never meant to come at all. He could not decide which of the three theories was the most distressing.

His mood became morbidly introspective. He was weighed down by a sense of his own unworthiness. He submitted himself to a thorough examination, and the conclusion to which he came was that, as an aspirant to the regard, of a girl like Betty, he did not score a single point. No wonder she had ignored the appointment.

A cold sweat broke out on him. This was the snub! She had not administered it in the Casino simply in order that, by being delayed, its force might be the more overwhelming.

He looked at his watch again, and the world grew black. It was twelve minutes after ten.

John, in his time, had thought and read a good deal about love. Ever since he had grown up, he had wanted to fall in love. He had imagined love as a perpetual exhilaration, something that flooded life with a golden glow as if by the pressing of a button or the pulling of a switch, and automatically removed from it everything mean and hard and uncomfortable; a something that made a man feel grand and god-like, looking down (benevolently, of course) on his fellow men as from some lofty mountain.

That it should make him feel a worm-like humility had not entered his calculations. He was beginning to see something of the possibilities of love. His tentative excursions into the unknown emotion, while at college, had never really deceived him; even at the time a sort of second self had looked on and sneered at the poor imitation.

This was different. This had nothing to do with moonlight and soft music. It was raw and hard. It hurt. It was a thing sharp and jagged, tearing at the roots of his soul.

He turned his head, and looked up the path for the hundredth time, and this time he sprang to his feet. Between the pines on the hillside his eye had caught the flutter of a white dress.

CHAPTER VII
MR. SCOBELL IS FRANK

Much may happen in these rapid times in the course of an hour and a half. While John was keeping his vigil on the sandstone rock, Betty was having an interview with Mr. Scobell which was to produce far-reaching results, and which, incidentally, was to leave her angrier and more at war with the whole of her world than she could remember to have been in the entire course of her life.

The interview began, shortly after breakfast, in a gentle and tactful manner, with Aunt Marion at the helm. But Mr. Scobell was not the man to stand by silently while persons were being tactful. At the end of the second minute he had plunged through his sister's mild monologue like a rhinoceros through a cobweb, and had stated definitely, with an economy of words, the exact part which Betty was to play in Mervian affairs.

"You say you want to know why you were cabled for. I'll tell you. There's no use talking for half a day before you get to the point. I guess you've heard that there's a prince here instead of a republic now? Well, that's where you come in."

"Do you mean—?" she hesitated.

"Yes, I do," said Mr. Scobell. There was a touch of doggedness in his voice. He was not going to stand any nonsense, by Heck, but there was no doubt that Betty's wide-open eyes were not very easy to meet. He went on rapidly. "Cut out any fool notions about romance." Miss Scobell, who was knitting a sock, checked her needles for a moment in order to sigh. Her brother eyed her morosely, then resumed his remarks. "This is a matter of state. That's it. You gotta cut out fool notions and act for good of state. You gotta look at it in the proper spirit. Great honor—see what I mean? Princess and all that. Chance of a lifetime—dynasty—you gotta look at it that way."

Miss Scobell heaved another sigh, and dropped a stitch.

"For the love of Mike," said her brother, irritably, "don't snort like that, Marion."

"Very well, dear."

Betty had not taken her eyes off him from his first word. An unbiased observer would have said that she made a pretty picture, standing there, in her white dress, but in the matter of pictures, still life was evidently what Mr. Scobell preferred for his gaze never wandered from the cigar stump which he had removed from his mouth in order to knock off the ash.

Betty continued to regard him steadfastly. The shock of his words had to some extent numbed her. At this moment she was merely thinking, quite dispassionately, what a singularly nasty little man he looked, and wondering—not for the first time—what strange quality, invisible to everybody else, it had been in him that had made her mother his adoring slave during the whole of their married life.

Then her mind began to work actively once more. She was a Western girl, and an insistence on freedom was the first article in her creed. A great rush of anger filled her, that this man should set himself up to dictate to her.

"Do you mean that you want me to marry this Prince?" she said.

"That's right."

"I won't do anything of the sort."

"Pshaw! Don't be foolish. You make me tired."

Betty's eye shone mutinously. Her cheeks were flushed, and her slim, boyish figure quivered. Her chin, always determined, became a silent Declaration of Independence.

"I won't," she said.

Aunt Marion, suspending operations on the sock, went on with tact at the point where her brother's interruption had forced her to leave off.

"I'm sure he's a very nice young man. I have not seen him, but everybody says so. You like him, Bennie, don't you?"

"Sure, I like him. He's a corker. Wait till you see him, Betty. Nobody's asking you to marry him before lunch. You'll have plenty of time to get acquainted. It beats me what you're kicking at. You give me a pain in the neck. Be reasonable."

Betty sought for arguments to clinch her refusal.

"It's ridiculous," she said. "You talk as if you had just to wave your hand. Why should your prince want to marry a girl he has never seen?"

"He will," said Mr. Scobell confidently.

"How do you know?"

"Because I know he's a sensible young skeesicks. That's how. See here, Betty, you've gotten hold of wrong ideas about this place. You don't understand the position of affairs. Your aunt didn't till I put her wise."

"He bit my head off, my dear," murmured Miss Scobell, knitting placidly.

"You're thinking that Mervo is an ordinary state, and that the Prince is one of those independent, all-wool, off-with-his-darned-head rulers like you read about in the best sellers. Well, you've got another guess coming. If you want to know who's the big noise here, it's me—me! This Prince guy is my hired man. See? Who sent for him? I did. Who put him on the throne? I did. Who pays him his salary? I do, from the profits of the Casino. Now do you understand? He knows his job. He knows which side his bread's buttered. When I tell him about this marriage, do you know what he'll say? He'll say 'Thank you, sir!' That's how things are in this island."

Betty shuddered. Her face was white with humiliation. She half-raised her hands with an impulsive movement to hide it.

"I won't. I won't. I won't!" she gasped.

Mr. Scobell was pacing the room in an ecstasy of triumphant rhetoric.

"There's another thing," he said, swinging round suddenly and causing his sister to drop another stitch. "Maybe you think he's some kind of a Dago, this guy? Maybe that's what's biting you. Let me tell you that he's an American—pretty near as much an American as you are yourself."

Betty stared at him.

"An American!"

"Don't believe it, eh? Well, let me tell you that his mother was born and raised in Jersey, and that he has lived all his life in the States. He's no little runt of a Dago. No, sir. He's a Harvard man, six-foot high and weighs two hundred pounds. That's the sort of man he is. I guess that's not American enough for you, maybe? No?"

"You do shout so, Bennie!" murmured Miss Scobell. "I'm sure there's no need."

Betty uttered a cry. Something had told her who he was, this Harvard man who had sold himself. That species of sixth sense which lies undeveloped at the back of our minds during the ordinary happenings of life wakes sometimes in moments of keen emotion. At its highest, it is prophecy; at its lowest, a vague presentiment. It woke in Betty now. There was no particular reason why she should have connected her stepfather's words with John. The term he had used was an elastic one. Among the visitors to the island there were probably several Harvard men. But somehow she knew.

"Who is he?" she cried. "What was his name before he—when he—?"

"His name?" said Mr. Scobell. "John Maude. Maude was his mother's name._She was a Miss Westley. Here, where are you going?"

Betty was walking slowly toward the door. Something in her face checked_Mr. Scobell.

"I want to think," she said quietly. "I'm going out."

* * * * *

In days of old, in the age of legend, omens warned heroes of impending doom. But to-day the gods have grown weary, and we rush unsuspecting on our fate. No owl hooted, no thunder rolled from the blue sky as John went up the path to meet the white dress that gleamed between the trees.

His heart was singing within him. She had come. She had not forgotten, or changed her mind, or willfully abandoned him. His mood lightened swiftly. Humility vanished. He was not such an outcast, after all. He was someone. He was the man Betty Silver had come to meet.

But with the sight of her face came reaction.

Her face was pale and cold and hard. She did not speak or smile. As she drew near she looked at him, and there was that in her look which set a chill wind blowing through the world and cast a veil across the sun.

And in this bleak world they stood silent and motionless while eons rolled by.

Betty was the first to speak.

"I'm late," she said.

John searched in his brain for words, and came empty away. He shook his head dumbly.

"Shall we sit down?" said Betty.

John indicated silently the sandstone rock on which he had been communing with himself.

They sat down. A sense of being preposterously and indecently big obsessed John. There seemed no end to him. Wherever he looked, there were hands and feet and legs. He was a vast blot on the face of the earth. He glanced out of the corner of his eye at Betty. She was gazing out to sea.

He dived into his brain again. It was absurd! There must be something to say.

And then he realized that a worse thing had befallen. He had no voice. It had gone. He knew that, try he never so hard to speak, he would not be able to utter a word. A nightmare feeling of unreality came upon him. Had he ever spoken? Had he ever done anything but sit dumbly on that rock, looking at those sea gulls out in the water?

He shot another swift glance at Betty, and a thrill went through him._There were tears in her eyes.

The next moment—the action was almost automatic—his left hand was clasping her right, and he was moving along the rock to her side.

She snatched her hand away.

His brain, ransacked for the third time, yielded a single word.

"Betty!"

She got up quickly.

In the confused state of his mind, John found it necessary if he were to speak at all, to say the essential thing in the shortest possible way. Polished periods are not for the man who is feeling deeply.

He blurted out, huskily, "I love you!" and finding that this was all that he could say, was silent.

Even to himself the words, as he spoke them, sounded bald and meaningless. To Betty, shaken by her encounter with Mr. Scobell, they sounded artificial, as if he were forcing himself to repeat a lesson. They jarred upon her.

"Don't!" she said sharply. "Oh, don't!"

Her voice stabbed him. It could not have stirred him more if she had uttered a cry of physical pain.

"Don't! I know. I've been told."

"Been told?"

She went on quickly.

"I know all about it. My stepfather has just told me. He said—he said you were his—" she choked—"his hired man; that he paid you to stay here and advertise the Casino. Oh, it's too horrible! That it should be you! You, who have been—you can't understand what you—have been to me—ever since we met; you couldn't understand. I can't tell you—a sort of help—something—something that—I can't put it into words. Only it used to help me just to think of you. It was almost impersonal. I didn't mind if I never saw you again. I didn't expect ever to see you again. It was just being able to think of you. It helped—you were something I could trust. Something strong—solid." She laughed bitterly. "I suppose I made a hero of you. Girls are fools. But it helped me to feel that there was one man alive who—who put his honor above money—"

She broke off. John stood motionless, staring at the ground. For the first time in his easy-going life he knew shame. Even now he had not grasped to the full the purport of her words. The scales were falling from his eyes, but as yet he saw but dimly.

She began to speak again, in a low, monotonous voice, almost as if she were talking to herself. She was looking past him, at the gulls that swooped and skimmed above the glittering water.

"I'm so tired of money—money—money. Everything's money. Isn't there a man in the world who won't sell himself? I thought that you—I suppose I'm stupid. It's business, I suppose. One expects too much."

She looked at him wearily.

"Good-by," she said. "I'm going."

He did not move.

She turned, and went slowly up the path. Still he made no movement. A spell seemed to be on him. His eyes never left her as she passed into the shadow of the trees. For a moment her white dress stood out clearly. She had stopped. With his whole soul he prayed that she would look back. But she moved on once more, and was gone. And suddenly a strange weakness came upon John. He trembled. The hillside flickered before his eyes for an instant, and he clutched at the sandstone rock to steady himself.

Then his brain cleared, and he found himself thinking swiftly. He could not let her go like this. He must overtake her. He must stop her. He must speak to her. He must say—he did not know what it was that he would say—anything, so that he spoke to her again.

He raced up the path, calling her name. No answer came to his cries. Above him lay the hillside, dozing in the noonday sun; below, the Mediterranean, sleek and blue, without a ripple. He stood alone in a land of silence and sleep.

CHAPTER VIII

AN ULTIMATUM FROM THE THRONE

At half-past twelve that morning business took Mr. Benjamin Scobell to the royal Palace. He was not a man who believed in letting the grass grow under his feet. He prided himself on his briskness of attack. Every now and then Mr. Crump, searching the newspapers, would discover and hand to him a paragraph alluding to his "hustling methods." When this happened, he would preserve the clipping and carry it about in his vest-pocket with his cigars till time and friction wore it away. He liked to think of himself as swift and sudden—the Human Thunderbolt.

In this matter of the royal alliance, it was his intention to have at it and clear it up at once. Having put his views clearly before Betty, he now proposed to lay them with equal clarity before the Prince. There was no sense in putting the thing off. The sooner all parties concerned understood the position of affairs, the sooner the business would be settled.

That Betty had not received his information with joy did not distress him. He had a poor opinion of the feminine intelligence. Girls got their minds full of nonsense from reading novels and seeing plays—like Betty. Betty objected to those who were wiser than herself providing a perfectly good prince for her to marry. Some fool notion of romance, of course. Not that he was angry. He did not blame her any more than the surgeon blames a patient for the possession of an unsuitable appendix. There was no animus in the matter. Her mind was suffering from foolish ideas, and he was the surgeon whose task it was to operate upon it. That was all. One had to expect foolishness in women. It was their nature. The only thing to do was to tie a rope to them and let them run around till they were tired of it, then pull them in. He saw his way to managing Betty.

Nor did he anticipate trouble with John. He had taken an estimate of John's character, and it did not seem to him likely that it contained unsuspected depths. He set John down, as he had told Betty, as a young man acute enough to know when he had a good job and sufficiently sensible to make concessions in order to retain it. Betty, after the manner of woman, might make a fuss before yielding to the inevitable, but from level-headed John he looked for placid acquiescence.

His mood, as the automobile whirred its way down the hill toward the town, was sunny. He looked on life benevolently and found it good. The view appealed to him more than it had managed to do on other days. As a rule, he was the man of blood and iron who had no time for admiring scenery, but to-day he vouchsafed it a not unkindly glance. It was certainly a dandy little place, this island of his. A vineyard on the right caught his eye. He made a mental note to uproot it and run up a hotel in its place. Further down the hill, he selected a site for a villa, where the mimosa blazed, and another where at present there were a number of utterly useless violets. A certain practical element was apt, perhaps, to color Mr. Scobell's half-hours with nature.

The sight of the steamboat leaving the harbor on its journey to Marseilles gave him another idea. Now that Mervo was a going concern, a real live proposition, it was high time that it should have an adequate service of boats. The present system of one a day was absurd. He made a note to look into the matter. These people wanted waking up.

Arriving at the Palace, he was informed that His Highness had gone out shortly after breakfast, and had not returned. The majordomo gave the information with a tinkle of disapproval in his voice. Before taking up his duties at Mervo, he had held a similar position in the household of a German prince, where rigid ceremonial obtained, and John's cheerful disregard of the formalities frankly shocked him. To take the present case for instance: When His Highness of Swartzheim had felt inclined to enjoy the air of a morning, it had been a domestic event full of stir and pomp. He had not merely crammed a soft hat over his eyes and strolled out with his hands in his pockets, but without a word to his household staff as to where he was going or when he might be expected to return.

Mr. Scobell received the news equably, and directed his chauffeur to return to the villa. He could not have done better, for, on his arrival, he was met with the information that His Highness had called to see him shortly after he had left, and was now waiting in the morning-room.

The sound of footsteps came to Mr. Scobell's ears as he approached the room. His Highness appeared to be pacing the floor like a caged animal at the luncheon hour. The resemblance was heightened by the expression in the royal eye as His Highness swung round at the opening of the door and faced the financier.

"Why, say, Prince," said Mr. Scobell, "this is lucky. I been looking for you. I just been to the Palace, and the main guy there told me you had gone out."

"I did. And I met your stepdaughter."

Mr. Scobell was astonished. Fate was certainly smoothing his way if it arranged meetings between Betty and the Prince before he had time to do it himself. There might be no need for the iron hand after all.

"You did?" he said. "Say, how the Heck did you come to do that? What did you know about Betty?"

"Miss Silver and I had met before, in America, when I was in college."

Mr. Scobell slapped his thigh joyously.

"Gee, it's all working out like a fiction story in the magazines!"

"Is it?" said John. "How? And, for the matter of that, what?"

Mr. Scobell answered question with question. "Say, Prince, you and_Betty were pretty good friends in the old days, I guess?"

John looked at him coldly.

"We won't discuss that, if you don't mind," he said.

His tone annoyed Mr. Scobell. Off came the velvet glove, and the iron hand displayed itself. His green eyes glowed dully and the tip of his nose wriggled, as was its habit in times of emotion.

"Is that so?" he cried, regarding John with disfavor. "Well, I guess!_Won't discuss it! You gotta discuss it, Your Royal Texas League_Highness! You want making a head shorter, my bucko. You—"

John's demeanor had become so dangerous that he broke off abruptly, and with an unostentatious movement, as of a man strolling carelessly about his private sanctum, put himself within easy reach of the door handle.

He then became satirical.

"Maybe Your Serene, Imperial Two-by-Fourness would care to suggest a subject we can discuss?"

John took a step forward.

"Yes, I will," he said between his teeth. "You were talking to Miss Silver about me this morning. She told me one or two of the things you said, and they opened my eyes. Until I heard them, I had not quite understood my position. I do now. You said, among other things, that I was your hired man."

"It wasn't intended for you to hear," said Mr. Scobell, slightly mollified, "and Betty shouldn't oughter have handed it to you. I don't wonder you feel raw. I wouldn't say that sort of thing to a guy's face. Sure, no. Tact's my middle name. But, since you have heard it, well—!"

"Don't apologize. You were quite right. I was a fool not to see it before. No description could have been fairer. You might have said much more. You might have added that I was nothing more than a steerer for a gambling hell."

"Oh, come, Prince!"

There was a knock at the door. A footman entered, bearing, with a detached air, as if he disclaimed all responsibility, a letter on a silver tray.

Mr. Scobell slit the envelope, and began to read. As he did so his eyes grew round, and his mouth slowly opened till his cigar stump, after hanging for a moment from his lower lip, dropped off like an exhausted bivalve and rolled along the carpet.

"Prince," he gasped, "she's gone. Betty!"

"Gone! What do you mean?"

"She's beaten it. She's half-way to Marseilles by now. Gee, and I saw the darned boat going out!"

"She's gone!"

"This is from her. Listen what she says:

"*By the time you read this I shall be gone. I am going back to America as quickly as I can. I am giving this to a boy to take to you directly the boat has started. Please do not try to bring me back. I would sooner die than marry the Prince.*"

John started violently.

"What!" he cried.

Mr. Scobell nodded sympathy.

"That's what she says. She sure has it in bad for you. What does she mean? Seeing you and she are old friends—"

"I don't understand. Why does she say that to you? Why should she think that you knew that I had asked her to marry me?"

"Eh?" cried Mr. Scobell. "You asked her to marry you? And she turned you down! Prince, this beats the band. Say, you and I must get together and do something. The girl's mad. See here, you aren't wise to what's been happening. I been fixing this thing up. I fetched you over here, and then I fetched Betty, and I was going to have you two marry. I told Betty all about it this morning."

John cut through his explanations with a sudden sharp cry. A blinding blaze of understanding had flashed upon him. It was as if he had been groping his way in a dark cavern and had stumbled unexpectedly into brilliant sunlight. He understood everything now. Every word that Betty had spoken, every gesture that she had made, had become amazingly clear. He saw now why she had shrunk back from him, why her eyes had worn that look. He dared not face the picture of himself as he must have appeared in those eyes, the man whom Mr. Benjamin Scobell's Casino was paying to marry her, the hired man earning his wages by speaking words of love.

A feeling of physical sickness came over him. He held to the table for support as he had held to the sandstone rock. And then came rage, rage such as he had never felt before, rage that he had not thought himself capable of feeling. It swept over him in a wave, pouring through his veins and blinding him, and he clung to the table till his knuckles whitened under the strain, for he knew that he was very near to murder.

A minute passed. He walked to the window, and stood there, looking out. Vaguely he heard Mr. Scobell's voice at his back, talking on, but the words had no meaning for him.

He had begun to think with a curious coolness. His detachment surprised him. It was one of those rare moments in a man's life when, from the outside, through a breach in that wall of excuses and self-deception which he has been at such pains to build, he looks at himself impartially.

The sight that John saw through the wall was not comforting. It was not a heroic soul that, stripped of its defenses, shivered beneath the scrutiny. In another mood he would have mended the breach, excusing and extenuating, but not now. He looked at himself without pity, and saw himself weak, slothful, devoid of all that was clean and fine, and a bitter contempt filled him.

Outside the window, a blaze of color, Mervo smiled up at him, and suddenly he found himself loathing its exotic beauty. He felt stifled. This was no place for a man. A vision of clean winds and wide spaces came to him.

And just then, at the foot of the hill, the dome of the Casino caught the sun, and flashed out in a blaze of gold.

He swung round and faced Mr. Scobell. He had made up his mind.

The financier was still talking.

"So that's how it stands, Prince," he was saying, "and it's up to us to get busy."

John looked at him.

"I intend to," he said.

"Good boy!" said the financier.

"To begin with, I shall run you out of this place, Mr. Scobell."

The other gasped.

"There is going to be a cleaning-up," John went on. "I've thought it out. There will be no more gambling in Mervo."

"You're crazy with the heat!" gasped Mr. Scobell. "Abolish gambling?_You can't."

"I can. That concession of yours isn't worth the paper it's written on. The Republic gave it to you. The Republic's finished. If you want to conduct a Casino in Mervo, there's only one man who can give you permission, and that's myself. The acts of the Republic are not binding on me. For a week you have been gambling on this island without a concession and now it's going to stop. Do you understand?"

"But, Prince, talk sense." Mr. Scobell's voice was almost tearful. "It's you who don't understand. Do, for the love of Mike, come down off the roof and talk sense. Do you suppose that these guys here will stand for this? Not on your life. Not for a minute. See here. I'm not blaming you. I know you don't know what you're saying. But listen here. You must cut out this kind of thing. You mustn't get these ideas in your head. You stick to your job, and don't butt in on other folks'. Do you know how long you'd stay Prince of this joint if you started in to monkey with my Casino? Just about long enough to let you pack a collar-stud and a toothbrush into your grip. And after that there wouldn't be any more Prince, sonnie. You stick to your job and I'll stick to mine. You're a mighty good Prince for all that's required of you. You're ornamental, and you've got get-up in you. You just keep right on being a good boy, and don't start trying stunts off your own beat, and you'll do fine. Don't forget that I'm the big noise here. I'm old Grayback from 'way back in Mervo. See! I've only to twiddle my fingers and there'll be a revolution and you for the Down-and-Out Club. Don't you forget it, sonnie."

John shrugged his shoulders.

"I've said all I have to say. You've had your notice to quit. After to-night the Casino is closed."

"But don't I tell you the people won't stand for it?"

"That's for them to decide. They may have some self-respect."

"They'll fire you!"

"Very well. That will prove that they have not."

"Prince, talk sense! You can't mean that you'll throw away a hundred thousand dollars a year as if it was dirt!"

"It is dirt when it's made that way. We needn't discuss it any more."

"But, Prince!"

"It's finished."

"But, say—!"

John had left the room.

He had been gone several minutes before the financier recovered full possession of his faculties.

When he did, his remarks were brief and to the point.

"Bug-house!" he gasped. "Abso-lutely bug-house!"

CHAPTER IX
MERVO CHANGES ITS CONSTITUTION

Humor, if one looks into it, is principally a matter of retrospect. In after years John was wont to look back with amusement on the revolution which ejected him from the throne of his ancestors. But at the time its mirthfulness did not appeal to him. He was in a frenzy of restlessness. He wanted Betty. He wanted to see her and explain. Explanations could not restore him to the place he had held in her mind, but at least they would show her that he was not the thing he had appeared.

Mervo had become a prison. He ached for America. But, before he could go, this matter of the Casino must be settled. It was obvious that it could only be settled in one way. He did not credit his subjects with the high-mindedness that puts ideals first and money after. That military and civilians alike would rally to a man round Mr. Scobell and the Casino he was well aware. But this did not affect his determination to remain till the last. If he went now, he would be like a boy who makes a runaway ring at the doorbell. Until he should receive formal notice of dismissal, he must stay, although every day had forty-eight hours and every hour twice its complement of weary minutes.

So he waited, chafing, while Mervo examined the situation, turned it over in its mind, discussed it, slept upon it, discussed it again, and displayed generally that ponderous leisureliness which is the Mervian's birthright.

Indeed, the earliest demonstration was not Mervian at all. It came from the visitors to the island, and consisted of a deputation of four, headed by the wizened little man, who had frowned at John in the Dutch room on the occasion of his meeting with Betty, and a stolid individual with a bald forehead and a walrus mustache.

The tone of the deputation was, from the first, querulous. The wizened man had constituted himself spokesman. He introduced the party—the walrus as Colonel Finch, the others as Herr von Mandelbaum and Mr. Archer-Cleeve. His own name was Pugh, and the whole party, like the other visitors whom they represented, had, it seemed, come to Mervo, at great trouble and expense, to patronize the tables, only to find these suddenly, without a word of warning, withdrawn from their patronage. And what the deputation wished to know was, What did it all mean?

"We were amazed, sir—Your Highness," said Mr. Pugh. "We could not—we cannot—understand it. The entire thing is a baffling mystery to us. We asked the soldiers at the door. They referred us to Mr. Scobell. We asked Mr. Scobell. He referred us to you. And now we have come, as the representatives of our fellow visitors to this island, to ask Your Highness what it means!"

"Have a cigar," said John, extending the box. Mr. Pugh waved aside the preferred gift impatiently. Not so Herr von Mandelbaum, who slid forward after the manner of one in quest of second base and retired with his prize to the rear of the little army once more.

Mr. Archer-Cleeve, a young man with carefully parted fair hair and the expression of a strayed sheep, contributed a remark.

"No, but I say, by Jove, you know, I mean really, you know, what?"

That was Mr. Archer-Cleeve upon the situation.

"We have not come here for cigars," said Mr. Pugh. "We have come here,_Your Highness, for an explanation."

"Of what?" said John.

Mr. Pugh made an impatient gesture.

"Do you question my right to rule this massive country as I think best,_Mr. Pugh?"

"It is a high-handed proceeding," said the wizened little man.

The walrus spoke for the first time.

"What say?" he murmured huskily.

"I said," repeated Mr. Pugh, raising his voice, "that it was a high-handed proceeding, Colonel."

The walrus nodded heavily, in assent, with closed eyes.

"Yah," said Herr von Mandelbaum through the smoke.

John looked at the spokesman.

"You are from England, Mr. Pugh?"

"Yes, sir. I am a British citizen."

"Suppose some enterprising person began to run a gambling hell in_Piccadilly, would the authorities look on and smile?"

"That is an entirely different matter, sir. You are quibbling. In_England gambling is forbidden by law."

"So it is in Mervo, Mr. Pugh."

"Tchah!"

"What say?" said the walrus.

"I said 'Tchah!' Colonel."

"Why?" said the walrus.

"Because His Highness quibbled."

The walrus nodded approvingly.

"His Highness did nothing of the sort," said John. "Gambling is forbidden in Mervo for the same reason that it is forbidden in England, because it demoralizes the people."

"This is absurd, sir. Gambling has been permitted in Mervo for nearly a year."

"But not by me, Mr. Pugh. The Republic certainly granted Mr. Scobell a concession. But, when I came to the throne, it became necessary for him to get a concession from me. I refused it. Hence the closed doors."

Mr. Archer-Cleeve once more. "But—" He paused. "Forgotten what I was going to say," he said to the room at large.

Herr von Mandelbaum made some remark at the back of his throat, but was ignored.

John spoke again.

"If you were a prince, Mr. Pugh, would you find it pleasant to be in the pay of a gambling hell?"

"That is neither here nor—"

"On the contrary, it is, very much. I happen to have some self-respect. I've only just found it out, it's true, but it's there all right. I don't want to be a prince—take it from me, it's a much overrated profession—but if I've got to be one, I'll specialize. I won't combine it with being a bunco steerer on the side. As long as I am on the throne, this high-toned crap-shooting will continue a back number."

"What say?" said the walrus.

"I said that, while I am on the throne here, people who feel it necessary to chant 'Come, little seven!' must do it elsewhere."

"I don't understand you," said Mr. Pugh. "Your remarks are absolutely unintelligible."

"Never mind. My actions speak for themselves. It doesn't matter how I describe it—what it comes to is that the Casino is closed. You can follow that? Mervo is no longer running wide open. The lid is on."

"Then let me tell you, sir—" Mr. Pugh brought a bony fist down with a thump on the table—"that you are playing with fire. Understand me, sir, we are not here to threaten. We are a peaceful deputation of visitors. But I have observed your people, sir. I have watched them narrowly. And let me tell you that you are walking on a volcano. Already there are signs of grave discontent."

"Already!" cried John. "Already's good. I guess they call it going some in this infernal country if they can keep awake long enough to take action within a year after a thing has happened. I don't know if you have any influence with the populace, Mr. Pugh—you seem a pretty warm and important sort of person—but, if you have, do please ask them as a favor to me to get a move on. It's no good saying that I'm walking on a volcano. I'm from Missouri. I want to be shown. Let's see this volcano. Bring it out and make it trot around."

"You may jest—"

"Who's jesting? I'm not. It's a mighty serious thing for me. I want to get away. The only thing that's keeping me in this forsaken place is this delay. These people are obviously going to fire me sooner or later. Why on earth can't they do it at once?"

"What say?" said the walrus.

"You may well ask, Colonel," said Mr. Pugh, staring amazed at John._"His Highness appears completely to have lost his senses."

The walrus looked at John as if expecting some demonstration of practical insanity, but, finding him outwardly calm, closed his eyes and nodded heavily again.

"I must say, don't you know," said Mr. Archer-Cleeve, "it beats me, what?"

The entire deputation seemed to consider that John's last speech needed footnotes.

John was in no mood to supply them. His patience was exhausted.

"I guess we'll call this conference finished," he said. "You've been told all you came to find out,—my reason for closing the Casino. If it doesn't strike you as a satisfactory reason, that's up to you. Do what you like about it. The one thing you may take as a solid fact—and you can spread it around the town as much as ever you please—is that it is closed, and is not going to be reopened while I'm ruler here."

The deputation then withdrew, reluctantly.

* * * * *

On the following morning there came a note from Mr. Scobell. It was brief. "Come on down before the shooting begins," it ran. John tore it up.

It was on the same evening that definite hostilities may be said to have begun.

Between the Palace and the market-place there was a narrow street of flagged stone, which was busy during the early part of the day but deserted after sundown. Along this street, at about seven o'clock, John was strolling with a cigarette, when he was aware of a man crouching, with his back toward him. So absorbed was the man in something which he was writing on the stones that he did not hear John's approach, and the latter, coming up from behind was enabled to see over his shoulder. In large letters of chalk he read the words: *"Conspuez le Prince."*

John's knowledge of French was not profound, but he could understand this, and it annoyed him.

As he looked, the man, squatting on his heels, bent forward to touch up one of the letters. If he had been deliberately posing, he could not have assumed a more convenient attitude.

John had been a footballer before he was a prince. The temptation was too much for him. He drew back his foot—

There was a howl and a thud, and John resumed his stroll. The first gun from Fort Sumter had been fired.

* * * * *

Early next morning a window at the rear of the palace was broken by a stone, and toward noon one of the soldiers on guard in front of the Casino was narrowly missed by an anonymous orange. For Mervo this was practically equivalent to the attack on the Bastille, and John, when the report of the atrocities was brought to him, became hopeful.

But the effort seemed temporarily to have exhausted the fury of the mob. The rest of that day and the whole of the next passed without sensation.

After breakfast on the following morning Mr. Crump paid a visit to the Palace. John was glad to see him. The staff of the Palace were loyal, but considered as cheery companions, they were handicapped by the fact that they spoke no English, while John spoke no French.

Mr. Crump was the bearer of another note from Mr. Scobell. This time John tore it up unread, and, turning to the secretary, invited him to sit down and make himself at home.

Sipping a cocktail and smoking one of John's cigars, Mr. Crump became confidential.

"This is a queer business," he said. "Old Ben is chewing pieces out of the furniture up there. He's mad clean through. He's losing money all the while the people are making up their minds about this thing, and it beats him why they're so slow."

"It beats me, too. I don't believe these hook-worm victims ever turned my father out. Or, if they did, somebody must have injected radium into them first. I'll give them another couple of days, and, if they haven't fixed it by then, I'll go, and leave them to do what they like about it."

"Go! Do you want to go?"

"Of course I want to go! Do you think I like stringing along in this musical comedy island? I'm crazy to get back to America. I don't blame you, Crump, because it was not your fault, but, by George! if I had known what you were letting me in for when you carried me off here, I'd have called up the police reserves. Hello! What's this?"

He rose to his feet as the sound of agitated voices came from the other_side of the door. The next moment it flew open, revealing General_Poineau and an assorted group of footmen and other domestics._Excitement seemed to be in the air.

General Poineau rushed forward into the room, and flung his arms above his head. Then he dropped them to his side, and shrugged his shoulders, finishing in an attitude reminiscent of Plate 6 ("Despair") in "The Home Reciter."

"*Mon Prince!*" he moaned.

A perfect avalanche of French burst from the group outside the door.

"Crump!" cried John. "Stand by me, Crump! Get busy! This is where you make your big play. Never mind the chorus gentlemen in the passage. Concentrate yourself on Poineau. What's he talking about? I believe he's come to tell me the people have wakened up. Offer him a cocktail. What's the French for corpse-reviver? Get busy, Crump."

The general had begun to speak rapidly, with a wealth of gestures. It astonished John that Mr. Crump could follow the harangue as apparently he did.

"Well?" said John.

Mr. Crump looked grave.

"He says there is a large mob in the market-place. They are talking—"

"They would be!"

"—of moving in force on the Palace. The Palace Guards have gone over to the people. General Poineau urges you to disguise yourself and escape while there is time. You will be safe at his villa till the excitement subsides, when you can be smuggled over to France during the night—"

"Not for mine," said John, shaking his head. "It's mighty good of you, General, and I appreciate it, but I can't wait till night. The boat leaves for Marseilles in another hour. I'll catch that. I can manage it comfortably. I'll go up and pack my grip. Crump, entertain the General while I'm gone, will you? I won't be a moment."

But as he left the room there came through the open window the mutter of a crowd. He stopped. General Poineau whipped out his sword, and brought it to the salute. John patted him on the shoulder.

"You're a sport, General," he said, "but we sha'n't want it. Come along, Crump. Come and help me address the multitude."

The window of the room looked out on to a square. There was a small balcony with a stone parapet. As John stepped out, a howl of rage burst from the mob.

John walked on to the balcony, and stood looking down on them, resting his arms on the parapet. The howl was repeated, and from somewhere at the back of the crowd came the sharp crack of a rifle, and a shot, the first and last of the campaign, clipped a strip of flannel from the collar of his coat and splashed against the wall.

A broad smile spread over his face.

If he had studied for a year, he could not have hit on a swifter or more effective method of quieting the mob. There was something so engaging and friendly in his smile that the howling died away and fists that has been shaken unclenched themselves and fell. There was an expectant silence in the square.

John beckoned to Crump, who came on to the balcony with some reluctance, being mistrustful of the unseen sportsman with the rifle.

"Tell 'em it's all right, Crump, and that there's no call for any fuss._From their manner I gather that I am no longer needed on this throne._Ask them if that's right?"

A small man, who appeared to be in command of the crowd, stepped forward as the secretary finished speaking, and shouted some words which drew a murmur of approval from his followers.

"He wants to know," interpreted Mr. Crump, "if you will allow the_Casino to open again."

"Tell him no, but add that I shall be tickled to death to abdicate, if that's what they want. Speed them up, old man. Tell them to make up their minds on the jump, because I want to catch that boat. Don't let them get to discussing it, or they'll stand there talking till sunset. Yes or no. That's the idea."

There was a moment's surprised silence when Mr. Crump had spoken. The Mervian mind was unused to being hustled in this way. Then a voice shouted, as it were tentatively, "*Vive la Republique!*" and at once the cry was taken up on all sides.

John beamed down on them.

"That's right," he said. "Bully! I knew you could get a move on as quick as anyone else, if you gave your minds to it. This is what I call something like a revolution. It's a model to every country in the world. But I guess we must close down the entertainment now, or I shall be missing the boat. Will you tell them, Crump, that any citizen who cares for a drink and a cigar will find it in the Palace. Tell the household staff to stand by to pull corks. It's dry work revolutionizing. And now I really must be going. I've run it mighty fine. Slip one of these fellows down there half a dollar and send him to fetch a cab. I must step lively."

* * * * *

Five minutes later the revolutionists, obviously embarrassed and ill at ease, were sheepishly gulping down their refreshment beneath the stony eye of the majordomo and his assistants, while upstairs in the state bedroom the deposed Prince was whistling "Dixie" and packing the royal pajamas into a suitcase.

CHAPTER X
MRS. OAKLEY

Betty, when she stepped on board the boat for Marseilles, had had no definite plan of action. She had been caught up and swept away by an over-mastering desire for escape that left no room in her mind for thoughts of the morrow. It was not till the train was roaring its way across southern France that she found herself sufficiently composed to review her position and make plans.

She would not go back. She could not. The words she had used in her letter to Mr. Scobell were no melodramatic rhetoric. They were a plain and literal statement of the truth. Death would be infinitely preferable to life at Mervo on her stepfather's conditions.

But, that settled, what then? What was she to do? The gods are businesslike. They sell; they do not give. And for what they sell they demand a heavy price. We may buy life of them in many ways: with our honor, our health, our independence, our happiness, with our brains or with our hands. But somehow or other, in whatever currency we may choose to pay it, the price must be paid.

Betty faced the problem. What had she? What could she give? Her independence? That, certainly. She saw now what a mockery that fancied independence had been. She had come and gone as she pleased, her path smoothed by her stepfather's money, and she had been accustomed to consider herself free. She had learned wisdom now, and could understand that it was only by sacrificing such artificial independence that she could win through to freedom. The world was a market, and the only independent people in it were those who had a market value.

What was her market value? What could she do? She looked back at her life, and saw that she had dabbled. She had a little of most things—enough of nothing. She could sketch a little, play a little, sing a little, write a little. Also—and, as she remembered it, she felt for the first time a tremor of hope—she could use a typewriter reasonably well. That one accomplishment stood out in the welter of her thoughts, solid and comforting, like a rock in a quicksand. It was something definite, something marketable, something of value for which persons paid.

The tremor of hope did not comfort her long. Her mood was critical, and she saw that in this, her one accomplishment, she was, as in everything else, an amateur. She could not compete against professionals. She closed her eyes, and had a momentary vision of those professionals, keen of face, leathern of finger, rattling out myriads of words at a dizzy speed. And, at that, all her courage suddenly broke; she drooped forlornly, and, hiding her face on the cushioned arm-rest, she began to cry.

Tears are the Turkish bath of the soul. Nature never intended woman to pass dry-eyed through crises of emotion. A casual stranger, meeting Betty on her way to the boat, might have thought that she looked a little worried,—nothing more. The same stranger, if he had happened to enter the compartment at this juncture, would have set her down at sight as broken-hearted beyond recovery. Yet such is the magic of tears that it was at this very moment that Betty was beginning to be conscious of a distinct change for the better. Her heart still ached, and to think of John even for an instant was to feel the knife turning in the wound, but her brain was clear; the panic fear had gone, and she faced the future resolutely once more. For she had just remembered the existence of Mrs. Oakley.

* * * * *

Only once in her life had Betty met her stepfather's celebrated aunt, and the meeting had taken place nearly twelve years ago. The figure that remained in her memory was of a pale-eyed, grenadier-like old lady, almost entirely surrounded by clocks. It was these clocks that had impressed her most. She was too young to be awed by the knowledge that the tall old woman who stared at her just like a sandy cat she had once possessed was one of the three richest women in the whole wide world. She only remembered thinking that the finger which emerged from the plaid shawl and prodded her cheek was unpleasantly bony. But the clocks had absorbed her. It was as if all the clocks in the world had been gathered together into that one room. There had been big clocks, with almost human faces; small, perky clocks; clocks of strange shape; and one dingy, medium-sized clock in particular which had made her cry out with delight. Her visit had chanced to begin shortly before eleven in the morning, and she had not been in the room ten minutes before there was a whirring, and the majority of the clocks began to announce the hour, each after its own fashion—some with a slow bloom, some with a rapid, bell-like sound. But the medium-sized clock, unexpectedly belying its appearance of being nothing of particular importance, had performed its task in a way quite distinct from the others. It had suddenly produced from its interior a shabby little gold man with a trumpet, who had blown eleven little blasts before sliding backward into his house and shutting the door after him. Betty had waited in rapt silence till he finished, and had then shouted eagerly for more.

Just as the beginner at golf may effect a drive surpassing that of the expert, so may a child unconsciously eclipse the practised courtier. There was no soft side to Mrs. Oakley's character, as thousands of suave would-be borrowers had discovered in their time, but there was a soft spot. To general praise of her collection of clocks she was impervious; it was unique, and she did not require you to tell her so, but exhibit admiration for the clock with the little trumpeter, and she melted. It was the one oasis of sentiment in the Sahara of her mental outlook, the grain of radium in the pitchblende. Years ago it had stood in a little New England farmhouse, and a child had clapped her hands and shouted, even as Betty had done, when the golden man slid from his hiding-place. Much water had flowed beneath the bridge since those days. Many things had happened to the child. But she still kept her old love for the trumpeter. The world knew nothing of this. The world, if it had known, would have been delighted to stand before the clock and admire it volubly, by the day. But it had no inkling of the trumpeter's importance, and, when it came to visit Mrs. Oakley, was apt to waste its time showering compliments on the obvious beauties of the queens of the collection.

But Betty, ignoring these, jumped up and down before the dingy clock, demanding further trumpetings, and, turning to Mrs. Oakley, as one possessing influence, she was aware of a curious, intent look in the old lady's eyes.

"Do you like that clock, my dear?" said Mrs. Oakley.

"Yes! Oh, yes!"

"Perhaps you shall have it some day, honey."

Betty was probably the only person who had been admitted to that room who would not, on the strength of this remark, have steered the conversation gently to the subject of a small loan. Instead, she ran to the old lady, and kissed her. And, as to what had happened after that, memory was vague. There had been some talk, she remembered, of a dollar to buy candy, but it had come to nothing, and now that she had grown older and had read the frequent paragraphs and anecdotes that appeared in the papers about her stepfather's aunt, she could understand why. She knew now what everybody knew of Mrs. Oakley—her history, her eccentricities, and the miserliness of which the papers spoke with a satirical lightness that seemed somehow but a thin disguise for what was almost admiration.

Mrs. Oakley was one of two children, a son and a daughter, of a Vermont farmer. Of her early life no records remain. Her public history begins when she was twenty-two and came to New York. After two years' struggling, she found a position in the firm of one Redgrave. Those who knew her then speak of her as a tall, handsome girl, hard and intensely ambitious. From contemporary accounts she seems to have out-Nietzsched Nietzsche. Nietzsche's vision stopped short at the superman. Jane Scobell was a superwoman. She had all the titanic selfishness and indifference to the comfort of others which marks the superman, and, in addition, undeniable good looks and a knowledge of the weaknesses of men. Poor Mr. Redgrave had not had a chance from the start. She married him within a year. Two years later, catching the bulls in an unguarded moment, Mr. Redgrave despoiled them of a trifle over three million dollars, and died the same day of an apoplectic stroke caused by the excitement of victory. His widow, after a tour in Europe, returned to the United States and visited Pittsburg. Any sociologist will support the statement that it is difficult, almost impossible, for an attractive widow, visiting Pittsburg, not to marry a millionaire, even if she is not particularly anxious to do so. If such an act is the primary object of her visit, the thing becomes a certainty. Groping through the smoke, Jane Redgrave seized and carried off no less a quarry than Alexander Baynes Oakley, a widower, whose income was one of the seven wonders of the world. In the fullness of time he, too, died, and Jane Oakley was left with the sole control of two vast fortunes.

She did not marry again, though it was rumored that it took three secretaries, working nine hours a day, to cope with the written proposals, and that butler after butler contracted clergyman's sore throat through denying admittance to amorous callers. In the ten years after Alexander Baynes' death, every impecunious aristocrat in the civilized world must have made his dash for the matrimonial pole. But her pale eyes looked them over, and dismissed them.

During those early years she was tempted once or twice to speculation. A failure in a cotton deal not only cured her of this taste, but seems to have marked the point in her career when her thoughts began to turn to parsimony. Until then she had lived in some state, but now, gradually at first, then swiftly, she began to cut down her expenses. Now we find her in an apartment in West Central Park, next in a Washington Square hotel, then in a Harlem flat, and finally—her last, fixed abiding-place—in a small cottage on Staten Island.

It was a curious life that she led, this woman who could have bought kingdoms if she had willed it. A Swedish maid-of-all-work was her only companion. By day she would walk in her little garden, or dust, arrange and wind up her clocks. At night, she would knit, or read one of the frequent reports that arrived at the cottage from charity workers on the East Side. Those were her two hobbies, and her only extravagances—clocks and charity.

Her charity had its limitations. In actual money she expended little. She was a theoretical philanthropist. She lent her influence, her time, and her advice, but seldom her bank balance. Arrange an entertainment for the delectation of the poor, and you would find her on the platform, but her name would not be on the list of subscribers to the funds. She would deliver a lecture on thrift to an audience of factory girls, and she would give them a practical example of what she preached.

Yet, with all its limitations, her charity was partly genuine. Her mind was like a country in the grip of civil war. One-half of her sincerely pitied the poor, burned at any story of oppression, and cried "Give!" but the other cried "Halt!" and held her back, and between the two she fell.

* * * * *

It was to this somewhat unpromising haven of refuge that Betty's mind now turned in her trouble. She did not expect great things. She could not have said exactly what she did expect. But, at least, the cottage on Staten Island offered a resting-place on her journey, even if it could not be the journey's end. Her mad dash from Mervo ceased to be objectless. It led somewhere.

CHAPTER XI
A LETTER OF INTRODUCTION

New York, revisited, had much the same effect on Betty as it had had on John during his first morning of independence. As the liner came up the bay, and the great buildings stood out against the clear blue of the sky, she felt afraid and lonely. That terror which is said to attack immigrants on their first sight of the New York sky-line came to her, as she leaned on the rail, and with it a feeling of utter misery. By a continual effort during the voyage she had kept her thoughts from turning to John, but now he rose up insistently before her, and she realized all that had gone out of her life.

She rebelled against the mad cruelty of the fate which had brought them together again. It seemed to her now that she must always have loved him, but it had been such a vague, gentle thing, this love, before that last meeting—hardly more than a pleasant accompaniment to her life, something to think about in idle moments, a help and a support when things were running crosswise. She had been so satisfied with it, so content to keep him a mere memory. It seemed so needless and wanton to destroy her illusion.

Of love as a wild-beast passion, tearing and torturing quite ordinary persons like herself, she had always been a little sceptical. The great love poems of the world, when she read them, had always left her with the feeling that their authors were of different clay from herself and had no common meeting ground with her. She had seen her friends fall in love, as they called it, and it had been very pretty and charming, but as far removed from the frenzies of the poets as an amateur's snapshot of Niagara from the cataract itself. Elsa Keith, for instance, was obviously very fond and proud of Marvin, but she seemed perfectly placid about it. She loved, but she could still spare half an hour for the discussion of a new frock. Her soul did not appear to have been revolutionized in any way.

Gradually Betty had come to the conclusion that love, in the full sense of the word, was one of the things that did not happen. And now, as if to punish her presumption, it had leaped from hiding and seized her.

There was nothing exaggerated or unintelligible in the poets now. They ceased to be inhabitants of another world, swayed by curiously complex emotions. They were her brothers—ordinary men with ordinary feelings and a strange gift for expressing them. She knew now that it was possible to hate the man you loved and to love the man you hated, to ache for the sight of someone even while you fled from him.

It did not take her long to pass the Customs. A small grip constituted her entire baggage. Having left this in the keeping of the amiable proprietor of a near-by delicatessen store, she made her way to the ferry.

Her first enquiry brought her to the cottage. Mrs. Oakley was a celebrity on

Staten Island.

At the door she paused for a moment, then knocked.

The Swede servant, she who had been there at her former visit, twelve years ago, received her stolidly. Mrs. Oakley was dusting her clocks.

"Ask her if she can see me," said Betty. "I'm—" great step-niece sounded too ridiculous—"I'm her niece," she said.

The handmaid went and returned, stolid as ever. "Ay tal her vat yu say about niece, and she say she not knowing any niece," she announced.

Betty amended the description, and presently the Swede returned once more, and motioned her to enter.

Like so many scenes of childhood, the room of the clocks was sharply stamped on Betty's memory, and, as she came into it now, it seemed to her that nothing had changed. There were the clocks, all round the walls, of every shape and size, the big clocks with the human faces and the small, perky clocks. There was the dingy, medium-sized clock that held the trumpeter. And there, looking at her with just the old sandy-cat expression in her pale eyes, was Mrs. Oakley.

Even the possession of an income of eighteen million dollars and a unique collection of clocks cannot place a woman above the making of the obvious remark.

"How you have grown!" said Mrs. Oakley.

The words seemed to melt the chill that had gathered around Betty's heart. She had been prepared to enter into long explanations, and the knowledge that these would not be required was very comforting.

"Do you remember me?" she exclaimed.

"You are the little girl who clapped her hands at the trumpeter, but you are not little now."

"I'm not so very big," said Betty, smiling. She felt curiously at home, and pity for the loneliness of this strange old woman caused her to forget her own troubles.

"You look pretty when you smile," said Mrs. Oakley thoughtfully. She continued to look closely at her. "You are in trouble," she said.

Betty met her eyes frankly.

"Yes," she said.

The old woman bent her head over a Sevres china clock, and stroked it tenderly with her feather duster.

"Why did you run away?" she asked without looking up.

Betty had a feeling that the ground was being cut from beneath her feet. She had expected to have to explain who she was and why she had come, and behold, both were unnecessary. It was uncanny. And then the obvious explanation occurred to her.

"Did my stepfather cable?" she asked.

Mrs. Oakley laid down the feather duster and, opening a drawer, produced some sheets of paper—to the initiated eye plainly one of Mr. Scobell's lengthy messages.

"A wickedly extravagant cable," she said, frowning at it. "He could have expressed himself perfectly well at a quarter of the expense."

Betty began to read. The dimple on her chin appeared for a moment as she did so. The tone of the message was so obsequious. There was no trace of the old peremptory note in it. The words "dearest aunt" occurred no fewer than six times in the course of the essay, its author being apparently reckless of the fact that it was costing him half a dollar a time. Mrs. Oakley had been quite right in her criticism. The gist of the cable was, "*Betty has run away to America dearest aunt ridiculous is sure to visit you please dearest aunt do not encourage her.*" The rest was pure padding.

Mrs. Oakley watched her with a glowering eye. "If Bennie Scobell," she soliloquized, "imagines that he can dictate to me—" She ceased, leaving an impressive hiatus. Unhappy Mr. Scobell, convicted of dictation even after three dollars' worth of "dearest aunt!"

Betty handed back the cable. Her chin, emblem of war, was tilted and advanced.

"I'll tell you why I ran away, Aunt," she said.

Mrs. Oakley listened to her story in silence. Betty did not relate it at great length, for with every word she spoke, the thought of John stabbed her afresh. She omitted much that has been told in this chronicle. But she disclosed the essential fact, that Napoleonic Mr. Scobell had tried to force her into a marriage with a man she did not—she hesitated at the word—did not respect, she concluded.

Mrs. Oakley regarded her inscrutably for a while before replying.

"Respect!" she said at last. "I have never met a man in my life whom I could respect. Harpies! Every one of them! Every one of them! Every one of them!"

She was muttering to herself. It is possible that her thoughts were back with those persevering young aristocrats of her second widowhood. Certainly, if she had sometimes displayed a touch of the pirate in her dealings with man, man, it must be said in fairness, had not always shown his best side to her.

"Respect!" she muttered again. "Did you like him, this Prince of yours?"

Betty's eyes filled. She made no reply.

"Well, never mind," said Mrs. Oakley. "Don't cry, child! I'm not going to press you. You must have hated him or else loved him very much, or you would never have run away…. Dictate to me!" she broke off, half-aloud, her mind evidently once more on Mr. Scobell's unfortunate cable.

Betty could bear it no longer.

"I loved him!" she cried. "I loved him!"

She was shaking with dry sobs. She felt the old woman's eyes upon her, but she could not stop.

A sudden whirr cut through the silence. One of the large clocks near the door was beginning to strike the hour. Instantly the rest began to do the same, till the room was full of the noise. And above the din there sounded sharp and clear the note of the little trumpet.

The noise died away with metallic echoings.

"Honey!"

It was a changed voice that spoke. Betty looked up, and saw that the eyes that met hers were very soft. She moved quickly to the old woman's side.

"Honey, I'm going to tell you something about myself that nobody dreams of. Betty, when I was your age, *I* ran away from a man because I loved him. It was just a little village tragedy, my dear. I think he was fond of me, but father was poor and her folks were the great people of the place, and he married her. And I ran away, like you, and went to New York."

Betty pressed her hand. It was trembling.

"I'm so sorry," she whispered.

"I went to New York because I wanted to kill my heart. And I killed it. There's only one way. Work! Work! Work!" She was sitting bolt upright, and the soft look had gone out of her eyes. They were hard and fiery under the drawn brows. "Work! Ah, I worked! I never rested. For two years. Two whole years. It fought back at me. It tore me to bits. But I wouldn't stop. I worked on, I killed it."

She stopped, quivering. Betty was cold with a nameless dismay. She felt as if she were standing in the dark on the brink of an abyss.

The old woman began to speak again.

"Child, it's the same with you. Your heart's tearing you. Don't let it!_It will get worse and worse if you are afraid of it. Fight it! Kill it!_Work!"

She stopped again, clenching and unclenching her fingers, as if she were strangling some living thing. There was silence for a long moment.

"What can you do?" she asked suddenly.

Her voice was calm and unemotional again. The abruptness of the transition from passion to the practical took Betty aback. She could not speak.

"There must be something," continued Mrs. Oakley. "When I was your age I had taught myself bookkeeping, shorthand, and typewriting. What can you do? Can you use a typewriter?"

Blessed word!

"Yes," said Betty promptly.

"Well?"

"Not very well?"

"H'm. Well, I expect you will do it well enough for Mr. Renshaw—on my recommendation. I'll give you a letter to him. He is the editor of a small weekly paper. I don't know how much he will offer you, but take it and *work!* You'll find him pleasant. I have met him at charity organization meetings on the East Side. He's useful at the entertainments—does conjuring tricks—stupid, but they seem to amuse people. You'll find him pleasant. There."

She had been writing the letter of introduction during the course of these remarks. At the last word she blotted it, and placed it in an envelope.

"That's the address," she said. "J. Brabazon Renshaw, Office of *Peaceful Moments*. Take it to him now. Good-by."

It was as if she were ashamed of her late display of emotion. She spoke abruptly, and her pale eyes were expressionless. Betty thanked her and turned to go.

"Tell me how you get on," said Mrs. Oakley.

"Yes," said Betty.

"And *work*. Keep on working!"

There was a momentary return of her former manner as she spoke the words, and Betty wavered. She longed to say something comforting, something that would show that she understood.

Mrs. Oakley had taken up the feather duster again.

"Steena will show you out," she said curtly. And Betty was aware of the stolid Swede in the doorway. The interview was plainly at an end.

"Good-by, Aunt," she said, "and thank you ever so much—for everything."

CHAPTER XII
"PEACEFUL MOMENTS"

The man in the street did not appear to know it, but a great crisis was imminent in New York journalism.

Everything seemed much as usual in the city. The cars ran blithely on Broadway. Newsboys shouted their mystic slogan, "Wuxtry!" with undiminished vim. Society thronged Fifth Avenue without a furrow on its brow. At a thousand street corners a thousand policemen preserved their air of massive superiority to the things of this world. Of all the four million not one showed the least sign of perturbation.

Nevertheless, the crisis was at hand. Mr. J. Brabazon Renshaw, Editor-in-chief of *Peaceful Moments*, was about to leave his post and start on a three-months' vacation.

Peaceful Moments, as its name (an inspiration of Mr. Renshaw's own) was designed to imply, was a journal of the home. It was the sort of paper which the father of the family is expected to take back with him from the office and read aloud to the chicks before bedtime under the shade of the rubber plant.

Circumstances had left the development of the paper almost entirely to Mr. Renshaw. Its contents were varied. There was a "Moments in the Nursery" page, conducted by Luella Granville Waterman and devoted mainly to anecdotes of the family canary, by Jane (aged six), and similar works of the younger set. There was a "Moments of Meditation" page, conducted by the Reverend Edwin T. Philpotts; a "Moments among the Masters" page, consisting of assorted chunks looted from the literature of the past, when foreheads were bulged and thoughts profound, by Mr. Renshaw himself; one or two other special pages; a short story; answers to correspondents on domestic matters; and a "Moments of Mirth" page, conducted by one B. Henderson Asher—a very painful affair.

The proprietor of this admirable journal was that Napoleon of finance, Mr. Benjamin Scobell.

That this should have been so is but one proof of the many-sidedness of that great man.

Mr. Scobell had founded *Peaceful Moments* at an early stage in his career, and it was only at very rare intervals nowadays that he recollected that he still owned it. He had so many irons in the fire now that he had no time to waste his brain tissues thinking about a paper like *Peaceful Moments*. It was one of his failures. It certainly paid its way and brought him a small sum each year, but to him it was a failure, a bombshell that had fizzled.

He had intended to do big things with *Peaceful Moments*. He had meant to start a new epoch in the literature of Manhattan.

"I gottan idea," he had said to Miss Scobell. "All this yellow journalism—red blood and all that—folks are tired of it. They want something milder. Wholesome, see what I mean? There's money in it. Guys make a roll too big to lift by selling soft drinks, don't they? Well, I'm going to run a soft-drink paper. See?"

The enterprise had started well. To begin with, he had found the ideal editor. He had met Mr. Renshaw at a down-East gathering presided over by Mrs. Oakley, and his Napoleonic eye had seen in J. Brabazon the seeds of domestic greatness. Before they parted, he had come to terms with him. Nor had the latter failed to justify his intuition. He made an admirable editor. It was not Mr. Renshaw's fault that the new paper had failed to electrify America. It was the public on whom the responsibility for the failure must be laid. They spoiled the whole thing. Certain of the faithful subscribed, it is true, and continued to subscribe, but the great heart of the public remained untouched. The great heart of the public declined to be interested in the meditations of Mr. Philpotts and the humor of Mr. B. Henderson Asher, and continued to spend its money along the bad old channels. The thing began to bore Mr. Scobell. He left the conduct of the journal more and more to Mr. Renshaw, until finally—it was just after the idea for extracting gold from sea water had struck him—he put the whole business definitely out of his mind. (His actual words were that he never wanted to see or hear of the darned thing again, inasmuch as it gave him a pain in the neck.) Mr. Renshaw was given a free hand as to the editing, and all matters of finance connected with the enterprise were placed in the hands of Mr. Scobell's solicitors, who had instructions to sell the journal, if, as its owner crisply put it, they could find any chump who was enough of a darned chump to give real money for it. Up to the present the great army of chumps had fallen short of this ideal standard of darned chumphood.

Ever since this parting of the ways, Mr. Renshaw had been in his element. Under his guidance *Peaceful Moments* had reached a level of domesticity which made other so-called domestic journals look like sporting supplements. But at last the work had told upon him. Whether it was the effort of digging into the literature of the past every week, or the strain of reading B. Henderson Asher's "Moments of Mirth" is uncertain. At any rate, his labors had ended in wrecking his health to such an extent that the doctor had ordered him three months' complete rest, in the woods or mountains, whichever he preferred; and, being a farseeing man, who went to the root of things, had absolutely declined to consent to Mr. Renshaw's suggestion that he keep in touch with the paper during his vacation. He was adamant. He had seen copies of *Peaceful Moments* once or twice, and refused to permit a man in Mr. Renshaw's state of health to come in contact with Luella Granville Waterman's "Moments in the Nursery" and B. Henderson Asher's "Moments of Mirth."

"You must forget that such a paper exists," he said. "You must dismiss the whole thing from your mind, live in the open, and develop some flesh and muscle."

Mr. Renshaw had bowed before the sentence, howbeit gloomily, and now, on the morning of Betty's departure from Mrs. Oakley's house with the letter of introduction, was giving his final instructions to his temporary successor.

This temporary successor in the editorship was none other than John's friend, Rupert Smith, late of the *News*.

Smith, on leaving Harvard, had been attracted by newspaper work, and had found his first billet on a Western journal of the type whose society column consists of such items as "Jim Thompson was to town yesterday with a bunch of other cheap skates. We take this opportunity of once more informing Jim that he is a liar and a skunk," and whose editor works with a pistol on his desk and another in his hip-pocket. Graduating from this, he had proceeded to a reporter's post on a daily paper in Kentucky, where there were blood feuds and other Southern devices for preventing life from becoming dull. All this was good, but even while he enjoyed these experiences, New York, the magnet, had been tugging at him, and at last, after two eventful years on the Kentucky paper, he had come East, and eventually won through to the staff of the *News*.

His presence in the office of *Peaceful Moments* was due to the uncomfortable habit of most of the New York daily papers of cutting down their staff of reporters during the summer. The dismissed had, to sustain them, the knowledge that they would return, like the swallows, anon, and be received back into their old places; but in the meantime they suffered the inconvenience of having to support themselves as best they could. Smith, when, in the company of half-a-dozen others, he had had to leave the *News*, had heard of the vacant post of assistant editor on *Peaceful Moments*, and had applied for and received it. Whereby he was more fortunate than some of his late colleagues; though, as the character of his new work unrolled itself before him, he was frequently doubtful on that point. For the atmosphere of *Peaceful Moments*, however wholesome, was certainly not exciting, and his happened to be essentially a nature that needed the stimulus of excitement. Even in Park Row, the denizens of which street are rarely slaves to the conventional and safe, he had a well-established reputation in this matter. Others of his acquaintances welcomed excitement when it came to them in the course of the day's work, but it was Smith's practise to go in search of it. He was a young man of spirit and resource.

His appearance, to those who did not know him, hardly suggested this. He was very tall and thin, with a dark, solemn face. He was a purist in the matter of clothes, and even in times of storm and stress presented an immaculate appearance to the world. In his left eye, attached to a cord, he wore a monocle.

Through this, at the present moment, he was gazing benevolently at Mr. Renshaw, as the latter fussed about the office in the throes of departure. To the editor's rapid fire of advice and warning he listened with the pleased and indulgent air of a father whose infant son frisks before him. Mr. Renshaw interested him. To Smith's mind Mr. Renshaw, put him in any show you pleased, would alone have been worth the price of admission.

"Well," chirruped the holiday-maker—he was a little man with a long neck, and he always chirruped—"Well, I think that is all, Mr. Smith. Oh, ah, yes! The stenographer. You will need a new stenographer."

The *Peaceful Moments* stenographer had resigned her position three days before, in order to get married.

"Unquestionably, Comrade Renshaw," said Smith. "A blonde."

Mr. Renshaw looked annoyed.

"I have told you before, Mr. Smith, I object to your addressing me as_Comrade. It is not—it is not—er—fitting."

Smith waved a deprecating hand.

"Say no more," he said. "I will correct the habit. I have been studying the principles of Socialism somewhat deeply of late, and I came to the conclusion that I must join the cause. It looked good to me. You work for the equal distribution of property, and start in by swiping all you can and sitting on it. A noble scheme. Me for it. But I am interrupting you."

Mr. Renshaw had to pause for a moment to reorganize his ideas.

"I think—ah, yes. I think it would be best perhaps to wait for a day or two in case Mrs. Oakley should recommend someone. I mentioned the vacancy in the office to her, and she said she would give the matter her attention. I should prefer, if possible, to give the place to her nominee. She—"

"—has eighteen million a year," said Smith. "I understand. Scatter seeds of kindness."

Mr. Renshaw looked at him sharply. Smith's face was solemn and thoughtful.

"Nothing of the kind," the editor said, after a pause. "I should prefer Mrs. Oakley's nominee because Mrs. Oakley is a shrewd, practical woman who—er—who—who, in fact—"

"Just so," said Smith, eying him gravely through the monocle._"Entirely."

The scrutiny irritated Mr. Renshaw.

"Do put that thing away, Mr. Smith," he said.

"That thing?"

"Yes, that ridiculous glass. Put it away."

"Instantly," said Smith, replacing the monocle in his vest-pocket. "You object to it? Well, well, many people do. We all have these curious likes and dislikes. It is these clashings of personal taste which constitute what we call life. Yes. You were saying?"

Mr. Renshaw wrinkled his forehead.

"I have forgotten what I intended to say," he said querulously. "You have driven it out of my head."

Smith clicked his tongue sympathetically. Mr. Renshaw looked at his watch.

"Dear me," he said, "I must be going. I shall miss my train. But I think I have covered the ground quite thoroughly. You understand everything?"

"Absolutely," said Smith. "I look on myself as some engineer controlling a machine with a light hand on the throttle. Or like some faithful hound whose master—"

"Ah! There is just one thing. Mrs. Julia Burdett Parslow is a little inclined to be unpunctual with her 'Moments with Budding Girlhood.' If this should happen while I am away, just write her a letter, quite a pleasant letter, you understand, pointing out the necessity of being in good time. She must realize that we are a machine."

"Exactly," murmured Smith.

"The machinery of the paper cannot run smoothly unless contributors are in good time with their copy."

"Precisely," said Smith. "They are the janitors of the literary world._Let them turn off the steam heat, and where are we? If Mrs. Julia_Burdett Parslow is not up to time with the hot air, how shall our_'Girlhood' escape being nipped in the bud?"

"And there is just one other thing. I wish you would correct a slight tendency I have noticed lately in Mr. Asher to be just a trifle—well, not precisely risky, but perhaps a shade broad in his humor."

"Young blood!" sighed Smith. "Young blood!"

"Mr. Asher is a very sensible man, and he will understand. Well, that is all, I think. Now, I really must be going. Good-by, Mr. Smith."

"Good-by."

At the door Mr. Renshaw paused with the air of an exile bidding farewell to his native land, sighed and trotted out.

Smith put his feet upon the table, flicked a speck of dust from his coat-sleeve, and resumed his task of reading the proofs of Luella Granville Waterman's "Moments in the Nursery."

* * * * *

He had not been working long, when Pugsy Maloney, the office boy, entered.

"Say!" said Pugsy.

"Say on, Comrade Maloney."

"Dere's a loidy out dere wit a letter for Mr. Renshaw."

"Have you acquainted her with the fact that Mr. Renshaw has passed to other climes?"

"Huh?"

"Have you, in the course of your conversation with this lady, mentioned that Mr. Renshaw has beaten it?"

"Sure, I did. And she says can she see you?"

Smith removed his feet from the table.

"Certainly," he said. "Who am I that I should deny people these little treats? Ask her to come in, Comrade Maloney."

CHAPTER XIII

BETTY MAKES A FRIEND

Betty had appealed to Master Maloney's esthetic sense of beauty directly she appeared before him. It was with regret, therefore, rather than with the usual calm triumph of the office boy, that he informed her that the editor was not in. Also, seeing that she was evidently perturbed by the information, he had gone out of his way to suggest that she lay her business, whatever it might be, before Mr. Renshaw's temporary successor.

Smith received her with Old-World courtesy.

"Will you sit down?" he said. "Not to wait for Comrade Renshaw, of course. He will not be back for another three months. Perhaps I can help you. I am acting editor. The work is not light," he added gratuitously. "Sometimes the cry goes round New York, 'Can Smith get through it all? Will his strength support his unquenchable spirit?' But I stagger on. I do not repine. What was it that you wished to see Comrade Renshaw about?"

He swung his monocle lightly by its cord. For the first time since she had entered the office Betty was rather glad that Mr. Renshaw was away. Conscious of her defects as a stenographer she had been looking forward somewhat apprehensively to the interview with her prospective employer. But this long, solemn youth put her at her ease. His manner suggested in some indefinable way that the whole thing was a sort of round game.

"I came about the typewriting," she said.

Smith looked at her with interest.

"Are you the nominee?"

"I beg your pardon?"

"Do you come from Mrs. Oakley?"

"Yes."

"Then all is well. The decks have been cleared against your coming. Consider yourself engaged as our official typist. By the way, *can* you type?"

Betty laughed. This was certainly not the awkward interview she had been picturing in her mind.

"Yes," she said, "but I'm afraid I'm not very good at it."

"Never mind," said Smith. "I'm not very good at editing. Yet here I am. I foresee that we shall make an ideal team. Together, we will toil early and late till we whoop up this domestic journal into a shining model of what a domestic journal should be. What that is, at present, I do not exactly know. Excursion trains will be run from the Middle West to see this domestic journal. Visitors from Oshkosh will do it before going on to Grant's tomb. What exactly is your name?"

Betty hesitated. Yes, perhaps it would be better. "Brown," she said.

"Mine is Smith. The smiling child in the outer office is Pugsy Maloney, one of our most prominent citizens. Homely in appearance, perhaps, but one of us. You will get to like Comrade Maloney. And now, to touch on a painful subject—work. Would you care to start in now, or have you any other engagements? Perhaps you wish to see the sights of this beautiful little city before beginning? You would prefer to start in now? Excellent. You could not have come at a more suitable time, for I was on the very point of sallying out to purchase about twenty-five cents' worth of lunch. We editors, Comrade Brown, find that our tissues need constant restoration, such is the strenuous nature of our duties. You will find one or two letters on that table. Good-by, then, for the present."

He picked up his hat, smoothed it carefully and with a courtly inclination of his head, left the room.

Betty sat down, and began to think. So she was really earning her own living! It was a stimulating thought. She felt a little bewildered. She had imagined something so different. Mrs. Oakley had certainly said that *Peaceful Moments* was a small paper, but despite that, her imagination had conjured up visions of bustle and activity, and a peremptory, overdriven editor, snapping out words of command. Smith, with his careful speech and general air of calm detachment from the noisy side of life, created an atmosphere of restfulness. If this was a sample of life in the office, she thought, the paper had been well named. She felt soothed and almost happy.

Interesting and exciting things, New York things, began to happen at once. To her, meditating, there entered Pugsy Maloney, the guardian of the gate of this shrine of Peace, a nonchalant youth of about fifteen, with a freckled, mask-like face, the expression of which never varied, bearing in his arms a cat. The cat was struggling violently, but he appeared quite unconscious of it. Its existence did not seem to occur to him.

"Say!" said Pugsy.

Betty was fond of cats.

"Oh, don't hurt her!" she cried anxiously.

Master Maloney eyed the cat as if he were seeing it for the first time.

"I wasn't hoitin' her," he said, without emotion. "Dere was two fresh kids in the street sickin' a dawg on to her. And I comes up and says, 'G'wan! What do youse t'ink youse doin', fussin' de poor dumb animal?' An' one of de guys, he says,

'G'wan! Who do youse t'ink youse is?' An' I says, 'I'm de guy what's goin' to swat youse on de coco, smarty, if youse don't quit fussin' de poor dumb animal.' So wit' dat he makes a break at swattin' me one, but I swats him one, an' I swats de odder feller one, an' den I swats dem bote some more, an' I gits de kitty, an' I brings her in here, cos I t'inks maybe youse'll look after her. I can't be boddered myself. Cats is foolishness."

And, having finished this Homeric narrative, Master Maloney fixed an expressionless eye on the ceiling, and was silent.

"How splendid of you, Pugsy!" cried Betty. "She might have been killed, poor thing."

"She had it pretty fierce," admitted Master Maloney, gazing dispassionately at the rescued animal, which had escaped from his clutch and taken up a strong position on an upper shelf of the bookcase.

"Will you go out and get her some milk, Pugsy? She's probably starving._Here's a quarter. Will you keep the change?"

"Sure thing," assented Master Maloney.

He strolled slowly out, while Betty, mounting a chair, proceeded to chirrup and snap her fingers in the effort to establish the foundations of an *entente cordiale* with the cat.

By the time Pugsy returned, carrying a five-cent bottle of milk, the animal had vacated the shelf, and was sitting on the table, polishing her face. The milk having been poured into the lid of a tobacco tin, in lieu of a saucer, she suspended her operations and adjourned for refreshments, Pugsy, having no immediate duties on hand, concentrated himself on the cat.

"Say!" he said.

"Well?"

"Dat kitty. Pipe de leather collar she's wearin'."

Betty had noticed earlier in the proceedings that a narrow leather collar encircled the animal's neck.

"Guess I know where dat kitty belongs. Dey all has dose collars. I guess she's one of Bat Jarvis's kitties. He's got twenty-t'ree of dem, and dey all has dose collars."

"Bat Jarvis?"

"Sure."

"Who is he?"

Pugsy looked at her incredulously.

"Say! Ain't youse never heard of Bat Jarvis? He's—he's Bat Jarvis."

"Do you know him?"

"Sure, I knows him."

"Does he live near here?"

"Sure, he lives near here."

"Then I think the best thing for you to do is to run round and tell him that I am taking care of his cat, and that he had better come and fetch it. I must be getting on with my work, or I shall never finish it."

She settled down to type the letters Smith had indicated. She attacked her task cautiously. She was one of those typists who are at their best when they do not have to hurry.

She was putting the finishing touches to the last of the batch, when there was a shuffling of feet in the outer room, followed by a knock on the door. The next moment there entered a short, burly young man, around whom there hung, like an aroma, an indescribable air of toughness, partly due, perhaps, to the fact that he wore his hair in a well-oiled fringe almost down to his eyebrows, thus presenting the appearance of having no forehead at all. His eyes were small and set close together. His mouth was wide, his jaw prominent. Not, in short, the sort of man you would have picked out on sight as a model citizen. He blinked furtively, as his eyes met Betty's, and looked round the room. His face lighted up as he saw the cat.

"Say!" he said, stepping forward, and touching the cat's collar._"Ma'am, mine!"

"Are you Mr. Jarvis?" asked Betty.

The visitor nodded, not without a touch of complacency, as of a monarch abandoning his incognito.

For Mr. Jarvis was a celebrity.

By profession he was a dealer in animals, birds, and snakes. He had a fancier's shop on Groome Street, in the heart of the Bowery. This was on the ground floor. His living abode was in the upper story of that house, and it was there that he kept the twenty-three cats whose necks were adorned with leather collars.

But it was not the fact that he possessed twenty-three cats with leather collars that had made Mr. Jarvis a celebrity. A man may win a local reputation, if only for eccentricity, by such means. Mr. Jarvis' reputation was far from being purely local. Broadway knew him, and the Tenderloin. Tammany Hall knew him. Long Island City knew him. For Bat Jarvis was the leader of the famous Groome Street Gang, the largest and most influential of the four big gangs of the East Side.

To Betty, so little does the world often know of its greatest men, he was merely a decidedly repellent-looking young man in unbecoming clothes. But his evident affection for the cat gave her a feeling of fellowship toward him. She beamed upon him, and Mr. Jarvis, who was wont to face the glare of rivals without flinching, avoided her eye and shuffled with embarrassment.

"I'm so glad she's safe!" said Betty. "There were two boys teasing her in the street. I've been giving her some milk."

Mr. Jarvis nodded, with his eyes on the floor.

There was a pause. Then he looked up, and, fixing his gaze some three feet above her head, spoke.

"Say!" he said, and paused again. Betty waited expectantly.

He relaxed into silence again, apparently thinking.

"Say!" he said. "Ma'am, obliged. Fond of de kit. I am."

"She's a dear," said Betty, tickling the cat under the ear.

"Ma'am," went on Mr. Jarvis, pursuing his theme, "obliged. Sha'n't fergit it. Any time you're in bad, glad to be of service. Bat Jarvis. Groome Street. Anybody'll show youse where I live."

He paused, and shuffled his feet; then, tucking the cat more firmly under his arm, left the room. Betty heard him shuffling downstairs.

He had hardly gone, when the door opened again, and Smith came in.

"So you have had company while I was away?" he said. "Who was the grandee with the cat? An old childhood's friend? Was he trying to sell the animal to us?"

"That was Mr. Bat Jarvis," said Betty.

Smith looked interested.

"Bat! What was he doing here?"

Betty related the story of the cat. Smith nodded thoughtfully.

"Well," he said, "I don't know that Comrade Jarvis is precisely the sort of friend I would go out of my way to select. Still, you never know what might happen. He might come in useful. And now, let us concentrate ourselves tensely on this very entertaining little journal of ours, and see if we cannot stagger humanity with it."

CHAPTER XIV
A CHANGE OF POLICY

The feeling of tranquillity which had come to Betty on her first acquaintance with *Peaceful Moments* seemed to deepen as the days went by, and with each day she found the sharp pain at her heart less vehement. It was still there, but it was dulled. The novelty of her life and surroundings kept it in check. New York is an egotist. It will suffer no divided attention. "Look at me!" says the voice of the city imperiously, and its children obey. It snatches their thoughts from their inner griefs, and concentrates them on the pageant that rolls unceasingly from one end of the island to the other. One may despair in New York, but it is difficult to brood on the past; for New York is the City of the Present, the City of Things that are Going On.

To Betty everything was new and strange. Her previous acquaintance with the metropolis had not been extensive. Mr. Scobell's home—or, rather, the house which he owned in America—was on the outskirts of Philadelphia, and it was there that she had lived when she was not paying visits. Occasionally, during horse-show week, or at some other time of festivity, she had spent a few days with friends who lived in Madison or upper Fifth Avenue, but beyond that, New York was a closed book to her.

It would have been a miracle in the circumstances, if John and Mervo and the whole of the events since the arrival of the great cable had not to some extent become a little dream-like. When she was alone at night, and had leisure to think, the dream became a reality once more; but in her hours of work, or what passed for work in the office of *Peaceful Moments*, and in the hours she spent walking about the streets and observing the ways of this new world of hers, it faded. Everything was so bright and busy! Every moment had its fresh interest.

And, above all, there was the sense of adventure. She was twenty-four; she had health and an imagination; and almost unconsciously she was stimulated by the thrill of being for the first time in her life genuinely at large. The child's love of hiding dies hard in us. To Betty, to walk abroad in New York in the midst of hurrying crowds, just Betty Brown—one of four million and no longer the beautiful Miss Silver of the society column, was to taste the romance of disguise, or invisibility.

During office hours she came near to complete contentment. To an expert stenographer the amount of work to be done would have seemed ridiculously small, but Betty, who liked plenty of time for a task, generally managed to make it last comfortably through the day.

This was partly owing to the fact that her editor, when not actually at work himself, was accustomed to engage her in conversation, and to keep her so engaged until the entrance of Pugsy Maloney heralded the arrival of some caller.

Betty liked Smith. His odd ways, his conversation, and his extreme solicitude for his clothes amused her. She found his outlook on life refreshing. Smith was an optimist. Whatever cataclysm might occur, he never doubted for a moment that he would be comfortably on the summit of the debris when all was over. He amazed Betty with his stories of his reportorial adventures. He told them for the most part as humorous stories at his own expense, but the fact remained that in a considerable proportion of them he had only escaped a sudden and violent death by adroitness or pure good luck. His conversation opened up a new world to Betty. She began to see that in America, and especially in New York, anything may happen to anybody. She looked on Smith with new eyes.

"But surely all this," she said one morning, after he had come to the end of the story of a highly delicate piece of interviewing work in connection with some Cumberland Mountains feudists, "surely all this—" She looked round the room.

"Domesticity?" suggested Smith.

"Yes," said Betty. "Surely it all seems rather tame to you?"

Smith sighed.

"Comrade Brown," he said, "you have touched the spot with an unerring finger."

Since Mr. Renshaw's departure, the flatness of life had come home to Smith with renewed emphasis. Before, there had always been the quiet entertainment of watching the editor at work, but now he was feeling restless. Like John at Mervo, he was practically nothing but an ornament. *Peaceful Moments*, like Mervo, had been set rolling and had continued to roll on almost automatically. The staff of regular contributors sent in their various pages. There was nothing for the man in charge to do. Mr. Renshaw had been one of those men who have a genius for being as busy over nothing as if it were some colossal work, but Smith had not that gift. He liked something that he could grip and that gripped him. He was becoming desperately bored. He felt like a marooned sailor on a barren rock of domesticity.

A visitor who called at the office at this time did nothing to remove this sensation of being outside everything that made life worth living. Betty, returning to the office one afternoon, found Smith in the doorway, just parting from a thickset young man. There was a rather gloomy expression on the thickset young man's face.

Smith, too, she noted, when they were back in the inner office, seemed to have something on his mind. He was strangely silent.

"Comrade Brown," he said at last, "I wish this little journal of ours had a sporting page."

Betty laughed.

"Less ribaldry," protested Smith pained. "This is a sad affair. You saw the man I was talking to? That was Kid Brady. I used to know him when I was out West. He wants to fight anyone in the country at a hundred and thirty-three pounds. We all have our hobbies. That is Comrade Brady's."

"Is he a boxer?"

"He would like to be. Out West, nobody could touch him. He's in the championship class. But he has been pottering about New York for a month without being able to get a fight. If we had a sporting page on *Peaceful Moments* we could do him some good, but I don't see how we can write him up," said Smith, picking up a copy of the paper, and regarding it gloomily, "in 'Moments in the Nursery' or 'Moments with Budding Girlhood.'"

He put up his eyeglass, and stared at the offending journal with the air of a vegetarian who has found a caterpillar in his salad. Incredulity, dismay, and disgust fought for precedence in his expression.

"B. Henderson Asher," he said severely, "ought to be in some sort of a home. Cain killed Abel for telling him that story."

He turned to another page, and scrutinized it with deepening gloom.

"Is Luella Granville Waterman by any chance a friend of yours, Comrade Brown? No? I am glad. For it seems to me that for sheer, concentrated piffle, she is in a class by herself."

He read on for a few moments in silence, then looked up and fixed Betty with his monocle. There was righteous wrath in his eyes.

"And people," he said, "are paying money for this! *Money!* Even now they are sitting down and writing checks for a year's subscription. It isn't right! It's a skin game. I am assisting in a carefully planned skin game!"

"But perhaps they like it," suggested Betty.

Smith shook his head.

"It is kind of you to try and soothe my conscience, but it is useless. I see my position too clearly. Think of it, Comrade Brown! Thousands of poor, doddering, half-witted creatures in Brooklyn and Flatbush, who ought not really to have control of their own money at all, are getting buncoed out of whatever it is per annum in exchange for—how shall I put it in a forcible yet refined and gentlemanly manner?—for cat's meat of this description. Why, selling gold bricks is honest compared with it. And I am temporarily responsible for the black business!"

He extended a lean hand with melodramatic suddenness toward Betty. The unexpectedness of the movement caused her to start back in her chair with a little exclamation of surprise. Smith nodded with a kind of mournful satisfaction.

"Exactly!" he said. "As I expected! You shrink from me. You avoid my polluted hand. How could it be otherwise? A conscientious green-goods man would do the same." He rose from his seat. "Your attitude," he said, "confirms me in a decision that has been in my mind for some days. I will no longer calmly accept this terrible position. I will try to make amends. While I am in charge, I will give our public something worth reading. All these Watermans and Ashers and Parslows must go!"

"Go!"

"Go!" repeated Smith firmly. "I have been thinking it over for days. You cannot look me in the face, Comrade Brown, and say that there is a single feature which would not be better away. I mean in the paper, not in my face. Every one of these punk pages must disappear. Letters must be despatched at once, informing Julia Burdett Parslow and the others, and in particular B. Henderson Asher, who, on brief acquaintance, strikes me as an ideal candidate for a lethal chamber—that, unless they cease their contributions instantly, we shall call up the police reserves. Then we can begin to move."

Betty, like most of his acquaintances, seldom knew whether Smith was talking seriously or not. She decided to assume, till he should dismiss the idea, that he meant what he said.

"But you can't!" she exclaimed.

"With your kind cooperation, nothing easier. You supply the mechanical work. I will compose the letters. First, B. Henderson Asher. 'Dear Sir'—"

"But—" she fell back on her original remark—"but you can't. What will Mr. Renshaw say when he comes back?"

"Sufficient unto the day. I have a suspicion that he will be the first to approve. His vacation will have made him see things differently—purified him, as it were. His conscience will be alive once more."

"But—"

"Why should we worry ourselves because the end of this venture is wrapped in obscurity? Why, Columbus didn't know where he was going to when he set out. All he knew was some highly interesting fact about an egg. What that was, I do not at the moment recall, but I understand it acted on Columbus like a tonic. We are the Columbuses of the journalistic world. Full steam ahead, and see what happens. If Comrade Renshaw is not pleased, why, I shall have been a martyr to a good cause. It is a far, far better thing that I do than I have ever done, so to speak. Why should I allow possible inconvenience to myself to stand in the way of the happiness which we propose to inject into those Brooklyn and Flatbush homes? Are you ready then, once more? 'Dear Sir—'"

Betty gave in.

When the letters were finished, she made one more objection.

"They are certain to call here and make a fuss," she said, "Mr. Asher and the rest."

"You think they will not bear the blow with manly fortitude?"

"I certainly do. And I think it's hard on them, too. Suppose they depend for a living on what they make from *Peaceful Moments?*"

"They don't," said Smith reassuringly. "I've looked into that. Have no pity for them. They are amateurs—degraded creatures of substance who take the cocktails out of the mouths of deserving professionals. B. Henderson Asher, for instance, is largely interested in gents' haberdashery. And so with the others. We touch their pride, perhaps, but not their purses."

Betty's soft heart was distinctly relieved by the information.

"I see," she said. "But suppose they do call, what will you do? It will be very unpleasant."

Smith pondered.

"True," he said. "True. I think you are right there. My nervous system is so delicately attuned that anything in the shape of a brawl would reduce it to a frazzle. I think that, for this occasion only, we will promote Comrade Maloney to the post of editor. He is a stern, hard, rugged man who does not care how unpopular he is. Yes, I think that would be best."

He signed the letters with a firm hand, "per pro P. Maloney, editor."

Then he lit a cigarette, and leaned back in his chair.

"An excellent morning's work," he said. "Already I begin to feel the dawnings of a new self-respect."

Betty, thinking the thing over, a little dazed by the rapidity of_Smith's method of action, had found a fresh flaw in the scheme.

"If you send Mr. Asher and the others away, how are you going to bring the paper out at all? You can't write it all yourself."

Smith looked at her with benevolent admiration.

"She thinks of everything," he murmured. "That busy brain is never still. No, Comrade Brown, I do not propose to write the whole paper myself. I do not shirk work when it gets me in a corner and I can't side-step, but there are limits. I propose to apply to a few of my late companions of Park Row, bright boys who will be delighted to come across with red-hot stuff for a moderate fee."

"And the proprietor of the paper? Won't he make any objection?"

Smith shook his head with a touch of reproof.

"You seem determined to try to look on the dark side. Do you insinuate that we are not acting in the proprietor's best interests? When he gets his check for the receipts, after I have handled the paper awhile, he will go singing about the streets. His beaming smile will be a byword. Visitors will be shown it as one of the sights. His only doubt will be whether to send his money to the bank or keep it in tubs and roll in it. And anyway," he added, "he's in Europe somewhere, and never sees the paper, sensible man."

He scratched a speck of dust off his coat-sleeve with his finger nail.

"This is a big thing," he resumed. "Wait till you see the first number of the new series. My idea is that *Peaceful Moments* shall become a pretty warm proposition. Its tone shall be such that the public will wonder why we do not print it on asbestos. We shall comment on all the live events of the week—murders, Wall Street scandals, glove fights, and the like, in a manner which will make our readers' spines thrill. Above all, we shall be the guardians of the people's rights. We shall be a spot light, showing up the dark places and bringing into prominence those who would endeavor in any way to put the people in Dutch. We shall detect the wrongdoer, and hand him such a series of resentful wallops that he will abandon his little games and become a model citizen. In this way we shall produce a bright, readable little sheet which will make our city sit up and take notice. I think so. I think so. And now I must be hustling about and seeing our new contributors. There is no time to waste."

CHAPTER XV
THE HONEYED WORD

The offices of Peaceful Moments were in a large building in a street off Madison Avenue. They consisted of a sort of outer lair, where Pugsy Maloney spent his time reading tales of life on the prairies and heading off undesirable visitors; a small room, into which desirable but premature visitors were loosed, to wait their turn for admission into the Presence; and a larger room beyond, which was the editorial sanctum.

Smith, returning from luncheon on the day following his announcement of the great change, found both Betty and Pugsy waiting in the outer lair, evidently with news of import.

"Mr. Smith," began Betty.

"Dey're in dere," said Master Maloney with his customary terseness.

"Who, exactly?" asked Smith.

"De whole bunch of dem."

Smith inspected Pugsy through his eyeglass. "Can you give me any particulars?" he asked patiently. "You are well-meaning, but vague, Comrade Maloney. Who are in there?"

"About 'steen of dem!" said Pugsy.

"Mr. Asher," said Betty, "and Mr. Philpotts, and all the rest of them." She struggled for a moment, but, unable to resist the temptation, added, "I told you so."

A faint smile appeared upon Smith's face.

"Dey just butted in," said Master Maloney, resuming his narrative. "I was sittin' here, readin' me book, when de foist of de guys blows in. 'Boy,' says he, 'is de editor in?' 'Nope,' I says. 'I'll go in and wait,' says he. 'Nuttin' doin',' says I. 'Nix on de goin'-in act.' I might as well have saved me breat'! In he butts. In about t'ree minutes along comes another gazebo. 'Boy,' says he, 'is de editor in?' 'Nope,' I says. 'I'll wait,' says he, lightin' out for de door, and in he butts. Wit' dat I sees de proposition's too fierce for muh. I can't keep dese big husky guys out if dey bucks center like dat. So when de rest of de bunch comes along, I don't try to give dem de trun down. I says, 'Well, gent,' I says, 'it's up to youse. De editor ain't in, but, if you feels lonesome, push t'roo. Dere's plenty dere to keep youse company. I can't be boddered!'"

"And what more could you have said?" agreed Smith approvingly. "Tell me, did these gentlemen appear to be gay and light-hearted, or did they seem to be looking for someone with a hatchet?"

"Dey was hoppin' mad, de whole bunch of dem."

"Dreadfully," attested Betty.

"As I suspected," said Smith, "but we must not repine. These trifling contretemps are the penalties we pay for our high journalistic aims. I fancy that with the aid of the diplomatic smile and the honeyed word I may manage to win out. Will you come and give me your moral support, Comrade Brown?"

He opened the door of the inner room for Betty, and followed her in.

Master Maloney's statement that "about 'steen" visitors had arrived proved to be a little exaggerated. There were five men in the room.

As Smith entered, every eye was turned upon him. To an outside spectator he would have seemed rather like a very well-dressed Daniel introduced into a den of singularly irritable lions. Five pairs of eyes were smoldering with a long-nursed resentment. Five brows were corrugated with wrathful lines. Such, however, was the simple majesty of Smith's demeanor that for a moment there was dead silence. Not a word was spoken as he paced, wrapped in thought, to the editorial chair. Stillness brooded over the room as he carefully dusted that piece of furniture, and, having done so to his satisfaction, hitched up the knees of his trousers and sank gracefully into a sitting position.

This accomplished, he looked up and started. He gazed round the room.

"Ha! I am observed!" he murmured.

The words broke the spell. Instantly the five visitors burst simultaneously into speech.

"Are you the acting editor of this paper?"

"I wish to have a word with you, sir."

"Mr. Maloney, I presume?"

"Pardon me!"

"I should like a few moments' conversation."

The start was good and even, but the gentleman who said "Pardon me!" necessarily finished first, with the rest nowhere.

Smith turned to him, bowed, and fixed him with a benevolent gaze through his eyeglass.

"Are you Mr. Maloney, may I ask?" enquired the favored one.

The others paused for the reply. Smith shook his head. "My name is_Smith."

"Where is Mr. Maloney?"

Smith looked across at Betty, who had seated herself in her place by the typewriter.

"Where did you tell me Mr. Maloney had gone to, Miss Brown? Ah, well, never mind. Is there anything *I* can do for you, gentlemen? I am on the editorial staff of this paper."

"Then, maybe," said a small, round gentleman who, so far, had done only chorus work, "you can tell me what all this means? My name is Waterman, sir. I am here on behalf of my wife, whose name you doubtless know."

"Correct me if I am wrong," said Smith, "but I should say it, also, was_Waterman."

"Luella Granville Waterman, sir!" said the little man proudly. "My wife," he went on, "has received this extraordinary communication from a man signing himself P. Maloney. We are both at a loss to make head or tail of it."

"It seems reasonably clear to me," said Smith, reading the letter.

"It's an outrage. My wife has been a contributor to this journal since its foundation. We are both intimate friends of Mr. Renshaw, to whom my wife's work has always given complete satisfaction. And now, without the slightest warning, comes this peremptory dismissal from P. Maloney. Who is P. Maloney? Where is Mr. Renshaw?"

The chorus burst forth. It seemed that that was what they all wanted to know. Who was P. Maloney? Where was Mr. Renshaw?

"I am the Reverend Edwin T. Philpott, sir," said a cadaverous-looking man with light blue eyes and a melancholy face. "I have contributed 'Moments of Meditation' to this journal for some considerable time."

Smith nodded.

"I know, yours has always seemed to me work which the world will not willingly let die."

The Reverend Edwin's frosty face thawed into a bleak smile.

"And yet," continued Smith, "I gather that P. Maloney, on the other hand, actually wishes to hurry on its decease. Strange!"

A man in a serge suit, who had been lurking behind Betty, bobbed into the open.

"Where's this fellow Maloney? P. Maloney. That's the man we want to see. I've been working for this paper without a break, except when I had the grip, for four years, and now up comes this Maloney fellow, if you please, and tells me in so many words that the paper's got no use for me."

"These are life's tragedies," sighed Smith.

"What does he mean by it? That's what I want to know. And that's what these gentlemen want to know. See here—"

"I am addressing—" said Smith.

"Asher's my name. B. Henderson Asher. I write 'Moments of Mirth.'"

A look almost of excitement came into Smith's face, such a look as a visitor to a foreign land might wear when confronted with some great national monument. He stood up and shook Mr. Asher reverently by the hand.

"Gentlemen," he said, reseating himself, "this is a painful case. The circumstances, as you will admit when you have heard all, are peculiar. You have asked me where Mr. Renshaw is. I don't know."

"You don't know!" exclaimed Mr. Asher.

"Nobody knows. With luck you may find a black cat in a coal cellar on a moonless night, but not Mr. Renshaw. Shortly after I joined this journal, he started out on a vacation, by his doctor's orders, and left no address. No letters were to be forwarded. He was to enjoy complete rest. Who can say where he is now? Possibly racing down some rugged slope in the Rockies with two grizzlies and a wildcat in earnest pursuit. Possibly in the midst of Florida Everglades, making a noise like a piece of meat in order to snare alligators. Who can tell?"

Silent consternation prevailed among his audience.

"Then, do you mean to say," demanded Mr. Asher, "that this fellow_Maloney's the boss here, and that what he says goes?"

Smith bowed.

"Exactly. A man of intensely masterful character, he will brook no opposition. I am powerless to sway him. Suggestions from myself as to the conduct of the paper would infuriate him. He believes that radical changes are necessary in the policy of *Peaceful Moments*, and he will carry them through if it snows. Doubtless he would gladly consider your work if it fitted in with his ideas. A rapid-fire impression of a glove fight, a spine-shaking word picture of a railway smash, or something on those lines, would be welcomed. But—"

"I have never heard of such a thing," said Mr. Waterman indignantly.

"In this life," said Smith, shaking his head, "we must be prepared for every emergency. We must distinguish between the unusual and the impossible. It is unusual for the acting editor of a weekly paper to revolutionize its existing policy, and you have rashly ordered your life on the assumption that it is impossible. You are unprepared. The thing comes on you as a surprise. The cry goes round New York, 'Comrades Asher, Waterman, Philpotts, and others have been taken unawares. They cannot cope with the situation.'"

"But what is to be done?" cried Mr. Asher.

"Nothing, I fear, except to wait. It may be that when Mr. Renshaw, having dodged the bears and eluded the wildcat, returns to his post, he will decide not to continue the paper on the lines at present mapped out. He should be back in about ten weeks."

"Ten weeks!"

"Till then, the only thing to do is to wait. You may rely on me to keep a watchful eye on your interests. When your thoughts tend to take a gloomy turn say to yourselves, 'All is well. Smith is keeping a watchful eye on our interests.'"

"All the same, I should like to see this P. Maloney," said Mr. Asher.

"I shouldn't," said Smith. "I speak in your best interests. P. Maloney is a man of the fiercest passions. He cannot brook interference. If you should argue with him, there is no knowing what might not happen. He would be the first to regret any violent action, when once he had cooled off, but— Of course, if you wish it I could arrange a meeting. No? I think you are wise. And now, gentlemen, as I have a good deal of work to get through—

"All very disturbing to the man of culture and refinement," said Smith, as the door closed behind the last of the malcontents. "But I think that we may now consider the line clear. I see no further obstacle in our path. I fear I have made Comrade Maloney perhaps a shade unpopular with our late contributors, but these things must be. We must clench our teeth and face them manfully. He suffers in an excellent cause."

CHAPTER XVI

TWO VISITORS TO THE OFFICE

There was once an editor of a paper in the Far West who was sitting at his desk, musing pleasantly on life, when a bullet crashed through the window and imbedded itself in the wall at the back of his head. A happy smile lighted up the editor's face. "Ah!" he said complacently, "I knew that personal column of ours would make a hit!"

What the bullet was to the Far West editor, the visit of Mr. Martin_Parker to the offices of *Peaceful Moments* was to Smith.

It occurred shortly after the publication of the second number of the new series, and was directly due to Betty's first and only suggestion for the welfare of the paper.

If the first number of the series had not staggered humanity, it had at least caused a certain amount of comment. The warm weather had begun, and there was nothing much going on in New York. The papers were consequently free to take notice of the change in the policy of *Peaceful Moments*. Through the agency of Smith's newspaper friends, it received some very satisfactory free advertisement, and the sudden increase in the sales enabled Smith to bear up with fortitude against the numerous letters of complaint from old subscribers who did not know what was good for them. Visions of a large new public which should replace these Brooklyn and Flatbush ingrates filled his mind.

The sporting section of the paper pleased him most. The personality of Kid Brady bulked large in it. A photograph of the ambitious pugilist, looking moody and important in an attitude of self-defense, filled half a page, and under the photograph was the legend, "Jimmy Garvin must meet this boy." Jimmy was the present holder of the light-weight title. He had won it a year before, and since then had confined himself to smoking cigars as long as walking sticks and appearing nightly in a vaudeville sketch entitled, "A Fight for Honor." His reminiscences were being published in a Sunday paper. It was this that gave Smith the idea of publishing Kid Brady's autobiography in *Peaceful Moments*, an idea which won the Kid's whole-hearted gratitude. Like most pugilists he had a passion for bursting into print. Print is the fighter's accolade. It signifies that he has arrived. He was grateful to Smith, too, for not editing his contributions. Jimmy Garvin groaned under the supervision of a member of the staff of his Sunday paper, who deleted his best passages and altered the rest into Addisonian English. The readers of *Peaceful Moments* got their Brady raw.

"Comrade Brady," said Smith meditatively to Betty one morning, "has a singularly pure and pleasing style. It is bound to appeal powerfully to the many-headed. Listen to this. Our hero is fighting one Benson in the latter's home town, San Francisco, and the audience is rooting hard for the native son. Here is

Comrade Brady on the subject: 'I looked around that house, and I seen I hadn't a friend in it. And then the gong goes, and I says to myself how I has one friend, my old mother down in Illinois, and I goes in and mixes it, and then I seen Benson losing his goat, so I gives him a half-scissor hook, and in the next round I picks up a sleep-producer from the floor and hands it to him, and he takes the count.' That is what the public wants. Crisp, lucid, and to the point. If that does not get him a fight with some eminent person, nothing will."

He leaned back in his chair.

"What we really need now," he said thoughtfully, "is a good, honest, muck-raking series. That's the thing to put a paper on the map. The worst of it is that everything seems to have been done. Have you by any chance a second 'Frenzied Finance' at the back of your mind? Or proofs that nut sundaes are composed principally of ptomaine and outlying portions of the American workingman? It would be the making of us."

Now it happened that in the course of her rambles through the city Betty had lost herself one morning in the slums. The experience had impressed itself on her mind with an extraordinary vividness. Her lot had always been cast in pleasant places, and she had never before been brought into close touch with this side of life. The sight of actual raw misery had come home to her with an added force from that circumstance. Wandering on, she had reached a street which eclipsed in cheerlessness even its squalid neighbors. All the smells and noises of the East Side seemed to be penned up here in a sort of canyon. The masses of dirty clothes hanging from the fire-escapes increased the atmosphere of depression. Groups of ragged children covered the roadway.

It was these that had stamped the scene so indelibly on her memory. She loved children, and these seemed so draggled and uncared-for.

Smith's words gave her an idea.

"Do you know Broster Street, Mr. Smith?" she asked.

"Down on the East Side? Yes, I went there once to get a story, one red-hot night in August, when I was on the *News*. The Ice Company had been putting up their prices, and trouble was expected down there. I was sent to cover it."

He did not add that he had spent a week's salary that night, buying ice and distributing it among the denizens of Broster Street.

"It's an awful place," said Betty, her eyes filling with tears. "Those poor children!"

Smith nodded.

"Some of those tenement houses are fierce," he said thoughtfully. Like Betty, he found himself with a singularly clear recollection of his one visit to Broster Street. "But you can't do anything."

"Why not?" cried Betty. "Oh, why not? Surely you couldn't have a better subject for your series? It's wicked. People only want to be told about them to make them better. Why can't we draw attention to them?"

"It's been done already. Not about Broster Street, but about other tenements. Tenements as a subject are played out. The public isn't interested in them. Besides, it wouldn't be any use. You can't tree the man who is really responsible, unless you can spend thousands scaring up evidence. The land belongs in the first place to some corporation or other. They lease it to a lessee. When there's a fuss, they say they aren't responsible, it's up to the lessee. And he, bright boy, lies so low you can't find out who it is."

"But we could try," urged Betty.

Smith looked at her curiously. The cause was plainly one that lay near to her heart. Her face was flushed and eager. He wavered, and, having wavered, he did what no practical man should do. He allowed sentiment to interfere with business. He knew that a series of articles on Broster Street would probably be so much dead weight on the paper, something to be skipped by the average reader, but he put the thought aside.

"Very well," he said. "If you care to turn in a few crisp remarks on the subject, I'll print them."

Betty's first instalment was ready on the following morning. It was a curious composition. A critic might have classed it with Kid Brady's reminiscences, for there was a complete absence of literary style. It was just a wail of pity, and a cry of indignation, straight from the heart and split up into paragraphs.

Smith read it with interest, and sent it off to the printer unaltered.

"Have another ready for next week, Comrade Brown," he said. "It's a long shot, but this might turn out to be just what we need."

And when, two days after the publication of the number containing the article, Mr. Martin Parker called at the office, he felt that the long shot had won out.

He was holding forth on life in general to Betty shortly before the luncheon hour when Pugsy Maloney entered bearing a card.

"Martin Parker?" said Smith, taking it. "I don't know him. We make new friends daily."

"He's a guy wit' a tall-shaped hat," volunteered Master Maloney, "an' he's wearing a dude suit an' shiny shoes."

"Comrade Parker," said Smith approvingly, "has evidently not been blind to the importance of a visit to *Peaceful Moments*. He has dressed himself in his best. He has felt, rightly, that this is no occasion for the flannel suit and the old straw hat. I would not have it otherwise. It is the right spirit. Show the guy in. We will give him audience."

Pugsy withdrew.

Mr. Martin Parker proved to be a man who might have been any age between thirty-five and forty-five. He had a dark face and a black mustache. As Pugsy had stated, in effect, he wore a morning coat, trousers with a crease which brought a smile of kindly approval to Smith's face, and patent-leather shoes of pronounced shininess.

"I want to see the editor," he said.

"Will you take a seat?" said Smith.

He pushed a chair toward the visitor, who seated himself with the care inspired by a perfect trouser crease. There was a momentary silence while he selected a spot on the table on which to place his hat.

"I have come about a private matter," he said, looking meaningly at Betty, who got up and began to move toward the door. Smith nodded to her, and she went out.

"Say," said Mr. Parker, "hasn't something happened to this paper these last few weeks? It used not to take such an interest in things, used it?"

"You are very right," responded Smith. "Comrade Renshaw's methods were good in their way. I have no quarrel with Comrade Renshaw. But he did not lead public thought. He catered exclusively to children with water on the brain and men and women with solid ivory skulls. I feel that there are other and larger publics. I cannot content myself with ladling out a weekly dole of predigested mental breakfast food. I—"

"Then you, I guess," said Mr. Parker, "are responsible for this Broster_Street thing?"

"At any rate, I approve of it and put it in the paper. If any husky guy, as Comrade Maloney would put it, is anxious to aim a swift kick at the author of that article, he can aim it at me."

"I see," said Mr. Parker. He paused. "It said 'Number one' in the paper. Does that mean there are going to be more of them?"

"There is no flaw in your reasoning. There are to be several more."

Mr. Parker looked at the door. It was closed. He bent forward.

"See here," he said, "I'm going to talk straight, if you'll let me."

"Assuredly, Comrade Parker. There must be no secrets, no restraint between us. I would not have you go away and say to yourself, 'Did I make my meaning clear? Was I too elusive?'"

Mr. Parker scratched the floor with the point of a gleaming shoe. He seemed to be searching for words.

"Say on," urged Smith. "Have you come to point out some flaw in that article? Does it fall short in any way of your standard for such work?"

Mr. Parker came to the point.

"If I were you," he said, "I should quit it. I shouldn't go on with those articles."

"Why?" enquired Smith.

"Because," said Mr. Parker.

He looked at Smith, and smiled slowly, an ingratiating smile. Smith did not respond.

"I do not completely gather your meaning," he said. "I fear I must ask you to hand it to me with still more breezy frankness. Do you speak from purely friendly motives? Are you advising me to discontinue the series because you fear that it will damage the literary reputation of the paper? Do you speak solely as a literary connoisseur? Or are there other reasons?"

Mr. Parker leaned forward.

"The gentleman whom I represent—"

"Then this is no matter of your own personal taste? There is another?"

"See here, I'm representing a gentleman who shall be nameless, and I've come on his behalf to tip you off to quit this game. These articles of yours are liable to cause him inconvenience."

"Financial? Do you mean that he may possibly have to spend some of his spare doubloons in making Broster Street fit to live in?"

"It's not so much the money. It's the publicity. There are reasons why he would prefer not to have it made too public that he's the owner of the tenements down there."

"Well, he knows what to do. If he makes Broster Street fit for a not-too-fastidious pig to live in—"

Mr. Parker coughed. A tentative cough, suggesting that the situation was now about to enter upon a more delicate phase.

"Now, see here, sir," he said, "I'm going to be frank. I'm going to put my cards on the table, and see if we can't fix something up. Now, see here. We don't want any unpleasantness. You aren't in this business for your health, eh? You've got your living to make, same as everybody else, I guess. Well, this is how it stands. To a certain extent, I don't mind owning, since we're being frank with one another, you've got us—that's to say, this gentleman I'm speaking of—in a cleft stick. Frankly, that Broster Street story of yours has attracted attention—I saw it myself in two Sunday papers—and if there's going to be any more of them—Well, now, here's a square proposition. How much do you want to stop those articles? That's straight. I've been frank with you, and I want you to be frank with me. What's your figure? Name it, and if you don't want the earth I guess we needn't quarrel."

He looked expectantly at Smith. Smith, gazing sadly at him through his monocle, spoke quietly, with the restrained dignity of some old Roman senator dealing with the enemies of the Republic.

"Comrade Parker," he said, "I fear that you have allowed your intercourse with this worldly city to undermine your moral sense. It is useless to dangle rich bribes before the editorial eyes. *Peaceful Moments* cannot be muzzled. You doubtless mean well, according to your somewhat murky lights, but we are not for sale, except at fifteen cents weekly. From the hills of Maine to the Everglades of Florida, from Portland, Oregon, to Melonsquashville, Tennessee, one sentence is in every man's mouth. And what is that sentence? I give you three guesses. You give it up? It is this: '*Peaceful Moments* cannot be muzzled!'"

Mr. Parker rose.

"Nothing doing, then?" he said.

"Nothing."

Mr. Parker picked up his hat.

"See here," he said, a grating note in his voice, hitherto smooth and conciliatory, "I've no time to fool away talking to you. I've given you your chance. Those stories are going to be stopped. And if you've any sense in you at all, you'll stop them yourself before you get hurt. That's all I've got to say, and that goes."

He went out, closing the door behind him with a bang that added emphasis to his words.

"All very painful and disturbing," murmured Smith. "Comrade Brown!" he called.

Betty came in.

"Did our late visitor bite a piece out of you on his way out? He was in the mood to do something of the sort."

"He seemed angry," said Betty.

"He *was* angry," said Smith. "Do you know what has happened, Comrade Brown? With your very first contribution to the paper you have hit the bull's-eye. You have done the state some service. Friend Parker came as the representative of the owner of those Broster Street houses. He wanted to buy us off. We've got them scared, or he wouldn't have shown his hand with such refreshing candor. Have you any engagements at present?"

"I was just going out to lunch, if you could spare me."

"Not alone. This lunch is on the office. As editor of this journal I will entertain you, if you will allow me, to a magnificent banquet. *Peaceful Moments* is grateful to you. *Peaceful Moments,"* he added, with the contented look the Far West editor must have worn as the bullet came through the window, "is, owing to you, going some now."

* * * * *

When they returned from lunch, and reentered the outer office, Pugsy Maloney, raising his eyes for a moment from his book, met them with the information that another caller had arrived and was waiting in the inner room.

"Dere's a guy in dere waitin' to see youse," he said, jerking his head towards the door.

"Yet another guy? This is our busy day. Did he give a name?"

"Says his name's Maude," said Master Maloney, turning a page.

"Maude!" cried Betty, falling back.

Smith beamed.

"Old John Maude!" he said. "Great! I've been wondering what on earth he's been doing with himself all this time. Good-old John! You'll like him," he said, turning, and stopped abruptly, for he was speaking to the empty air. Betty had disappeared.

"Where's Miss Brown, Pugsy?" he said. "Where did she go?"

Pugsy vouchsafed another jerk of the head, in the direction of the outer door.

"She's beaten it," he said. "I seen her make a break for de stairs. Guess she's forgotten to remember somet'ing," he added indifferently, turning once more to his romance of prairie life. "Goils is bone-heads."

CHAPTER XVII

THE MAN AT THE ASTOR

Refraining from discussing with Master Maloney the alleged bone-headedness of girls, Smith went through into the inner room, and found John sitting in the editorial chair, glancing through the latest number of *Peaceful Moments*.

"Why, John, friend of my youth," he said, "where have you been hiding all this time? I called you up at your office weeks ago, and an acid voice informed me that you were no longer there. Have you been fired?"

"Yes," said John. "Why aren't you on the *News* any more? Nobody seemed to know where you were, till I met Faraday this morning, who told me you were here."

Smith was conscious of an impression that in some subtle way John had changed since their last meeting. For a moment he could not have said what had given him this impression. Then it flashed upon him. Before, John had always been, like Mrs. Fezziwig in "The Christmas Carol," one vast substantial smile. He had beamed cheerfully on what to him was evidently the best of all possible worlds. Now, however, it would seem that doubts had occurred to him as to the universal perfection of things. His face was graver. His eyes and his mouth alike gave evidence of disturbing happenings.

In the matter of confidences, Smith was not a believer in spade-work. If they were offered to him, he was invariably sympathetic, but he never dug for them. That John had something on his mind was obvious, but he intended to allow him, if he wished to reveal it, to select his own time for the revelation.

John, for his part, had no intention of sharing this particular trouble even with Smith. It was too new and intimate for discussion.

It was only since his return to New York that the futility of his quest had really come home to him. In the belief of having at last escaped from Mervo he had been inclined to overlook obstacles. It had seemed to him, while he waited for his late subjects to dismiss him, that, once he could move, all would be simple. New York had dispelled that idea. Logically, he saw with perfect clearness, there was no reason why he and Betty should ever meet again.

To retain a spark of hope beneath this knowledge was not easy and John, having been in New York now for nearly three weeks without any encouragement from the fates, was near the breaking point. A gray apathy had succeeded the frenzied restlessness of the first few days. The necessity for some kind of work that would to some extent occupy his mind was borne in upon him, and the thought of Smith had followed naturally. If anybody could supply distraction, it would be Smith. Faraday, another of the temporary exiles from the *News*, whom he had met by chance in Washington Square, had informed him of Smith's new position and of the renaissance of *Peaceful Moments*, and he had hurried to the office to present himself as an unskilled but willing volunteer to the cause. Inspection of the current number of the paper had convinced him that the *Peaceful Moments* atmosphere, if it could not cure, would at least relieve.

"Faraday told me all about what you had done to this paper," he said._"I came to see if you would let me in on it. I want work."

"Excellent!" said Smith. "Consider yourself one of us."

"I've never done any newspaper work, of course, but—"

"Never!" cried Smith. "Is it so long since the deaf old college days that you forget the *Gridiron?*"

In their last year at Harvard, Smith and John, assisted by others of a congenial spirit, had published a small but lively magazine devoted to college topics, with such success—from one point of view—that on the appearance of the third number it was suppressed by the authorities.

"You were the life and soul of the *Gridiron,*" went on Smith. "You shall be the life and soul of *Peaceful Moments*. You have special qualifications for the post. A young man once called at the office of a certain newspaper, and asked for a job. 'Have you any specialty?' enquired the editor. 'Yes,' replied the bright boy, 'I am rather good at invective.' 'Any particular kind of invective?' queried the man up top. 'No,' replied our hero, 'just general invective.' Such is your case, my son. You have a genius for general invective. You are the man *Peaceful Moments* has been waiting for."

"If you think so—"

"I do think so. Let us consider it settled. And now, tell me, what do you think of our little journal?"

"Well—aren't you asking for trouble? Isn't the proprietor—?"

Smith waved his hand airily.

"Dismiss him from your mind," he said. "He is a gentleman of the name of Benjamin Scobell, who—"

"Benjamin Scobell!"

"Who lives in Europe and never sees the paper. I happen to know that he is anxious to get rid of it. His solicitors have instructions to accept any reasonable offer. If only I could close in on a small roll, I would buy it myself, for by the time we have finished our improvements, it will be a sound investment for the young speculator. Have you read the Broster Street story? It has hit somebody already. Already some unknown individual is grasping the lemon in his unwilling fingers. And—to remove any diffidence you may still have about lending your sympathetic aid—that was written by no hardened professional, but by our stenographer. She'll be in soon, and I'll introduce you. You'll like her. I do not despair, later on, of securing an epoch-making contribution from Comrade Maloney."

As he spoke, that bulwark of the paper entered in person, bearing an envelope.

"Ah, Comrade Maloney," said Smith. "Is that your contribution? What is the subject? 'Mustangs I have Met?'"

"A kid brought dis," said Pugsy. "Dere ain't no answer."

Smith read the letter with raised eyebrows.

"We shall have to get another stenographer," he said. "The gifted author of our Broster Street series has quit."

"Oh!" said John, not interested.

"Quit at a moment's notice and without explanation. I can't understand it."

"I guess she had some reason," said John, absently. He was inclined to be absent during these days. His mind was always stealing away to occupy itself with the problem of the discovery of Betty. The motives that might have led a stenographer to resign her position had no interest for him.

Smith shrugged his shoulders.

"Oh, Woman, Woman!" he said resignedly.

"She says she will send in some more Broster Street stuff, though, which is a comfort. But I'm sorry she's quit. You would have liked her."

"Yes?" said John.

At this moment there came from the outer office a piercing squeal. It penetrated into the editorial sanctum, losing only a small part of its strength on the way. Smith looked up with patient sadness.

"If Comrade Maloney," he said, "is going to take to singing during business hours, I fear this journal must put up its shutters. Concentrated thought will be out of the question."

He moved to the door and flung it open as a second squeal rent the air, and found Master Maloney writhing in the grip of a tough-looking person in patched trousers and a stained sweater. His left ear was firmly grasped between the stranger's finger and thumb.

The tough person released Pugsy, and, having eyed Smith keenly for a moment, made a dash for the stairs, leaving the guardian of the gate rubbing his ear resentfully.

"He blows in," said Master Maloney, aggrieved, "an' asks is de editor in. I tells him no, an' he nips me by the ear when I tries to stop him buttin' t'roo."

"Comrade Maloney," said Smith, "you are a martyr. What would Horatius have done if somebody had nipped him by the ear when he was holding the bridge? It might have made all the difference. Did the gentleman state his business?"

"Nope. Just tried to butt t'roo."

"One of these strong, silent men. The world is full of us. These are the perils of the journalistic life. You will be safer and happier when you are a cowboy, Comrade Maloney."

Smith was thoughtful as he returned to the inner room.

"Things are warming up, John," he said. "The sport who has just left evidently came just to get a sight of me. Otherwise, why should he tear himself away without stopping for a chat. I suppose he was sent to mark me down for whichever gang Comrade Parker is employing."

"What do you mean?" said John. "All this gets past me. Who is Parker?"

Smith related the events leading up to Mr. Parker's visit, and described what had happened on that occasion.

"So, before you throw in your lot with this journal," he concluded, "it would be well to think the matter over. You must weigh the pros and cons. Is your passion for literature such that you do not mind being put out of business with a black-jack for the cause? Will the knowledge that a low-browed gentleman is waiting round the corner for you stimulate or hinder you in your work? There's no doubt now that we are up against a tough crowd."

"By Jove!" said John. "I hadn't a notion it was like that."

"You feel, then, that on the whole—"

"I feel that on the whole this is just the business I've been hunting for. You couldn't keep me out of it now with an ax."

Smith looked at him curiously, but refrained from enquiries. That there must be something at the back of this craving for adventure and excitement, he knew. The easy-going John he had known of old would certainly not have deserted the danger zone, but he would not have welcomed entry to it so keenly. It was plain that he was hungry for work that would keep him from thought. Smith was eminently a patient young man, and though the problem of what upheaval had happened to change John to such an extent interested him greatly, he was prepared to wait for explanations.

Of the imminence of the danger he was perfectly aware. He had known from the first that Mr. Parker's concluding words were not an empty threat. His experience as a reporter had given him the knowledge that is only given in its entirety to police and newspaper men: that there are two New Yorks—one, a modern, well-policed city, through which one may walk from end to end without encountering adventure; the other, a city as full of sinister intrigue, of whisperings and conspiracies, of battle, murder, and sudden death in dark byways, as any town of mediaeval Italy. Given certain conditions, anything may happen in New York. And Smith realized that these conditions now prevailed in his own case. He had come into conflict with New York's underworld. Circumstances had placed him below the surface, where only his wits could help him.

He would have been prepared to see the thing through by himself, but there was no doubt that John as an ally would be a distinct comfort.

Nevertheless, he felt compelled to give his friend a last chance of withdrawing.

"You know," he said, "there is really no reason why you should—"

"But I'm going to," interrupted John. "That's all there is to it. What's going to happen, anyway? I don't know anything about these gangs. I thought they spent all their time shooting each other up."

"Not all, unfortunately, Comrade John. They are always charmed to take on a small job like this on the side."

"And what does it come to? Do we have an entire gang camping on our trail in a solid mass, or only one or two toughs?"

"Merely a section, I should imagine. Comrade Parker would go to the main boss of the gang—Bat Jarvis, if it was the Groome Street gang, or Spider Reilly and Dude Dawson if he wanted the Three Points or the Table Hill lot. The boss would chat over the matter with his own special partners, and they would fix it up among themselves. The rest of the gang would probably know nothing about it. The fewer in the game, you see, the fewer to divide the Parker dollars. So what we have to do is to keep a lookout for a dozen or so aristocrats of that dignified deportment which comes from constant association with the main boss, and, if we can elude these, all will be well."

* * * * *

It was by Smith's suggestion that the editorial staff of *Peaceful_Moments* dined that night at the Astor roof-garden.

"The tired brain," he said, "needs to recuperate. To feed on such a night as this in some low-down hostelry on the level of the street, with German waiters breathing heavily down the back of one's neck and two fiddles and a piano hitting up ragtime about three feet from one's tympanum, would be false economy. Here, fanned by cool breezes and surrounded by passably fair women and brave men, one may do a certain amount of tissue-restoring. Moreover, there is little danger up here of being slugged by our moth-eaten acquaintance of this afternoon. We shall probably find him waiting for us at the main entrance with a black-jack, but till then—"

He turned with gentle grace to his soup. It was a warm night, and the roof-garden was full. From where they sat they could see the million twinkling lights of the city. John, watching them, as he smoked a cigarette at the conclusion of the meal, had fallen into a dream. He came to himself with a start, to find Smith in conversation with a waiter.

"Yes, my name is Smith," he was saying.

The waiter retired to one of the tables and spoke to a young man sitting there. John, recollected having seen this solitary diner looking in their direction once or twice during dinner, but the fact had not impressed him.

"What's the matter?" he asked.

"The man at that table sent over to ask if my name was Smith. It was. He is now coming along to chat in person. I wonder why. I don't know him from Adam."

The stranger was threading his way between the tables.

"Can I have a word with you, Mr. Smith?" he said. The waiter brought a chair and he seated himself.

"By the way," said Smith, "my friend, Mr. Maude. Your own name will doubtless come up in the course of general chitchat over the coffee-cups."

"Not on your tintype it won't," said the stranger decidedly. "It won't be needed. Is Mr. Maude on your paper? That's all right, then. I can go ahead."

He turned to Smith.

"It's about that Broster Street thing."

"More fame!" murmured Smith. "We certainly are making a hit with the great public over Broster Street."

"Well, you understand certain parties have got it in against you?"

"A charming conversationalist, one Comrade Parker, hinted at something of the sort in a recent conversation. We shall endeavor, however, to look after ourselves."

"You'll need to. The man behind is a big bug."

"Who is he?"

The stranger shrugged his shoulders.

"Search me. You wouldn't expect him to give that away."

"Then on what system have you estimated the size of the gentleman's bug-hood? What makes you think that he's a big bug?"

"By the number of dollars he was ready to put up to have you put through."

Smith's eyes gleamed for an instant, but he spoke as coolly as ever.

"Oh!" he said. "And which gang has he hired?"

"I couldn't say. He—his agent, that is—came to Bat Jarvis. Bat for some reason turned the job down."

"He did? Why?"

"Search me. Nobody knows. But just as soon as he heard who it was he was being asked to lay for, he turned it down cold. Said none of his fellows was going to put a finger on anyone who had anything to do with your paper. I don't know what you've been doing to Bat, but he sure is the long-lost brother to you."

"A powerful argument in favor of kindness to animals!" said Smith. "One of his celebrated stud of cats came into the possession of our stenographer. What did she do? Instead of having the animal made into a nourishing soup, she restored it to its bereaved owner. Observe the sequel. We are very much obliged to Comrade Jarvis."

"He sent me along," went on the stranger, "to tell you to watch out, because one of the other gangs was dead sure to take on the job. And he said you were to know that he wasn't mixed up in it. Well, that's all. I'll be pushing along. I've a date. Glad to have met you, Mr. Maude. Good-night."

For a few moments after he had gone, Smith and John sat smoking in silence.

"What's the time?" asked Smith suddenly. "If it's not too late—Hello, here comes our friend once more."

The stranger came up to the table, a light overcoat over his dress clothes. From the pocket of this he produced a watch.

"Force of habit," he said apologetically, handing it to John. "You'll pardon me. Good-night again."

CHAPTER XVIII
THE HIGHFIELD

John looked after him, open-mouthed. The events of the evening had been a revelation to him. He had not realized the ramifications of New York's underworld. That members of the gangs should appear in gorgeous raiment in the Astor roof-garden was a surprise. "And now," said Smith, "that our friend has so sportingly returned your watch, take a look at it and see the time. Nine? Excellent. We shall do it comfortably."

"What's that?" asked John.

"Our visit to the Highfield. A young friend of mine who is fighting there to-night sent me tickets a few days ago. In your perusal of *Peaceful Moments* you may have chanced to see mention of one Kid Brady. He is the man. I was intending to go in any case, but an idea has just struck me that we might combine pleasure with business. Has it occurred to you that these black-jack specialists may drop in on us at the office? And, if so, that Comrade Maloney's statement that we are not in may be insufficient to keep them out? Comrade Brady would be an invaluable assistant. And as we are his pugilistic sponsors, without whom he would not have got this fight at all, I think we may say that he will do any little thing we may ask of him."

It was certainly true that, from the moment the paper had taken up his cause, Kid Brady's star had been in the ascendant. The sporting pages of the big dailies had begun to notice him, until finally the management of the Highfield Club had signed him on for a ten-round bout with a certain Cyclone Dick Fisher.

"He should," continued Smith, "if equipped in any degree with the finer feelings, be bubbling over with gratitude toward us. At any rate, it is worth investigating."

* * * * *

Far away from the comfortable glare of Broadway, in a place of disheveled houses and insufficient street-lamps, there stands the old warehouse which modern enterprise has converted into the Highfield Athletic and Gymnastic Club. The imagination, stimulated by the title, conjures up picture-covered walls, padded chairs, and seas of white shirt front. The Highfield differs in some respects from this fancy picture. Indeed, it would be hard to find a respect in which it does not differ. But these names are so misleading! The title under which the Highfield used to be known till a few years back was "Swifty Bob's." It was a good, honest title. You knew what to export, and if you attended seances at Swifty Bob's you left your gold watch and your little savings at home. But a wave of anti-pugilistic feeling swept over the New York authorities. Promoters of boxing contests found themselves, to their acute disgust, raided by the police. The industry began to languish. Persons avoided places where at any moment the festivities might be marred by an inrush of large men in blue uniforms, armed with locust sticks.

And then some big-brained person suggested the club idea, which stands alone as an example of American dry humor. At once there were no boxing contests in New York; Swifty Bob and his fellows would have been shocked at the idea of such a thing. All that happened now was exhibition sparring bouts between members of the club. It is true that next day the papers very tactlessly reported the friendly exhibition spar as if it had been quite a serious affair, but that was not the fault of Swifty Bob.

Kid Brady, the chosen of *Peaceful Moments*, was billed for a "ten-round exhibition contest," to be the main event of the evening's entertainment.

* * * * *

A long journey on the subway took them to the neighborhood, and after considerable wandering they arrived at their destination.

Smith's tickets were for a ring-side box, a species of sheep pen of unpolished wood, with four hard chairs in it. The interior of the Highfield Athletic and Gymnastic Club was severely free from anything in the shape of luxury and ornament. Along the four walls were raised benches in tiers. On these were seated as tough-looking a collection of citizens as one might wish to see. On chairs at the ringside were the reporters with tickers at their sides. In the center of the room, brilliantly lighted by half-a-dozen electric chandeliers, was the ring.

There were preliminary bouts before the main event. A burly gentleman in shirt-sleeves entered the ring, followed by two slim youths in fighting costume and a massive person in a red jersey, blue serge trousers, and yellow braces, who chewed gum with an abstracted air throughout the proceedings.

The burly gentleman gave tongue in a voice that cleft the air like a cannon ball.

"Ex-hibit-i-on four-round bout between Patsy Milligan and Tommy_Goodley, members of this club. Patsy on my right, Tommy on my left._Gentlemen will kindly stop smokin'."

The audience did nothing of the sort. Possibly they did not apply the description to themselves. Possibly they considered the appeal a mere formula. Somewhere in the background a gong sounded, and Patsy, from the right, stepped briskly forward to meet Tommy, approaching from the left.

The contest was short but energetic. At intervals the combatants would cling affectionately to one another, and on these occasions the red-jerseyed man, still chewing gum and still wearing the same air of being lost in abstract thought, would split up the mass by the simple method of ploughing his way between the pair. Toward the end of the first round Thomas, eluding a left swing, put Patrick neatly to the floor, where the latter remained for the necessary ten seconds.

The remaining preliminaries proved disappointing. So much so that in the last of the series a soured sportsman on one of the benches near the roof began in satirical mood to whistle the "Merry Widow Waltz." It was here that the red-jerseyed thinker for the first and last time came out of his meditative trance. He leaned over the ropes, and spoke, without heat, but firmly:

"If that guy whistling back up yonder thinks he can do better than these boys, he can come right down into the ring."

The whistling ceased.

There was a distinct air of relief when the last preliminary was finished and preparations for the main bout began. It did not commence at once. There were formalities to be gone through, introductions and the like. The burly gentleman reappeared from nowhere, ushering into the ring a sheepishly grinning youth in a flannel suit.

"In-ter-*doo*-cin' Young Leary," he bellowed impressively, "a noo member of this club, who will box some good boy here in September."

He walked to the other side of the ring and repeated the remark. A raucous welcome was accorded to the new member.

Two other notable performers were introduced in a similar manner, and then the building became suddenly full of noise, for a tall youth in a bath robe, attended by a little army of assistants, had entered the ring. One of the army carried a bright green bucket, on which were painted in white letters the words "Cyclone Dick Fisher." A moment later there was another, though a far less, uproar, as Kid Brady, his pleasant face wearing a self-conscious smirk, ducked under the ropes and sat down in the opposite corner.

"Ex-hib-it-i-on ten-round bout," thundered the burly gentleman, "between Cyclone Dick Fisher—"

Loud applause. Mr. Fisher was one of the famous, a fighter with a reputation from New York to San Francisco. He was generally considered the most likely man to give the hitherto invincible Jimmy Garvin a hard battle for the light-weight championship.

"Oh, you Dick!" roared the crowd.

Mr. Fisher bowed benevolently.

"—and Kid Brady, member of this—"

There was noticeably less applause for the Kid. He was an unknown. A few of those present had heard of his victories in the West, but these were but a small section of the crowd. When the faint applause had ceased, Smith rose to his feet.

"Oh, you Kid!" he observed encouragingly. "I should not like Comrade Brady," he said, reseating himself, "to think that he has no friend but his poor old mother, as occurred on a previous occasion."

The burly gentleman, followed by the two armies of assistants, dropped down from the ring, and the gong sounded.

Mr. Fisher sprang from his corner as if somebody had touched a spring. He seemed to be of the opinion that if you are a cyclone, it is never too soon to begin behaving like one. He danced round the Kid with an india-rubber agility. The *Peaceful Moments* representative exhibited more stolidity. Except for the fact that he was in fighting attitude, with one gloved hand moving slowly in the neighborhood of his stocky chest, and the other pawing the air on a line with his square jaw, one would have said that he did not realize the position of affairs. He wore the friendly smile of the good-natured guest who is led forward by his hostess to join in some game to amuse the children.

Suddenly his opponent's long left shot out. The Kid, who had been strolling forward, received it under the chin, and continued to stroll forward as if nothing of note had happened. He gave the impression of being aware that Mr. Fisher had committed a breach of good taste and of being resolved to pass it off with ready tact.

The Cyclone, having executed a backward leap, a forward leap, and a feint, landed heavily with both hands. The Kid's genial smile did not even quiver, but he continued to move forward. His opponent's left flashed out again, but this time, instead of ignoring the matter, the Kid replied with a heavy right swing, and Mr. Fisher leaping back, found himself against the ropes. By the time he had got out of that uncongenial position, two more of the Kid's swings had found their mark. Mr. Fisher, somewhat perturbed, scuttled out into the middle of the ring, the Kid following in his self-contained, stolid way.

The Cyclone now became still more cyclonic. He had a left arm which seemed to open out in joints like a telescope. Several times when the Kid appeared well out of distance there was a thud as a brown glove ripped in over his guard and jerked his head back. But always he kept boring in, delivering an occasional right to the body with the pleased smile of an infant destroying a Noah's ark with a tack-hammer. Despite these efforts, however, he was plainly getting all the worst of it. Energetic Mr. Fisher, relying on his long left, was putting in three blows to his one. When the gong sounded, ending the first round, the house was practically solid for the Cyclone. Whoops and yells rose from everywhere. The building rang with shouts of, "Oh, you Dick!"

Smith turned sadly to John.

"It seems to me," he said, "that this merry meeting looks like doing Comrade Brady no good. I should not be surprised at any moment to see his head bounce off on to the floor."

Rounds two and three were a repetition of round one. The Cyclone raged almost unchecked about the ring. In one lightning rally in the third he brought his right across squarely on to the Kid's jaw. It was a blow which should have knocked any boxer out. The Kid merely staggered slightly, and returned to business still smiling.

With the opening of round four there came a subtle change. The Cyclone's fury was expending itself. That long left shot out less sharply. Instead of being knocked back by it, the *Peaceful Moments* champion now took the hits in his stride, and came shuffling in with his damaging body-blows. There were cheers and "Oh, you Dick's!" at the sound of the gong, but there was an appealing note in them this time. The gallant sportsmen whose connection with boxing was confined to watching other men fight and betting on what they considered a certainty, and who would have expired promptly if anyone had tapped them sharply on their well-filled vests, were beginning to fear that they might lose their money after all.

In the fifth round the thing became a certainty. Like the month of March, the Cyclone, who had come in like a lion, was going out like a lamb. A slight decrease in the pleasantness of the Kid's smile was noticeable. His expression began to resemble more nearly the gloomy importance of the *Peaceful Moments* photographs. Yells of agony from panic-stricken speculators around the ring began to smite the rafters. The Cyclone, now but a gentle breeze, clutched repeatedly, hanging on like a leech till removed by the red-jerseyed referee.

Suddenly a grisly silence fell upon the house. For the Kid, battered, but obviously content, was standing in the middle of the ring, while on the ropes the Cyclone, drooping like a wet sock, was sliding slowly to the floor.

"*Peaceful Moments* wins," said Smith. "An omen, I fancy, Comrade John."

Penetrating into the Kid's dressing-room some moments later, the editorial staff found the winner of the ten-round exhibition bout between members of the club seated on a chair having his right leg rubbed by a shock-headed man in a sweater, who had been one of his seconds during the conflict. The Kid beamed as they entered.

"Gents," he said, "come right in. Mighty glad to see you."

"It is a relief to me, Comrade Brady," said Smith, "to find that you can see us. I had expected to find that Comrade Fisher's purposeful wallops had completely closed your star-likes."

"Sure, I never felt them. He's a good, quick boy, is Dick, but," continued the Kid with powerful imagery "he couldn't hit a hole in a block of ice-cream, not if he was to use a coke-hammer."

"And yet at one period in the proceedings," said Smith, "I fancied that your head would come unglued at the neck. But the fear was merely transient. When you began to get going, why, then I felt like some watcher of the skies when a new planet swims into his ken, or like stout Cortez when with eagle eyes he stared at the Pacific."

The Kid blinked.

"How's that?" he enquired.

"And why did I feel like that, Comrade Brady? I will tell you. Because my faith in you was justified. Because there before me stood the ideal fighting editor of *Peaceful Moments*. It is not a post that any weakling can fill. Mere charm of manner cannot qualify a man for the position. No one can hold down the job simply by having a kind heart or being good at comic songs. No. We want a man of thews and sinews, a man who would rather be hit on the head with a half-brick than not. And you, Comrade Brady, are such a man."

The shock-headed man, who during this conversation had been concentrating himself on his subject's left leg now announced that he guessed that would about do, and having advised the Kid not to stop and pick daisies, but to get into his clothes at once before he caught a chill, bade the company goodnight and retired.

Smith shut the door.

"Comrade Brady," he said, "you know those articles about the tenements we've been having in the paper?"

"Sure. I read 'em. They're to the good. It was about time some strong josher came and put it across 'em."

"So we thought. Comrade Parker, however, totally disagreed with us."

"Parker?"

"That's what I'm coming to," said Smith. "The day before yesterday a man named Parker called at the office and tried to buy us off."

"You gave him the hook, I guess?" queried the interested Kid.

"To such an extent, Comrade Brady," said Smith, "that he left breathing threatenings and slaughter. And it is for that reason that we have ventured to call upon you. We're pretty sure by this time that Comrade Parker has put one of the gangs on to us."

"You don't say!" exclaimed the Kid. "Gee! They're tough propositions, those gangs."

"So we've come along to you. We can look after ourselves out of the office, but what we want is someone to help in case they try to rush us there. In brief, a fighting editor. At all costs we must have privacy. No writer can prune and polish his sentences to his satisfaction if he is compelled constantly to break off in order to eject boisterous toughs. We therefore offer you the job of sitting in the outer room and intercepting these bravoes before they can reach us. The salary we leave to you. There are doubloons and to spare in the old oak chest. Take what you need and put the rest—if any—back. How does the offer strike you, Comrade Brady?"

"Gents," said the Kid, "it's this way."

He slipped into his coat, and resumed.

"Now that I've made good by licking Dick, they'll be giving me a chance of a big fight. Maybe with Jimmy Garvin. Well, if that happens, see what I mean? I'll have to be going away somewhere and getting into training. I shouldn't be able to come and sit with you. But, if you gents feel like it, I'd be mighty glad to come in till I'm wanted to go into training camp."

"Great," said Smith. "And touching salary—"

"Shucks!" said the Kid with emphasis. "Nix on the salary thing. I wouldn't take a dime. If it hadn't 'a' been for you, I'd have been waiting still for a chance of lining up in the championship class. That's good enough for me. Any old thing you want me to do, I'll do it, and glad to."

"Comrade Brady," said Smith warmly, "you are, if I may say so, the goods. You are, beyond a doubt, supremely the stuff. We three, then, hand-in-hand, will face the foe, and if the foe has good, sound sense, he will keep right away. You appear to be ready. Shall we meander forth?"

The building was empty and the lights were out when they emerged from the dressing-room. They had to grope their way in darkness. It was raining when they reached the street, and the only signs of life were a moist policeman and the distant glare of saloon lights down the road.

They turned off to the left, and, after walking some hundred yards, found themselves in a blind alley.

"Hello!" said John. "Where have we come to?"

Smith sighed.

"In my trusting way," he said, "I had imagined that either you or Comrade Brady was in charge of this expedition and taking me by a known route to the nearest subway station. I did not think to ask. I placed myself, without hesitation, wholly in your hands."

"I thought the Kid knew the way," said John.

"I was just taggin' along with you gents," protested the light-weight. "I thought you was taking me right. This is the first time I been up here."

"Next time we three go on a little jaunt anywhere," said Smith resignedly, "it would be as well to take a map and a corps of guides with us. Otherwise we shall start for Broadway and finish up at Minneapolis."

They emerged from the blind alley and stood in the dark street, looking doubtfully up and down it.

"Aha!" said Smith suddenly. "I perceive a native. Several natives, in fact. Quite a little covey of them. We will put our case before them, concealing nothing, and rely on their advice to take us to our goal."

A little knot of men was approaching from the left. In the darkness it was impossible to say how many of them were there. Smith stepped forward, the Kid at his side.

"Excuse me, sir," he said to the leader, "but if you can spare me a moment of your valuable time—"

There was a sudden shuffle of feet on the pavement, a quick movement on the part of the Kid, a chunky sound as of wood striking wood, and the man Smith had been addressing fell to the ground in a heap.

As he fell, something dropped from his hand on to the pavement with a bump and a rattle. Stooping swiftly, the Kid picked it up, and handed it to Smith. His fingers closed upon it. It was a short, wicked-looking little bludgeon, the black-jack of the New York tough.

"Get busy," advised the Kid briefly.

CHAPTER XIX
THE FIRST BATTLE

The promptitude and despatch with which the Kid had attended to the gentleman with the black-jack had not been without its effect on the followers of the stricken one. Physical courage is not an outstanding quality of the New York gangsman. His personal preference is for retreat when it is a question of unpleasantness with a stranger. And, in any case, even when warring among themselves, the gangs exhibit a lively distaste for the hard knocks of hand-to-hand fighting. Their chosen method of battling is to lie down on the ground and shoot.

The Kid's rapid work on the present occasion created a good deal of confusion. There was no doubt that much had been hoped for from speedy attack. Also, the generalship of the expedition had been in the hands of the fallen warrior. His removal from the sphere of active influence had left the party without a head. And, to add to their discomfiture, they could not account for the Kid. Smith they knew, and John was to be accounted for, but who was this stranger with the square shoulders and the uppercut that landed like a cannon ball? Something approaching a panic prevailed among the gang.

It was not lessened by the behavior of the intended victims. John was the first to join issue. He had been a few paces behind the others during the black-jack incident, but, dark as it was, he had seen enough to show him that the occasion was, as Smith would have said, one for the shrewd blow rather than the prolonged parley. With a shout, he made a football rush into the confused mass of the enemy. A moment later Smith and the Kid followed, and there raged over the body of the fallen leader a battle of Homeric type.

It was not a long affair. The rules and conditions governing the encounter offended the delicate sensibilities of the gang. Like artists who feel themselves trammeled by distasteful conventions, they were damped and could not do themselves justice. Their forte was long-range fighting with pistols. With that they felt en rapport. But this vulgar brawling in the darkness with muscular opponents who hit hard and often with the clenched fist was distasteful to them. They could not develop any enthusiasm for it. They carried pistols, but it was too dark and the combatants were too entangled to allow them to use these.

There was but one thing to be done. Reluctant as they might be to abandon their fallen leader, it must be done. Already they were suffering grievously from John, the black-jack, and the lightning blows of the Kid. For a moment they hung, wavering, then stampeded in half-a-dozen different directions, melting into the night whence they had come.

John, full of zeal, pursued one fugitive some fifty yards down the street, but his quarry, exhibiting a rare turn of speed, easily outstripped him.

He came back, panting, to find Smith and the Kid examining the fallen leader of the departed ones with the aid of a match, which went out just as John arrived.

The Kid struck another. The head of it fell off and dropped upon the up-turned face. The victim stirred, shook himself, sat up, and began to mutter something in a foggy voice.

"He's still woozy," said the Kid.

"Still—what exactly, Comrade Brady?"

"In the air," explained the Kid. "Bats in the belfry. Dizzy. See what I mean? It's often like that when a feller puts one in with a bit of weight behind it just where that one landed. Gee! I remember when I fought Martin Kelly; I was only starting to learn the game then. Martin and me was mixing it good and hard all over the ring, when suddenly he puts over a stiff one right on the point. What do you think I done? Fall down and take the count? Not on your life. I just turns round and walks straight out of the ring to my dressing-room. Willie Harvey, who was seconding me, comes tearing in after me, and finds me getting into my clothes. 'What's doing, Kid?' he asks. 'I'm going fishin', Willie,' I says. 'It's a lovely day.' 'You've lost the fight,' he says. 'Fight?' says I. 'What fight?' See what I mean? I hadn't a notion of what had happened. It was half an hour and more before I could remember a thing."

During this reminiscence, the man on the ground had contrived to clear his mind of the mistiness induced by the Kid's upper cut. The first sign he showed of returning intelligence was a sudden dash for safety up the road. But he had not gone five yards when he sat down limply.

The Kid was inspired to further reminiscence.

"Guess he's feeling pretty poor," he said. "It's no good him trying to run for a while after he's put his chin in the way of a real live one. I remember when Joe Peterson put me out, way back when I was new to the game—it was the same year I fought Martin Kelly. He had an awful punch, had old Joe, and he put me down and out in the eighth round. After the fight they found me on the fire-escape outside my dressing-room. 'Come in, Kid,' says they. 'It's all right, chaps,' I says, 'I'm dying.' Like that. 'It's all right, chaps, I'm dying.' Same with this guy. See what I mean?"

They formed a group about the fallen black-jack expert.

"Pardon us," said Smith courteously, "for breaking in upon your reverie, but if you could spare us a moment of your valuable time, there are one or two things which we would like to know."

"Sure thing," agreed the Kid.

"In the first place," continued Smith, "would it be betraying professional secrets if you told us which particular bevy of energetic cutthroats it is to which you are attached?"

"Gent," explained the Kid, "wants to know what's your gang."

The man on the ground muttered something that to Smith and John was unintelligible.

"It would be a charity," said the former, "if some philanthropist would give this fellow elocution lessons. Can you interpret, Comrade Brady?"

"Says it's the Three Points," said the Kid.

"The Three Points? That's Spider Reilly's lot. Perhaps this *is* Spider Reilly?"

"Nope," said the Kid. "I know the Spider. This ain't him. This is some other mutt."

"Which other mutt in particular?" asked Smith. "Try and find out, Comrade Brady. You seem to be able to understand what he says. To me, personally, his remarks sound like the output of a gramophone with a hot potato in its mouth."

"Says he's Jack Repetto," announced the interpreter.

There was another interruption at this moment. The bashful Mr. Repetto, plainly a man who was not happy in the society of strangers, made another attempt to withdraw. Reaching out a pair of lean hands, he pulled the Kid's legs from under him with a swift jerk, and, wriggling to his feet, started off again down the road. Once more, however, desire outran performance. He got as far as the nearest street-lamp, but no further. The giddiness seemed to overcome him again, for he grasped the lamp-post, and, sliding slowly to the ground, sat there motionless.

The Kid, whose fall had jolted and bruised him, was inclined to be wrathful and vindictive. He was the first of the three to reach the elusive Mr. Repetto, and if that worthy had happened to be standing instead of sitting it might have gone hard with him. But the Kid was not the man to attack a fallen foe. He contented himself with brushing the dust off his person and addressing a richly abusive flow of remarks to Mr. Repetto.

Under the rays of the lamp it was possible to discern more closely the features of the black-jack exponent. There was a subtle but noticeable resemblance to those of Mr. Bat Jarvis. Apparently the latter's oiled forelock, worn low over the forehead, was more a concession to the general fashion prevailing in gang circles than an expression of personal taste. Mr. Repetto had it, too. In his case it was almost white, for the fallen warrior was an albino. His eyes, which were closed, had white lashes and were set as near together as Nature had been able to manage without actually running them into one another. His underlip protruded and drooped. Looking at him, one felt instinctively that no judging committee of a beauty contest would hesitate a moment before him.

It soon became apparent that the light of the lamp, though bestowing the doubtful privilege of a clearer view of Mr. Repetto's face, held certain disadvantages. Scarcely had the staff of *Peaceful Moments* reached the faint yellow pool of light, in the center of which Mr. Repetto reclined, than, with a suddenness which caused them to leap into the air, there sounded from the darkness down the road the crack-crack-crack of a revolver. Instantly from the opposite direction came other shots. Three bullets cut grooves in the roadway almost at John's feet. The Kid gave a sudden howl. Smith's hat, suddenly imbued with life, sprang into the air and vanished, whirling into the night.

The thought did not come to them consciously at the moment, there being little time to think, but it was evident as soon as, diving out of the circle of light into the sheltering darkness, they crouched down and waited for the next move, that a somewhat skilful ambush had been effected. The other members of the gang, who had fled with such remarkable speed, had by no means been eliminated altogether from the game. While the questioning of Mr. Repetto had been in progress, they had crept back, unperceived except by Mr. Repetto himself. It being too dark for successful shooting, it had become Mr. Repetto's task to lure his captors into the light, which he had accomplished with considerable skill.

For some minutes the battle halted. There was dead silence. The circle of light was empty now. Mr. Repetto had vanished. A tentative shot from nowhere ripped through the air close to where Smith lay flattened on the pavement. And then the pavement began to vibrate and give out a curious resonant sound. Somewhere—it might be near or far—a policeman had heard the shots, and was signaling for help to other policemen along the line by beating on the flagstones with his night stick. The noise grew, filling the still air. From somewhere down the road sounded the ring of running feet.

"De cops!" cried a voice. "Beat it!"

Next moment the night was full of clatter. The gang was "beating it."

Smith rose to his feet and felt his wet and muddy clothes ruefully.

The rescue party was coming up at the gallop.

"What's doing?" asked a voice.

"Nothing now," said the disgusted voice of the Kid from the shadows._"They've beaten it."

The circle of lamplight became as if by mutual consent a general rendezvous. Three gray-clad policemen, tough, clean-shaven men with keen eyes and square jaws, stood there, revolvers in one hand, night sticks in the other. Smith, hatless and muddy, joined them. John and the Kid, the latter bleeding freely from his left ear, the lobe of which had been chipped by a bullet, were the last to arrive.

"What's been the rough-house?" inquired one of the policemen, mildly interested.

"Do you know a sport of the name of Repetto?" enquired Smith.

"Jack Repetto? Sure."

"He belongs to the Three Points," said another intelligent officer, as one naming some fashionable club.

"When next you see him," said Smith, "I should be obliged if you would use your authority to make him buy me a new hat. I could do with another pair of trousers, too, but I will not press the trousers. A new hat is, however, essential. Mine has a six-inch hole in it."

"Shot at you, did they?" said one of the policemen, as who should say,_"Tut, tut!"

"Shot at us!" burst out the ruffled Kid. "What do you think's been happening? Think an aeroplane ran into my ear and took half of it off? Think the noise was somebody opening bottles of pop? Think those guys that sneaked off down the road was just training for a Marathon?"

"Comrade Brady," said Smith, "touches the spot. He—"

"Say, are you Kid Brady?" enquired one of the officers. For the first time the constabulary had begun to display real animation.

"Reckoned I'd seen you somewhere!" said another. "You licked Cyclone_Dick all right, Kid, I hear."

"And who but a bone-head thought he wouldn't?" demanded the third warmly. "He could whip a dozen Cyclone Dicks in the same evening with his eyes shut."

"He's the next champeen," admitted the first speaker.

"If he juts it over Jimmy Garvin," argued the second.

"Jimmy Garvin!" cried the third. "He can whip twenty Jimmy Garvins with his feet tied. I tell you—"

"I am loath," observed Smith, "to interrupt this very impressive brain barbecue, but, trivial as it may seem to you, to me there is a certain interest in this other little matter of my ruined hat. I know that it may strike you as hypersensitive of us to protest against being riddled with bullets, but—"

"Well, what's been doin'?" inquired the Force. It was a nuisance, this perpetual harping on trifles when the deep question of the light-weight championship of the world was under discussion, but the sooner it was attended to, the sooner it would be over.

John undertook to explain.

"The Three Points laid for us," he said. "This man, Jack Repetto, was bossing the crowd. The Kid put one over on to Jack Repetto's chin, and we were asking him a few questions when the rest came back, and started shooting. Then we got to cover quick, and you came up and they beat it."

"That," said Smith, nodding, "is a very fair *precis* of the evening's events. We should like you, if you will be so good, to corral this Comrade Repetto, and see that he buys me a new hat."

"We'll round Jack up," said one of the policemen indulgently.

"Do it nicely," urged Smith. "Don't go hurting his feelings."

The second policeman gave it as his opinion that Jack was getting too gay. The third policeman conceded this. Jack, he said, had shown signs for some time past of asking for it in the neck. It was an error on Jack's part, he gave his hearers to understand, to assume that the lid was completely off the great city of New York.

"Too blamed fresh he's gettin'," the trio agreed. They seemed to think it was too bad of Jack.

"The wrath of the Law," said Smith, "is very terrible. We will leave the matter, then, in your hands. In the meantime, we should be glad if you would direct us to the nearest subway station. Just at the moment, the cheerful lights of the Great White Way are what I seem chiefly to need."

* * * * *

So ended the opening engagement of the campaign, in a satisfactory but far from decisive victory for the *Peaceful Moments*' army.

"The victory," said Smith, "was not bloodless. Comrade Brady's ear, my hat—these are not slight casualties. On the other hand, the elimination of Comrade Repetto is pleasant. I know few men whom I would not rather meet on a lonely road than Comrade Repetto. He is one of nature's black-jackers. Probably the thing crept upon him slowly. He started, possibly, in a merely tentative way by slugging one of the family circle. His aunt, let us say, or his small brother. But, once started, he is unable to resist the craving. The thing grips him like dram-drinking. He black-jacks now not because he really wants to, but because he cannot help himself. There's something singularly consoling in the thought that Comrade Repetto will no longer be among those present."

"There are others," said John.

"As you justly remark," said Smith, "there are others. I am glad we have secured Comrade Brady's services. We may need them."

CHAPTER XX
BETTY AT LARGE

It was not till Betty found herself many blocks distant from the office of *Peaceful Moments* that she checked her headlong flight. She had run down the stairs and out into the street blindly, filled only with that passion for escape which had swept her away from Mervo. Not till she had dived into the human river of Broadway and reached Times Square did she feel secure. Then, with less haste, she walked on to the park, and sat down on a bench, to think.

Inevitably she had placed her own construction on John's sudden appearance in New York and at the spot where only one person in any way connected with Mervo knew her to be. She did not know that Smith and he were friends, and did not, therefore, suspect that the former and not herself might be the object of his visit. Nor had any word reached her of what had happened at Mervo after her departure. She had taken it for granted that things had continued as she had left them; and the only possible explanation to her of John's presence in New York was that, acting under orders from Mr. Scobell, he had come to try and bring her back.

She shuddered as she conjured up the scene that must have taken place if Pugsy had not mentioned his name and she had gone on into the inner room. In itself the thought that, after what she had said that morning on the island, after she had forced on him, stripping it of the uttermost rag of disguise, the realization of how his position appeared to her, he should have come, under orders, to bring her back, was well-nigh unendurable. But to have met him, to have seen the man she loved plunging still deeper into shame, would have been pain beyond bearing. Better a thousand times than that this panic flight into the iron wilderness of New York.

It was cool and soothing in the park. The roar of the city was hushed. It was pleasant to sit there and watch the squirrels playing on the green slopes or scampering up into the branches through which one could see the gleam of water. Her thoughts became less chaotic. The peace of the summer afternoon stole upon her.

It did not take her long to make up her mind that the door of *Peaceful Moments* was closed to her. John, not finding her, might go away, but he would return. Reluctantly, she abandoned the paper. Her heart was heavy when she had formed the decision. She had been as happy at *Peaceful Moments* as it was possible for her to be now. She would miss Smith and the leisurely work and the feeling of being one of a team, working in a good cause. And that, brought Broster Street back to her mind, and she thought of the children. No, she could not abandon them. She had started the tenement articles, and she would go on with them. But she must do it without ever venturing into the dangerous neighborhood of the office.

A squirrel ran up and sat begging for a nut. Betty searched in the grass in the hope of finding one, but came upon nothing but shells. The squirrel bounded away, with a disdainful flick of the tail.

Betty laughed.

"You think of nothing but food. You ought to be ashamed to be so greedy."

And then it came to her suddenly that it was no trifle, this same problem of food.

The warm, green park seemed to grow chill and gray. Once again she must deal with life's material side.

Her case was at the same time better and worse than it had been on that other occasion when she had faced the future in the French train; better, because then New York had been to her something vague and terrifying, while now it was her city; worse, because she could no longer seek help from Mrs. Oakley.

That Mrs. Oakley had given John the information which had enabled him to discover her hiding-place, Betty felt certain. By what other possible means could he have found it? Why Mrs. Oakley, whom she had considered an ally, should have done so, she did not know. She attributed it to a change of mind, a reconsideration of the case when uninfluenced by sentiment. And yet it seemed strange. Perhaps John had gone to her and the sight of him had won the old lady over to his side. It might be so. At any rate, it meant that the cottage on Staten Island, like the office of *Peaceful Moments*, was closed to her. She must look elsewhere for help, or trust entirely to herself.

She sat on, thinking, with grave, troubled eyes, while the shadows lengthened and the birds rustled sleepily in the branches overhead.

* * * * *

Among the good qualities, none too numerous, of Mr. Bat Jarvis, of Groome Street in the Bowery, early rising was not included. It was his habit to retire to rest at an advanced hour, and to balance accounts by lying abed on the following morning. This idiosyncrasy of his was well known in the neighborhood and respected, and it was generally bold to be both bad taste and unsafe to visit Bat's shop until near the fashionable hour for luncheon, when the great one, shirt-sleeved and smoking a short pipe, would appear in the doorway, looking out upon the world and giving it to understand that he was now open to be approached by deserving acquaintances.

When, therefore, at ten o'clock in the morning his slumbers were cut short by a sharp rapping at the front door, his first impression was that he had been dreaming. When, after a brief interval, the noise was resumed, he rose in his might and, knuckling the sleep from his eyes, went down, tight-lipped, to interview this person.

He had got as far as a preliminary "Say!" when speech was wiped from his lips as with a sponge, and he stood gaping and ashamed, for the murderer of sleep and untimely knocker on front doors was Betty.

Mr. Jarvis had not forgotten Betty. His meeting with her at the office of *Peaceful Moments* had marked an epoch in his life. Never before had anyone quite like her crossed his path, and at that moment romance had come to him. His was essentially a respectful admiration. He was content—indeed, he preferred to worship from afar. Of his own initiative he would never have met her again. In her presence, with those gray eyes of hers looking at him, tremors ran down his spine, and his conscience, usually a battered and downtrodden wreck, became fiercely aggressive. She filled him with novel emotions, and whether these were pleasant or painful was more than he could say. He had not the gift of analysis where his feelings were concerned. To himself he put it, broadly, that she made him feel like a nickel with a hole in it. But that was not entirely satisfactory. There were other and pleasanter emotions mixed in with this humility. The thought of her made him feel, for instance, vaguely chivalrous. He wanted to do risky and useful things for her. Thus, if any fresh guy should endeavor to get gay with her, it would, he felt, be a privilege to fix that same guy. If she should be in bad, he would be more than ready to get busy on her behalf.

But he had never expected to meet her again, certainly not on his own doorstep at ten in the morning. To Bat ten in the morning was included with the small hours.

Betty smiled at him, a little anxiously. She had no suspicion that she played star to Mr. Jarvis' moth in the latter's life, and, as she eyed him, standing there on the doorstep, her excuse for coming to him began to seem terribly flimsy. Not being aware that he was in reality a tough Bayard, keenly desirous of obeying her lightest word, she had staked her all on the chance of his remembering the cat episode and being grateful on account of it; and in the cold light of the morning this idea, born in the watches of the night, when things tend to lose their proportion, struck her as less happy than she had fancied. Suppose he had forgotten all about it! Suppose he should be violent! For a moment her heart sank. He certainly was not a pleasing and encouraging sight, as he stood there blinking at her. No man looks his best immediately on rising from bed, and Bat, even at his best, was not a hero of romance. His forelock drooped dankly over his brow; there was stubble on his chin; his eyes were red, like a dog's. He did not look like the Fairy Prince who was to save her in her trouble.

"I—I hope you remember me, Mr. Jarvis," she faltered. "Your cat. I—"

He nodded speechlessly. Hideous things happened to his face. He was really trying to smile pleasantly, but it seemed a scowl to Betty, and her voice died away.

Mr. Jarvis spoke.

"Ma'am—sure!—step 'nside."

Betty followed him into the shop. There were birds in cages on the walls, and, patroling the floor, a great company of cats, each with its leather collar. One rubbed itself against Betty's skirt. She picked it up, and began to stroke it. And, looking over its head at Mr. Jarvis, she was aware that he was beaming sheepishly.

His eyes darted away the instant they met hers, but Betty had seen enough to show her that she had mistaken nervousness for truculence. Immediately, she was at her ease, and womanlike, had begun to control the situation. She made conversation pleasantly, praising the cats, admiring the birds, touching lightly on the general subject of domestic pets, until her woman's sixth sense told her that her host's panic had passed, and that she might now proceed to discuss business.

"I hope you don't mind my coming to you, Mr. Jarvis," she said. "You know you told me to if ever I were in trouble, so I've taken you at your word. You don't mind?"

Mr. Jarvis gulped, and searched for words.

"Glad," he said at last.

"I've left *Peaceful Moments*. You know I used to be stenographer there."

She was surprised and gratified to see a look of consternation spread itself across Mr. Jarvis' face. It was a hopeful sign that he should take her cause to heart to such an extent.

But Mr. Jarvis' consternation was not due wholly to solicitude for her. His thoughts at that moment, put, after having been expurgated, into speech, might have been summed up in the line: "Of all sad words of tongue or pen the saddest are these, 'It might have been'!"

"Ain't youse woikin' dere no more? Is dat right?" he gasped. "Gee! I wisht I'd 'a' known it sooner. Why, a guy come to me and wants to give me half a ton of the long green to go to dat poiper what youse was woikin' on and fix de guy what's runnin' it. An' I truns him down 'cos I don't want you to be frown out of your job. Say, why youse quit woikin' dere?" His eyes narrowed as an idea struck him. "Say," he went on, "you ain't bin fired? Has de boss give youse de trundown? 'Cos if he has, say de woid and I'll fix him for youse, loidy. An' it won't set you back a nickel," he concluded handsomely.

"No, no," cried Betty, horrified. "Mr. Smith has been very kind to me._I left of my own free will."

Mr. Jarvis looked disappointed. His demeanor was like that of some mediaeval knight called back on the eve of starting out to battle with the Paynim for the honor of his lady.

"What was that you said about the man who came to you and offered you money?" asked Betty.

Her mind had flashed back to Mr. Parker's visit, and her heart was beating quickly.

"Sure! He come to me all right an' wants de guy on de poiper fixed. An' I truns him down."

"Oh! You won't dream of doing anything to hurt Mr. Smith, will you, Mr. Jarvis?" said Betty anxiously.

"Not if you say so, loidy."

"And your—friends? You won't let them do anything?"

"Nope."

Betty breathed freely again. Her knowledge of the East Side was small, and that there might be those there who acted independently of Mr. Jarvis, disdainful of his influence, did not occur to her. She returned to her own affairs, satisfied that danger no longer threatened.

"Mr. Jarvis, I wonder if you can help me. I want to find some work to do," she said.

"Woik?"

"I have to earn my living, you see, and I'm afraid I don't know how to begin."

Mr. Jarvis pondered. "What sort of woik?"

"Any sort," said Betty valiantly. "I don't care what it is."

Mr. Jarvis knitted his brows in thought. He was not used to being an employment agency. But Betty was Betty, and even at the cost of a headache he must think of something.

At the end of five minutes inspiration came to him.

"Say," he said, "what do youse call de guy dat sits an' takes de money at an eatin'-joint? Cashier? Well, say, could youse be dat?"

"It would be just the thing. Do you know a place?"

"Sure. Just around de corner. I'll take you dere."

Betty waited while he put on his coat, and they started out. Betty chatted as they walked, but Mr. Jarvis, who appeared a little self-conscious beneath the unconcealed interest of the neighbors, was silent. At intervals he would turn and glare ferociously at the heads that popped out of windows or protruded from doorways. Fame has its penalties, and most of the population of that portion of the Bowery had turned out to see their most prominent citizen so romantically employed as a squire of dames.

After a short walk Bat halted the expedition before a dingy restaurant. The glass window bore in battered letters the name, Fontelli.

"Dis is de joint," he said.

Inside the restaurant a dreamy-eyed Italian sat gazing at vacancy and twirling a pointed mustache. In a far corner a solitary customer was finishing a late breakfast.

Signor Fontelli, for the sad-eyed exile was he, sprang to his feet at the sight of Mr. Jarvis' well-known figure. An ingratiating, but nervous, smile came into view behind the pointed mustache.

"Hey, Tony," said Mr. Jarvis, coming at once to the point, "I want you to know dis loidy. She's going to be cashier at dis joint."

Signor Fontelli looked at Betty and shook his head. He smiled deprecatingly. His manner seemed to indicate that, while she met with the approval of Fontelli, the slave of her sex, to Fontelli, the employer, she appealed in vain. He gave his mustache a sorrowful twirl.

"Ah, no," he sighed. "Not da cashier do I need. I take-a myself da money."

Mr. Jarvis looked at him coldly. He continued to look at him coldly. His lower jaw began slowly to protrude, and his forehead retreated further behind its zareba of forelock.

There was a pause. The signor was plainly embarrassed.

"Dis loidy," repeated Mr. Jarvis, "is cashier at dis joint at six per—" He paused. "Does dat go?" he added smoothly.

Certainly there was magnetism about Mr. Jarvis. With a minimum of words he produced remarkable results. Something seemed to happen suddenly to Signor Fontelli's spine. He wilted like a tired flower. A gesture, in which were blended resignation, humility, and a desire to be at peace with all men, particularly Mr. Jarvis, completed his capitulation.

Mr. Jarvis waited while Betty was instructed in her simple duties, then drew her aside.

"Say," he remarked confidentially, "youse'll be all right here. Six per ain't all de dough dere is in de woild, but, bein' cashier, see, you can swipe a whole heap more whenever you feel like it. And if Tony registers a kick, I'll come around and talk to him—see? Dat's right. Good-morning, loidy."

And, having delivered these admirable hints to young cashiers in a hurry to get rich, Mr. Jarvis ducked his head in a species of bow, declined to be thanked, and shuffled out into the street, leaving Betty to open her new career by taking thirty-seven cents from the late breakfaster.

CHAPTER XXI
CHANGES IN THE STAFF

Three days had elapsed since the battle which had opened the campaign, and there had been no further movement on the part of the enemy. Smith was puzzled. A strange quiet seemed to be brooding over the other camp. He could not believe that a single defeat had crushed the foe, but it was hard to think of any other explanation.

It was Pugsy Maloney who, on the fourth morning, brought to the office the inner history of the truce. His version was brief and unadorned, as was the way with his narratives. Such things as first causes and piquant details he avoided, as tending to prolong the telling excessively, thus keeping him from the perusal of his cowboy stories. He gave the thing out merely as an item of general interest, a bubble on the surface of the life of a great city. He did not know how nearly interested were his employers in any matter touching that gang which is known as the Three Points.

Pugsy said: "Dere's been fuss'n going on down where I live. Dude_Dawson's mad at Spider Reilly, and now de Table Hills is layin' for de_T'ree Points, to soak it to 'em. Dat's right."

He then retired to his outer fastness, yielding further details jerkily and with the distrait air of one whose mind is elsewhere.

Skilfully extracted and pieced together, these details formed themselves into the following typical narrative of East Side life.

There were four really important gangs in New York at this time. There were other less important institutions besides, but these were little more than mere friendly gatherings of old boyhood chums for purposes of mutual companionship. They might grow into formidable organizations in time, but for the moment the amount of ice which good judges declared them to cut was but small. They would "stick up" an occasional wayfarer for his "cush," and they carried "canisters" and sometimes fired them off, but these things do not signify the cutting of ice. In matters political there were only four gangs which counted, the East Side, the Groome Street, the Three Points and the Table Hill. Greatest of these, by virtue of their numbers, were the East Side and the Groome Street, the latter presided over at the time of this story by Mr. Bat Jarvis. These two were colossal, and, though they might fight each other, were immune from attack at the hands of the rest.

But between the other gangs, and especially between the Table Hill and the Three Points, which were much of a size, warfare raged as frequently as among the Republics of South America. There had always been bad blood between the

Table Hill and the Three Points. Little events, trifling in themselves, had always occurred to shatter friendly relations just when there seemed a chance of their being formed. Thus, just as the Table Hillites were beginning to forgive the Three Points for shooting the redoubtable Paul Horgan down at Coney Island, a Three Pointer injudiciously wiped out a Table Hillite near Canal Street. He pleaded self-defense, and in any case it was probably mere thoughtlessness, but nevertheless the Table Hillites were ruffled.

That had been a month or so back. During that month things had been simmering down, and peace was just preparing to brood when there occurred the incident alluded to by Pugsy, the regrettable falling out between Dude Dawson and Spider Reilly.

To be as brief as possible, Dude Dawson had gone to spend a happy evening at a dancing saloon named Shamrock Hall, near Groome Street. Now, Shamrock Hall belonged to a Mr. Maginnis, a friend of Bat Jarvis, and was under the direct protection of that celebrity. It was, therefore, sacred ground, and Mr. Dawson visited it in a purely private and peaceful capacity. The last thing he intended was to spoil the harmony of the evening.

Alas for the best intentions! Two-stepping clumsily round the room—for he was a poor, though enthusiastic, dancer—Dude Dawson collided with and upset a certain Reddy Davis and his partner. Reddy Davis was a member of the Three Points, and his temper was the temper of a red-headed man. He "slugged" Mr. Dawson. Mr. Dawson, more skilful at the fray than at the dance, joined battle willingly, and they were absorbed in a stirring combat, when an interruption occurred. In the far corner of the room, surrounded by admiring friends, sat Spider Reilly, monarch of the Three Points. He had noticed that there was a slight disturbance at the other side of the hall, but had given it little attention till the dancing ceasing suddenly and the floor emptying itself of its crowd, he had a plain view of Mr. Dawson and Mr. Davis squaring up at each other for the second round.

We must assume that Mr. Reilly was not thinking of what he did, for his action was contrary to all rules of gang etiquette. In the street it would have been perfectly legitimate, even praiseworthy, but in a dance-hall under the protection of a neutral power it was unpardonable.

What he did was to produce his revolver, and shoot the unsuspecting Mr. Dawson in the leg. Having done which, he left hurriedly, fearing the wrath of Bat Jarvis.

Mr. Dawson, meanwhile, was attended to and helped home. Willing informants gave him the name of his aggressor, and before morning the Table Hill camp was in a ferment. Shooting broke out in three places, though there were no casualties.

When the day dawned there existed between the two gangs a state of war more bitter than any in their record, for this time it was chieftain who had assaulted chieftain, Royal blood had been spilt.

Such was the explanation of the lull in the campaign against *Peaceful Moments*. The new war had taken the mind of Spider Reilly and his warriors off the paper and its affairs for the moment, much as the unexpected appearance of a mad bull would make a man forget that he had come out snipe-shooting.

At present there had been no pitched battle. As was usual between the gangs, war had broken out in a somewhat tentative fashion at first. There had been skirmishes by the wayside, but nothing more. The two armies were sparring for an opening.

* * * * *

Smith was distinctly relieved at the respite, for necessitating careful thought. This was the defection of Kid Brady.

The Kid's easy defeat of Cyclone Dick Fisher had naturally created a sensation in sporting circles. He had become famous in a night. It was not with surprise, therefore, that Smith received from his fighting editor the information that he had been matched against one Eddie Wood, whose fame outshone even that of the late Cyclone.

The Kid, a white man to the core, exhibited quite a feudal loyalty to the paper which had raised him from the ruck and placed him on the road to eminence.

"Say the word," he said, "and I'll call it off. If you feel you need me around here, Mr. Smith, say so, and I'll side-step Eddie."

"Comrade Brady," said Smith with enthusiasm, "I have had occasion before to call you sport. I do so again. But I'm not going to stand in your way. If you eliminate this Comrade Wood, they will have to give you a chance against Jimmy Garvin, won't they?"

"I guess that's right," said the Kid. "Eddie stayed nineteen rounds against Jimmy, and, if I can put him away, it gets me clear into line with Jim, and he'll have to meet me."

"Then go in and win, Comrade Brady. We shall miss you. It will be as if a ray of sunshine had been removed from the office. But you mustn't throw a chance away."

"I'll train at White Plains," said the Kid, "so I'll be pretty near in case I'm wanted."

"Oh, we shall be all right," said Smith, "and if you win, we'll bring out a special number. Good luck, Comrade Brady, and many thanks for your help."

* * * * *

John, when he arrived at the office and learned the news, was for relying on their own unaided efforts.

"And, anyway," he said, "I don't see who else there is to help us. You could tell the police, I suppose," he went on doubtfully.

Smith shook his head.

"The New York policeman, Comrade John, is, like all great men, somewhat peculiar. If you go to a New York policeman and exhibit a black eye, he is more likely to express admiration for the handiwork of the citizen responsible for the same than sympathy. No; since coming to this city I have developed a habit of taking care of myself, or employing private help. I do not want allies who will merely shake their heads at Comrade Reilly and his merry men, however sternly. I want someone who, if necessary, will soak it to them good."

"Sure," said John. "But who is there now the Kid's gone?"

"Who else but Comrade Jarvis?" said Smith.

"Jarvis? Bat Jarvis?"

"The same. I fancy that we shall find, on enquiry, that we are ace high with him. At any rate, there is no harm in sounding him. It is true that he may have forgotten, or it may be that it is to Comrade Brown alone that he is—"

"Who's Brown?" asked John.

"Our late stenographer," explained Smith. "A Miss Brown. She entertained Comrade Jarvis' cat, if you remember. I wonder what has become of her. She has sent in three more corking efforts on the subject of Broster Street, but she gives no address. I wish I knew where she was. I'd have liked for you to meet her."

CHAPTER XXII

A GATHERING OF CAT SPECIALISTS

"It will probably be necessary," said Smith, as they set out for Groome Street, "to allude to you, Comrade John, in the course of this interview, as one of our most eminent living cat-fanciers. You have never met Comrade Jarvis, I believe? Well, he is a gentleman with just about enough forehead to prevent his front hair getting inextricably blended with his eyebrows, and he owns twenty-three cats, each with a leather collar round its neck. It is, I fancy, the cat note which we shall have to strike to-day. If only Comrade Brown were with us, we could appeal to his finer feelings. But he has seen me only once and you never, and I should not care to bet that he will feel the least particle of dismay at the idea of our occiputs getting all mussed up with a black-jack. But when I inform him that you are an English cat-fancier, and that in your island home you have seventy-four fine cats, mostly Angoras, that will be a different matter. I shall be surprised if he does not fall on your neck."

They found Mr. Jarvis in his fancier's shop, engaged in the intellectual occupation of greasing a cat's paws with butter. He looked up as they entered, and then resumed his task.

"Comrade Jarvis," said Smith, "we meet again. You remember me?"

"Nope," said Mr. Jarvis promptly.

Smith was not discouraged.

"Ah!" he said tolerantly, "the fierce rush of New York life! How it wipes from the retina to-day the image impressed on it but yesterday. Is it not so, Comrade Jarvis?"

The cat-expert concentrated himself on his patient's paws without replying.

"A fine animal," said Smith, adjusting his monocle. "To what particular family of the *Felis Domestica* does that belong? In color it resembles a Neapolitan ice more than anything."

Mr. Jarvis' manner became unfriendly.

"Say, what do youse want? That's straight, ain't it? If youse want to buy a boid or a snake, why don't youse say so?"

"I stand corrected," said Smith; "I should have remembered that time is money. I called in here partly in the hope that, though you only met me once—on the stairs of my office, you might retain pleasant recollections of me, but principally in order that I might make two very eminent cat-fanciers acquainted. This," he said, with a wave of his hand in the direction of John, "is Comrade Maude, possibly the best known of English cat-fanciers. Comrade Maude's stud of Angoras is celebrated wherever the English language is spoken."

Mr. Jarvis's expression changed. He rose, and, having inspected John with silent admiration for a while, extended a well-buttered hand towards him. Smith looked on benevolently.

"What Comrade Maude does not know about cats," he said, "is not knowledge. His information on Angoras alone would fill a volume."

"Say"—Mr. Jarvis was evidently touching on a point which had weighed deeply upon him—"why's catnip called catnip?"

John looked at Smith helplessly. It sounded like a riddle, but it was obvious that Mr. Jarvis's motive in putting the question was not frivolous. He really wished to know.

"The word, as Comrade Maude was just about to observe," said Smith, "is a corruption of catmint. Why it should be so corrupted I do not know. But what of that? The subject is too deep to be gone fully into at the moment. I should recommend you to read Mr. Maude's little brochure on the matter. Passing lightly on from that—"

"Did youse ever have a cat dat ate bettles?" enquired Mr. Jarvis.

"There was a time when many of Comrade Maude's *Felidae* supported life almost entirely on beetles."

"Did they git thin?"

John felt it was time, if he were to preserve his reputation, to assert himself.

"No," he replied firmly.

Mr. Jarvis looked astonished.

"English beetles," said Smith, "don't make cats thin. Passing lightly—"

"I had a cat oncst," said Mr. Jarvis, ignoring the remark and sticking to his point, "dat ate beetles and got thin and used to tie itself inter knots."

"A versatile animal," agreed Smith.

"Say," Mr. Jarvis went on, now plainly on a subject near to his heart, "dem beetles is fierce. Sure! Can't keep de cats off of eatin' dem, I can't. First t'ing you know dey've swallowed dem, and den dey gits thin and ties theirselves into knots."

"You should put them into strait-waistcoats," said Smith. "Passing, however, lightly—"

"Say, ever have a cross-eyed cat?"

"Comrade Maude's cats," said Smith, "have happily been almost entirely free from strabismus."

"Dey's lucky, cross-eyed cats is. You has a cross-eyed cat, and not'in' don't never go wrong. But, say, was dere ever a cat wit' one blue and one yaller one in your bunch? Gee! it's fierce when it's like dat. It's a skidoo, is a cat wit' one blue eye and one yaller one. Puts you in bad, surest t'ing you know. Oncst a guy give me a cat like dat, and first t'ing you know I'm in bad all round. It wasn't till I give him away to de cop on de corner and gets me one dat's cross-eyed dat I lifts de skidoo off of me."

"And what happened to the cop?" enquired Smith, interested.

"Oh, he got in bad, sure enough," said Mr. Jarvis without emotion. "One of de boys what he'd pinched and had sent up the road once lays for him and puts one over on him wit a black-jack. Sure. Dat's what comes of havin' a cat wit' one blue and one yaller one."

Mr. Jarvis relapsed into silence. He seemed to be meditating on the inscrutable workings of Fate. Smith took advantage of the pause to leave the cat topic and touch on matters of more vital import.

"Tense and exhilarating as is this discussion of the optical peculiarities of cats," he said, "there is another matter on which, if you will permit me, I should like to touch. I would hesitate to bore you with my own private troubles, but this is a matter which concerns Comrade Maude as well as myself, and I can see that your regard for Comrade Maude is almost an obsession."

"How's that?"

"I can see," said Smith, "that Comrade Maude is a man to whom you give the glad hand."

Mr. Jarvis regarded John with respectful affection.

"Sure! He's to the good, Mr. Maude is."

"Exactly," said Smith. "To resume, then. The fact is, Comrade Jarvis, we are much persecuted by scoundrels. How sad it is in this world! We look to every side. We look to north, east, south, and west, and what do we see? Mainly scoundrels. I fancy you have heard a little about our troubles before this. In fact, I gather that the same scoundrels actually approached you with a view to engaging your services to do us up, but that you very handsomely refused the contract. We are the staff of *Peaceful Moments*."

"*Peaceful Moments*," said Mr. Jarvis. "Sure, dat's right. A guy comes to me and says he wants you put through it, but I gives him de trundown."

"So I was informed," said Smith. "Well, failing you, they went to a gentleman of the name of Reilly—"

"Spider Reilly?"

"Exactly. Spider Reilly, the lessee and manager of the Three Points gang."

Mr. Jarvis frowned.

"Dose T'ree Points, dey're to de bad. Dey're fresh."

"It is too true, Comrade Jarvis."

"Say," went on Mr. Jarvis, waxing wrathful at the recollection, "what do youse t'ink dem fresh stiffs done de odder night? Started some rough woik in me own dance-joint."

"Shamrock Hall?" said Smith. "I heard about it."

"Dat's right, Shamrock Hall. Got gay, dey did, wit' some of the Table Hillers. Say, I got it in for dem gazebos, sure I have. Surest t'ing you know."

Smith beamed approval.

"That," he said, "is the right spirit. Nothing could be more admirable. We are bound together by our common desire to check the ever-growing spirit of freshness among the members of the Three Points. Add to that the fact that we are united by a sympathetic knowledge of the manners and customs of cats, and especially that Comrade Maude, England's greatest fancier, is our mutual friend, and what more do we want? Nothing."

"Mr. Maude's to de good," assented Mr. Jarvis, eying John once more in friendly fashion.

"We are all to the good," said Smith. "Now, the thing I wished to ask you is this. The office of the paper was, until this morning, securely guarded by Comrade Brady, whose name will be familiar to you."

"De Kid?"

"On the bull's-eye, as usual. Kid Brady, the coming light-weight champion of the world. Well, he has unfortunately been compelled to leave us, and the way into the office is consequently clear to any sand-bag specialist who cares to wander in. So what I came to ask was, will you take Comrade Brady's place for a few days?"

"How's that?"

"Will you come in and sit in the office for the next day or so and help hold the fort? I may mention that there is money attached to the job. We will pay for your services."

Mr. Jarvis reflected but a brief moment.

"Why, sure," he said. "Me fer dat."

"Excellent, Comrade Jarvis. Nothing could be better. We will see you tomorrow, then. I rather fancy that the gay band of Three Pointers who will undoubtedly visit the offices of *Peaceful Moments* in the next few days is scheduled to run up against the surprise of their lives."

"Sure t'ing. I'll bring me canister."

"Do," said Smith. "In certain circumstances one canister is worth a flood of rhetoric. Till to-morrow, then, Comrade Jarvis. I am very much obliged to you."

* * * * *

"Not at all a bad hour's work," he said complacently, as they turned out of Groome Street. "A vote of thanks to you, John, for your invaluable assistance."

"I didn't do much," said John, with a grin.

"Apparently, no. In reality, yes. Your manner was exactly right. Reserved, yet not haughty. Just what an eminent cat-fancier's manner should be. I could see that you made a pronounced hit with Comrade Jarvis. By the way, as he is going to show up at the office to-morrow, perhaps it would be as well if you were to look up a few facts bearing on the feline world. There is no knowing what thirst for information a night's rest may not give Comrade Jarvis. I do not presume to dictate, but if you were to make yourself a thorough master of the subject of catnip, for instance, it might quite possibly come in useful."

CHAPTER XXIII

THE RETIREMENT OF SMITH

The first member of the staff of *Peaceful Moments* to arrive at the office on the following morning was Master Maloney. This sounds like the beginning of a "Plod and Punctuality," or "How Great Fortunes have been Made" story, but, as a matter of fact, Master Maloney, like Mr. Bat Jarvis, was no early bird. Larks who rose in his neighborhood, rose alone. He did not get up with them. He was supposed to be at the office at nine o'clock. It was a point of honor with him, a sort of daily declaration of independence, never to put in an appearance before nine-thirty. On this particular morning he was punctual to the minute, or half an hour late, whichever way you choose to look at it.

He had only whistled a few bars of "My Little Irish Rose," and had barely got into the first page of his story of life on the prairie, when Kid Brady appeared. The Kid had come to pay a farewell visit. He had not yet begun training, and he was making the best of the short time before such comforts should be forbidden by smoking a big black cigar. Master Maloney eyed him admiringly. The Kid, unknown to that gentleman himself, was Pugsy's ideal. He came from the Plains, and had, indeed, once actually been a cowboy; he was a coming champion; and he could smoke big black cigars. There was no trace of his official well-what-is-it-now? air about Pugsy as he laid down his book and prepared to converse.

"Say, Mr. Smith around anywhere, Pugsy?" asked the Kid.

"Naw, Mr. Brady. He ain't came yet," replied Master Maloney respectfully.

"Late, ain't he?"

"Sure! He generally blows in before I do."

"Wonder what's keepin' him?"

As he spoke, John appeared. "Hello, Kid," he said. "Come to say good-by?"

"Yep," said the Kid. "Seen Mr. Smith around anywhere, Mr. Maude?"

"Hasn't he come yet? I guess he'll be here soon. Hello, who's this?"

A small boy was standing at the door, holding a note.

"Mr. Maude?" he said. "Cop at Jefferson Market give me dis fer you."

"What!" He took the letter, and gave the boy a dime. "Why, it's from_Smith. Great Scott!"

It was apparent that the Kid was politely endeavoring to veil his curiosity. Master Maloney had no such delicacy.

"What's in de letter, boss?" he enquired.

"The letter," said John slowly, "is from Mr. Smith. And it says that he was sentenced this morning to thirty days on the Island for resisting the police."

"He's de guy!" admitted Master Maloney approvingly.

"What's that?" said the Kid. "Mr. Smith been slugging cops! What's he been doin' that for?"

"I must go and find out at once. It beats me."

It did not take John long to reach Jefferson Market, and by the judicious expenditure of a few dollars he was enabled to obtain an interview with Smith in a back room.

The editor of *Peaceful Moments* was seated on a bench, looking remarkably disheveled. There was a bruise on his forehead, just where the hair began. He was, however, cheerful.

"Ah, John," he said. "You got my note all right, then?" John looked at him, concerned.

"What on earth does it all mean?"

Smith heaved a regretful sigh.

"I fear," he said, "I have made precisely the blamed fool of myself that Comrade Parker hoped I would."

"Parker!"

Smith nodded.

"I may be misjudging him, but I seem to see the hand of Comrade Parker in this. We had a raid at my house last night, John. We were pulled."

"What on earth—?"

"Somebody—if it was not Comrade Parker it was some other citizen dripping with public spirit—tipped the police off that certain sports were running a pool-room in the house where I live."

On his departure from the *News*, Smith, from motives of economy, had moved from his hotel in Washington Square and taken a furnished room on Fourteenth Street.

"There actually was a pool-room there," he went on, "so possibly I am wronging Comrade Parker in thinking that this was a scheme of his for getting me out of the way. At any rate, somebody gave the tip, and at about three o'clock this morning I was aroused from a dreamless slumber by quite a considerable hammering at my door. There, standing on the mat, were two policemen. Very cordially the honest fellows invited me to go with them. A conveyance, it seemed, waited in the street without. I disclaimed all connection with the bad gambling persons below, but they replied that they were cleaning up the house, and, if I wished to make any remarks, I had better make them to the magistrate. This seemed reasonable. I said I would put on some clothes and come along. They demurred. They said they couldn't wait about while I put on clothes. I pointed out that sky-blue pajamas with old-rose frogs were not the costume in which the editor of a great New York weekly paper should be seen abroad in one of the world's greatest cities, but they assured me—more by their manner than their words—that my misgivings were groundless, so I yielded. These men, I told myself, have lived longer in New York than I. They know what is done, and what is not done. I will bow to their views. So I was starting to go with them like a lamb, when one of them gave me a shove in the ribs with his night stick. And it was here that I fancy I may have committed a slight error of policy."

He smiled dreamily for a moment, then went on.

"I admit that the old Berserk blood of the Smiths boiled at that juncture. I picked up a sleep-producer from the floor, as Comrade Brady would say, and handed it to the big-stick merchant. He went down like a sack of coal over the bookcase, and at that moment I rather fancy the other gentleman must have got busy with his club. At any rate, somebody suddenly loosed off some fifty thousand dollars' worth of fireworks, and the next thing I knew was that the curtain had risen for the next act on me, discovered sitting in a prison cell, with an out-size in lumps on my forehead."

He sighed again.

"What *Peaceful Moments* really needs," he said, "is a *sitz-redacteur*. A *sitz-redacteur*, John, is a gentleman employed by German newspapers with a taste for *lese-majeste* to go to prison whenever required in place of the real editor. The real editor hints in his bright and snappy editorial, for instance, that the Kaiser's mustache gives him bad dreams. The police force swoops down in a body on the office of the journal, and are met by the *sitz-redacteur*, who goes with them cheerfully, allowing the editor to remain and sketch out plans for his next week's article on the Crown Prince. We need a *sitz-redacteur* on *Peaceful Moments* almost as much as a fighting editor. Not now, of course. This has finished the thing. You'll have to close down the paper now."

"Close it down!" cried John. "You bet I won't."

"My dear old son," said Smith seriously, "what earthly reason have you for going on with it? You only came in to help me, and I am no more. I am gone like some beautiful flower that withers in the night. Where's the sense of getting yourself beaten up then? Quit!"

John shook his head.

"I wouldn't quit now if you paid me."

"But—"

A policeman appeared at the door.

"Say, pal," he remarked to John, "you'll have to be fading away soon, I guess. Give you three minutes more. Say it quick."

He retired. Smith looked at John.

"You won't quit?" he said.

"No."

Smith smiled.

"You're an all-wool sport, John," he said. "I don't suppose you know how to spell quit. Well, then, if you are determined to stand by the ship like Comrade Casabianca, I'll tell you an idea that came to me in the watches of the night. If ever you want to get ideas, John, you spend a night in one of these cells. They flock to you. I suppose I did more profound thinking last night than I've ever done in my life. Well, here's the idea. Act on it or not, as you please. I was thinking over the whole business from soup to nuts, and it struck me that the queerest part of it all is that whoever owns these Broster Street tenements should care a Canadian dime whether we find out who he is or not."

"Well, there's the publicity," began John.

"Tush!" said Smith. "And possibly bah! Do you suppose that the sort of man who runs Broster Street is likely to care a darn about publicity? What does it matter to him if the papers soak it to him for about two days? He knows they'll drop him and go on to something else on the third, and he knows he's broken no law. No, there's something more in this business than that. Don't think that this bright boy wants to hush us up simply because he is a sensitive plant who can't bear to think that people should be cross with him. He has got some private reason for wanting to lie low."

"Well, but what difference—?"

"Comrade, I'll tell you. It makes this difference: that the rents are almost certainly collected by some confidential person belonging to his own crowd, not by an ordinary collector. In other words, the collector knows the name of the man he's collecting for. But for this little misfortune of mine, I was going to suggest that we waylay that collector, administer the Third Degree, and ask him who his boss is."

John uttered an exclamation.

"You're right! I'll do it."

"You think you can? Alone?"

"Sure! Don't you worry. I'll—"

The door opened and the policeman reappeared.

"Time's up. Slide, sonny."

John said good-by to Smith, and went out. He had a last glimpse of his late editor, a sad smile on his face, telling the policeman what was apparently a humorous story. Complete good will seemed to exist between them. John consoled himself as he went away with the reflection that Smith's was a temperament that would probably find a bright side even to a thirty-days' visit to Blackwell's Island.

He walked thoughtfully back to the office. There was something lonely, and yet wonderfully exhilarating, in the realization that he was now alone and in sole charge of the campaign. It braced him. For the first time in several weeks he felt positively light-hearted.

CHAPTER XXIV
THE CAMPAIGN QUICKENS

Mr. Jarvis was as good as his word. Early in the afternoon he made his appearance at the office of *Peaceful Moments*, his forelock more than usually well oiled in honor of the occasion, and his right coat-pocket bulging in a manner that betrayed to the initiated eye the presence of his trusty "canister." With him, in addition, he brought a long, thin young man who wore under his brown tweed coat a blue-and-red striped sweater. Whether he brought him as an ally in case of need or merely as a kindred soul with whom he might commune during his vigil, did not appear.

Pugsy, startled out of his wonted calm by the arrival of this distinguished company, gazed after the pair, as they passed into the inner office, with protruding eyes.

John greeted the allies warmly, and explained Smith's absence. Mr. Jarvis listened to the story with interest, and introduced his colleague.

"T'ought I'd let him chase along. Long Otto's his monaker."

"Sure!" said John. "The more the merrier. Take a seat. You'll find cigars over there. You won't mind my not talking for the moment? There's a wad of work to clear up."

This was an overstatement. He was comparatively free of work, press day having only just gone by; but he was keenly anxious to avoid conversation on the subject of cats, of his ignorance of which Mr. Jarvis's appearance had suddenly reminded him. He took up an old proof sheet and began to glance through it, frowning thoughtfully.

Mr. Jarvis regarded the paraphernalia of literature on the table with interest. So did Long Otto, who, however, being a man of silent habit, made no comment. Throughout the seance and the events which followed it he confined himself to an occasional grunt. He seemed to lack other modes of expression.

"Is dis where youse writes up pieces fer de poiper?" enquired Mr._Jarvis.

"This is the spot," said John. "On busy mornings you could hear our brains buzzing in Madison Square Garden. Oh, one moment."

He rose and went into the outer office.

"Pugsy," he said, "do you know Broster Street?"

"Sure."

"Could you find out for me exactly when the man comes round collecting the rents?"

"Surest t'ing you know. I knows a kid what knows anodder kid what lives dere."

"Then go and do it now. And, after you've found out, you can take the rest of the day off."

"Me fer dat," said Master Maloney with enthusiasm. "I'll take me goil to de Bronx Zoo."

"Your girl? I didn't know you'd got a girl, Pugsy. I always imagined you as one of those strong, stern, blood-and-iron men who despised girls. Who is she?"

"Aw, she's a kid," said Pugsy. "Her pa runs a delicatessen shop down our street. She ain't a bad mutt," added the ardent swain. "I'm her steady."

"Well, mind you send me a card for the wedding. And if two dollars would be a help—"

"Sure t'ing. T'anks, boss. You're all right."

It had occurred to John that the less time Pugsy spent in the outer office during the next few days, the better. The lull in the warfare could not last much longer, and at any moment a visit from Spider Reilly and his adherents might be expected. Their probable first move in such an event would be to knock Master Maloney on the head to prevent his giving warning of their approach.

Events proved that he had not been mistaken. He had not been back in the inner office for more than a quarter of an hour when there came from without the sound of stealthy movements. The handle of the door began—to revolve slowly and quietly. The next moment three figures tumbled into the room.

It was evident that they had not expected to find the door unlocked, and the absence of resistance when they applied their weight had surprising effects. Two of the three did not pause in their career till they cannoned against the table. The third checked himself by holding the handle.

John got up coolly.

"Come right in," he said. "What can we do for you?" It had been too dark on the other occasion of his meeting with the Three Pointers to take note of their faces, though he fancied that he had seen the man holding the door-handle before. The others were strangers. They were all exceedingly unprepossessing in appearance.

There was a pause. The three marauders had become aware of the presence of Mr. Jarvis and his colleague, and the meeting was causing them embarrassment, which may have been due in part to the fact that both had produced and were toying meditatively with ugly-looking pistols.

Mr. Jarvis spoke.

"Well," he said, "what's doin'?"

The man to whom the question was directly addressed appeared to have some difficulty in finding a reply. He shuffled his feet, and looked at the floor. His two companions seemed equally at a loss.

"Goin' to start anything?" enquired Mr. Jarvis, casually.

The humor of the situation suddenly tickled John. The embarrassment of the uninvited guests was ludicrous.

"You've just dropped in for a quiet chat, is that it?" he said. "Well, we're all delighted to see you. The cigars are on the table. Draw up your chairs."

Mr. Jarvis opposed the motion. He drew slow circles in the air with his revolver.

"Say! Youse had best beat it. See?"

Long Otto grunted sympathy with the advice.

"And youse had best go back to Spider Reilly," continued Mr. Jarvis, "and tell him there ain't nothin' doing in the way of rough-house wit' dis gent here. And you can tell de Spider," went on Bat with growing ferocity, "dat next time he gits fresh and starts in to shootin' up my dance-joint, I'll bite de head off'n him. See? Dat goes. If he t'inks his little two-by-four crowd can git way wit' de Groome Street, he's got anodder guess comin'. An' don't fergit dis gent here and me is friends, and anyone dat starts anyt'ing wit' dis gent is going to find trouble. Does dat go? Beat it."

He jerked his shoulder in the direction of the door.

The delegation then withdrew.

"Thanks," said John. "I'm much obliged to you both. You're certainly there with the goods as fighting editors. I don't know what I should have done without you."

"Aw, Chee!" said Mr. Jarvis, handsomely dismissing the matter. Long_Otto kicked the leg of a table, and grunted.

Pugsy Maloney's report on the following morning was entirely satisfactory. Rents were collected in Broster Street on Thursdays. Nothing could have been more convenient, for that very day happened to be Thursday.

"I rubbered around," said Pugsy, "an' done de sleut' act, an' it's this way. Dere's a feller blows in every T'ursday 'bout six o'clock, an' den it's up to de folks to dig down inter deir jeans for de stuff, or out dey goes before supper. I got dat from my kid frien' what knows a kid what lives dere. An' say, he has it pretty fierce, dat kid. De kid what lives dere. He's a wop kid, an Italian, an' he's in bad 'cos his pa comes over from Italy to woik on de subway."

"I don't see why that puts him in bad," said John wonderingly. "You don't construct your stories well, Pugsy. You start at the end, then go back to any part which happens to appeal to you at the moment, and eventually wind up at the beginning. Why is this kid in bad because his father has come to work on the subway?"

"Why, sure, because his pa got fired an' swatted de foreman one on de coco, an' dey gives him t'oity days. So de kid's all alone, an' no one to pay de rent."

"I see," said John. "Well, come along with me and introduce me, and_I'll look after that."

At half-past five John closed the office for the day, and, armed with a big stick and conducted by Master Maloney, made his way to Broster Street. To reach it, it was necessary to pass through a section of the enemy's country, but the perilous passage was safely negotiated. The expedition reached its unsavory goal intact.

The wop kid inhabited a small room at the very top of a building half-way down the street. He was out when John and Pugsy arrived.

It was not an abode of luxury, the tenement; they had to feel their way up the stairs in almost pitch darkness. Most of the doors were shut, but one on the second floor was ajar. Through the opening John had a glimpse of a number of women sitting on up-turned boxes. The floor was covered with little heaps of linen. All the women were sewing. Stumbling in the darkness, John almost fell against the door. None of the women looked up at the noise. In Broster Street time was evidently money.

On the top floor Pugsy halted before the open door of an empty room. The architect in this case had apparently given rein to a passion for originality, for he had constructed the apartment without a window of any sort whatsoever. The entire stock of air used by the occupants came through a small opening over the door.

It was a warm day, and John recoiled hastily.

"Is this the kid's room?" he said. "I guess the corridor's good enough for me to wait in. What the owner of this place wants," he went on reflectively, "is scalping. Well, we'll do it in the paper if we can't in any other way. Is this your kid?"

A small boy had appeared. He seemed surprised to see visitors. Pugsy undertook to do the honors. Pugsy, as interpreter, was energetic, but not wholly successful. He appeared to have a fixed idea that the Italian language was one easily mastered by the simple method of saying "da" instead of "the," and adding a final "a" to any word that seemed to him to need one.

"Say, kid," he began, "has da rent-a-man come yet-a?"

The black eyes of the wop kid clouded. He gesticulated, and said something in his native language.

"He hasn't got next," reported Master Maloney. "He can't git on to me curves.

Dese wop kids is all bone-heads. Say, kid, look-a here." He walked to the door, rapped on it smartly, and, assuming a look of extreme ferocity, stretched out his hand and thundered: "Unbelt-a! Slip-a me da stuff!"

The wop kid's puzzlement in the face of this address became pathetic.

"This," said John, deeply interested, "is getting exciting. Don't give in, Pugsy. I guess the trouble is that your too perfect Italian accent is making the kid homesick."

Master Maloney made a gesture of disgust.

"I'm t'roo. Dese Dagoes makes me tired. Dey don't know enough to go upstairs to take de elevated. Beat it, you mutt," he observed with moody displeasure, accompanying the words with a gesture which conveyed its own meaning. The wop kid, plainly glad to get away, slipped down the stairs like a shadow.

Pugsy shrugged his shoulders.

"Boss," he said resignedly, "it's up to youse."

John reflected.

"It's all right," he said. "Of course, if the collector had been here, the kid wouldn't be. All I've got to do is to wait."

He peered over the banisters into the darkness below.

"Not that it's not enough," he said; "for of all the poisonous places I ever met this is the worst. I wish whoever built it had thought to put in a few windows. His idea of ventilation was apparently to leave a hole about the size of a lima bean and let the thing go at that."

"I guess there's a door on to de roof somewhere," suggested Pugsy. "At de joint where I lives dere is."

His surmise proved correct. At the end of the passage a ladder, nailed against the wall, ended in a large square opening, through which was visible, if not "that narrow strip of blue which prisoners call the sky," at any rate a tall brick chimney and a clothesline covered with garments that waved lazily in the breeze.

John stood beneath it, looking up.

"Well," he said, "this isn't much, but it's better than nothing. I suppose the architect of this place was one of those fellows who don't begin to appreciate air till it's thick enough to scoop chunks out with a spoon. It's an acquired taste, I guess, like Limburger cheese. And now, Pugsy, old scout, you had better beat it. There may be a rough-house here any minute now."

Pugsy looked up, indignant.

"Beat it?"

"While your shoe-leather's good," said John firmly. "This is no place for a minister's son. Take it from me."

"I want to stop and pipe de fun," objected Master Maloney.

"What fun?"

"I guess you ain't here to play ball," surmised Pugsy shrewdly, eying the big stick.

"Never mind why I'm here," said John. "Beat it. I'll tell you all about it tomorrow."

Master Maloney prepared reluctantly to depart. As he did so there was a sound of well-shod feet on the stairs, and a man in a snuff-colored suit, wearing a brown Homburg hat and carrying a small notebook in one hand, walked briskly up the stairs. His whole appearance proclaimed him to be the long-expected collector of rents.

CHAPTER XXV
CORNERED

He did not see John for a moment, and had reached the door of the room when he became aware of a presence. He turned in surprise. He was a smallish, pale-faced man with protruding eyes and teeth which gave him a certain resemblance to a rabbit.

"Hello!" he said.

"Welcome to our city," said John, stepping unostentatiously between him and the stairs.

Master Maloney, who had taken advantage of the interruption to edge back into the center of things, now appeared to consider the question of his departure permanently shelved. He sidled to a corner of the landing, and sat down on an empty soap box with the air of a dramatic critic at the opening night of a new play. The scene looked good to him. It promised interesting developments. He was an earnest student of the drama, as exhibited in the theaters of the East Side, and few had ever applauded the hero of "Escaped from Sing Sing," or hissed the villain of "Nellie, the Beautiful Cloak-model" with more fervor. He liked his drama to have plenty of action, and to his practised eye this one promised well. There was a set expression on John's face which suggested great things.

His pleasure was abruptly quenched. John, placing a firm hand on his collar, led him to the top of the stairs and pushed him down.

"Beat it," he said.

The rent-collector watched these things with a puzzled eye. He now turned to John.

"Say, seen anything of the wops that live here?" he enquired. "My name's Gooch. I've come to take the rent."

John nodded.

"I don't think there's much chance of your seeing them to-night," he said. "The father, I hear, is in prison. You won't get any rent out of him."

"Then it's outside for theirs," said Mr. Gooch definitely.

"What about the kid?" said John. "Where's he to go?"

"That's up to him. Nothing to do with me. I'm only acting under orders from up top."

"Whose orders?" enquired John.

"The gent who owns this joint."

"Who is he?"

Suspicion crept into the protruding eyes of the rent-collector.

"Say!" he demanded. "Who are you anyway, and what do you think you're doing here? That's what I'd like to know. What do you want with the name of the owner of this place? What business is it of yours?"

"I'm a newspaper man."

"I guessed you were," said Mr. Gooch with triumph. "You can't bluff me. Well, it's no good, sonny. I've nothing for you. You'd better chase off and try something else."

He became more friendly.

"Say, though," he said, "I just guessed you were from some paper. I wish I could give you a story, but I can't. I guess it's this *Peaceful Moments* business that's been and put your editor on to this joint, ain't it? Say, though, that's a queer thing, that paper. Why, only a few weeks ago it used to be a sort of take-home-and-read-to-the-kids affair. A friend of mine used to buy it regular. And then suddenly it comes out with a regular whoop, and starts knocking these tenements and boosting Kid Brady, and all that. It gets past me. All I know is that it's begun to get this place talked about. Why, you see for yourself how it is. Here is your editor sending you down to get a story about it. But, say, those *Peaceful Moments* guys are taking big risks. I tell you straight they are, and I know. I happen to be wise to a thing or two about what's going on on the other side, and I tell you there's going to be something doing if they don't cut it out quick. Mr. Qem, the fellow who owns this place isn't the man to sit still and smile. He's going to get busy. Say, what paper do you come from?"

"*Peaceful Moments*," said John.

For a moment the inwardness of the information did not seem to come home to Mr. Gooch. Then it hit him. He spun round. John was standing squarely between him and the stairs.

"Hey, what's all this?" demanded Mr. Gooch nervously. The light was dim in the passage, but it was sufficiently light to enable him to see John's face, and it did not reassure him.

"I'll soon tell you," said John. "First, however, let's get this business of the kid's rent settled. Take it out of this and give me the receipt."

He pulled out a bill.

"Curse his rent," said Mr. Gooch. "Let me pass."

"Soon," said John. "Business before pleasure. How much does the kid have to pay for the privilege of suffocating in this infernal place? As much as that?

Well, give me a receipt, and then we can get on to more important things."

"Let me pass."

"Receipt," said John laconically.

Mr. Gooch looked at the big stick, then scribbled a few words in his notebook and tore out the page. John thanked him.

"I will see that it reaches him," he said. "And now will you kindly tell me the name of the man for whom you collected that money?"

"Let me pass," bellowed Mr. Gooch. "I'll bring an action against you for assault and battery. Playing a fool game like this! Get away from those stairs."

"There has been no assault and battery—yet," said John. "Well, are you going to tell me?"

Mr. Gooch shuffled restlessly. John leaned against the banisters.

"As you said a moment ago," he observed, "the staff of *Peaceful_Moments* is taking big risks. I knew it before you told me. I have_had practical demonstration of the fact. And that is why this Broster_Street thing has got to be finished quick. We can't afford to wait. So_I am going to have you tell me this man's name right now."

"Help!" yelled Mr. Gooch.

The noise died away, echoing against the walls. No answering cry came from below. Custom had staled the piquancy of such cries in Broster Street. If anybody heard it, nobody thought the matter worth investigation.

"If you do that again," said John, "I'll break you in half. Now then! I can't wait much longer. Get busy!"

He looked huge and sinister to Mr. Gooch, standing there in the uncertain light; it was very lonely on that top floor and the rest of the world seemed infinitely far away. Mr. Gooch wavered. He was loyal to his employer, but he was still more loyal to Mr. Gooch.

"Well?" said John.

There was a clatter on the stairs of one running swiftly, and Pugsy_Maloney burst into view. For the first time since John had known him,_Pugsy was openly excited.

"Say, boss," he cried, "dey's coming!"

"What? Who?"

"Why, dem. I seen dem T'ree Pointers—Spider Reilly an'—"

He broke off with a yelp of surprise. Mr. Gooch had seized his opportunity, and had made his dash for safety. With a rush he dived past John, nearly upsetting

Pugsy, who stood in his path, and sprang down the stairs. Once he tripped, but recovered himself, and in another instant only the faint sound of his hurrying footsteps reached them.

John had made a movement as if to follow, but the full meaning of Pugsy's words came upon him and he stopped.

"Spider Reilly?" he said.

"I guess it was Spider Reilly," said Pugsy, excitedly. "Dey called him Spider. I guess dey piped youse comin' in here. Gee! it's pretty fierce, boss, dis! What youse goin' to do?"

"Where did you see them, Pugsy?"

"On the street just outside. Dere was a bunch of dem spielin' togedder, and I hears dem say you was in here. Dere ain't no ways out but de front, so dey ain't hurryin'. Dey just reckon to pike along upstairs, peekin' inter each room till dey find you. An' dere's a bunch of dem goin' to wait on de street in case youse beat it past down de stairs while de odder guys is rubberin' for youse. Gee, ain't dis de limit!"

John stood thinking. His mind was working rapidly. Suddenly he smiled.

"It's all right, Pugsy," he said. "It looks bad, but I see a way out. I'm going up that ladder there and through the trapdoor on to the roof. I shall be all right there. If they find me, they can only get at me one at a time. And, while I'm there, here's what I want you to do."

"Shall I go for de cops, boss?"

"No, not the cops. Do you know where Dude Dawson lives?"

The light of intelligence began to shine in Master Maloney's face. His eye glistened with approval. This was strategy of the right sort.

"I can ask around," he said. "I'll soon find him all right."

"Do, and as quick as you can. And when you've found him tell him that his old chum, Spider Reilly, is here, with the rest of his crowd. And now I'd better be getting up on to my perch. Off you go, Pugsy, my son, and don't take a week about it. Good-by."

Pugsy vanished, and John, going to the ladder, climbed out on to the roof with his big stick. He looked about him. The examination was satisfactory. The trapdoor appeared to be the only means of access to the roof, and between this roof and that of the next building there was a broad gulf. The position was practically impregnable. Only one thing could undo him, and that was, if the enemy should mount to the next roof and shoot from there. And even then he would have cover in the shape of the chimney. It was a pity that the trap opened downward, for he had no means of securing it and was obliged to allow it to hang open. But, except for that, his position could hardly have been stronger.

As yet there was no sound of the enemy's approach. Evidently, as Pugsy had said, they were conducting the search, room by room, in a thorough and leisurely way. He listened with his ear close to the open trapdoor, but could hear nothing.

A startled exclamation directly behind him brought him to his feet in a flash, every muscle tense. He whirled his stick above his head as he turned, ready to strike, then let it fall with a clatter. For there, a bare yard away, stood Betty.

CHAPTER XXVI
JOURNEY'S END

The capacity of the human brain for surprise, like that of the human body for pain, is limited. For a single instant a sense of utter unreality struck John like a physical blow. The world flickered before his eyes and the air seemed full of strange noises. Then, quite suddenly, these things passed, and he found himself looking at her with a total absence of astonishment, mildly amused in some remote corner of his brain at his own calm. It was absurd, he told himself, that he should be feeling as if he had known of her presence there all the time. Yet it was so. If this were a dream, he could not be taking the miracle more as a matter of course. Joy at the sight of her he felt, keen and almost painful, but no surprise. The shock had stunned his sense of wonder.

She was wearing a calico apron over her dress, an apron that had evidently been designed for a large woman. Swathed in its folds, she suggested a child playing at being grown up. Her sleeves were rolled back to the elbow, and her slim arms dripped with water. Strands of brown hair were blowing loose in the evening breeze. To John she had never seemed so bewitchingly pretty. He stared at her till the pallor of her face gave way to a warm red glow.

As they stood there, speechless, there came from the other side of the chimney, softly at first, then swelling, the sound of a child's voice, raised in a tentative wail. Betty started violently. The next moment she was gone, and from the unseen parts beyond the chimney came the noise of splashing water.

And at the same instant, through the trap, came a trampling of feet and the sound of whispering. The enemy had reached the top floor.

John was conscious of a remarkable exhilaration. He felt insanely light-hearted. He laughed aloud at the thought that until then he had completely forgotten the very existence of these earnest seekers after his downfall. He threw back his head and shouted. There was something so ridiculous in their assumption that they mattered to a man who had found Betty again.

He thrust his head down through the trap, to see what was going on. The dark passage was full of indistinct forms, gathered together in puzzled groups. The mystery of the vanished object of their pursuit was being discussed in hoarse whispers.

Suddenly there was an excited shout, then a rush of feet. John drew back his head, and waited, gripping his stick.

Voices called to each other in the passage below.

"De roof!"

"On top de roof!"

"He's beaten it for de roof!"

Feet shuffled on the stone floor. The voices ceased abruptly. And then, like a jack-in-the-box, there popped through the trap a head and shoulders.

The new arrival was a young man with a shock of red hair, a broken nose, and a mouth from which force or the passage of time had removed three front teeth. He held on to the edge of the trap, and stared up at John.

John beamed down at him, and shifted his grip on the stick.

"Who's here?" he cried. "Historic picture. 'Old Dr. Cook discovers the_North Pole.'"

The red-headed young man blinked. The strong light of the open air was trying to his eyes.

"Youse had best come down," he observed coldly. "We've got youse."

"And," continued John, unmoved, "is instantly handed a gum-drop by his faithful Eskimo."

As he spoke, he brought the stick down on the knuckles which disfigured the edges of the trap. The intruder uttered a howl and dropped out of sight. In the passage below there were whisperings and mutterings, growing gradually louder till something resembling coherent conversation came to John's ears, as he knelt by the trap making meditative billiard shots with the stick at a small pebble.

"Aw g'wan! Don't be a quitter."

"Who's a quitter?"

"Youse a quitter. Get on top de roof. He can't hoit youse."

"De guy's gotten a big stick."

John nodded appreciatively.

"I and Theodore," he murmured.

A somewhat baffled silence on the part of the attacking force was followed by further conversation.

"Gee! Some guy's got to go up."

Murmur of assent from the audience.

A voice, in inspired tones: "Let Sam do it."

The suggestion made a hit. There was no doubt about that. It was a success from the start. Quite a little chorus of voices expressed sincere approval of the very happy solution to what had seemed an insoluble problem. John, listening from above, failed to detect in the choir of glad voices one that might belong to Sam himself. Probably gratification had rendered the chosen one dumb.

"Yes, let Sam do it," cried the unseen chorus. The first speaker, unnecessarily, perhaps—for the motion had been carried almost unanimously—but possibly with the idea of convincing the one member of the party in whose bosom doubts might conceivably be harbored, went on to adduce reasons.

"Sam bein' a coon," he argued, "ain't goin' to git hoit by no stick. Youse can't hoit a coon by soakin' him on de coco, can you, Sam?"

John waited with some interest for the reply, but it did not come. Possibly Sam did not wish to generalize on insufficient experience.

"We can but try," said John softly, turning the stick round in his fingers.

A report like a cannon sounded in the passage below. It was merely a revolver shot, but in the confined space it was deafening. The bullet sang up into the sky.

"Never hit me," said John cheerfully.

The noise was succeeded by a shuffling of feet. John grasped his stick more firmly. This was evidently the real attack. The revolver shot had been a mere demonstration of artillery to cover the infantry's advance.

Sure enough, the next moment a woolly head popped through the opening, and a pair of rolling eyes gleamed up at him.

"Why, Sam!" he said cordially, "this is great. Now for our interesting experiment. My idea is that you *can* hurt a coon's head with a stick if you hit it hard enough. Keep quite still. Now. What, are you coming up? Sam, I hate to do it, but—"

A yell rang out. John's theory had been tested and proved correct.

By this time the affair had begun to attract spectators. The noise of the revolver had proved a fine advertisement. The roof of the house next door began to fill up. Only a few of the occupants could get a clear view of the proceedings, for the chimney intervened. There was considerable speculation as to what was passing in the Three Points camp. John was the popular favorite. The early comers had seen his interview with Sam, and were relating it with gusto to their friends. Their attitude toward John was that of a group of men watching a dog at a rat hole. They looked to him to provide entertainment for them, but they realized that the first move must be with the attackers. They were fair-minded men, and they did not expect John to make any aggressive move.

Their indignation, when the proceedings began to grow slow, was directed entirely at the dilatory Three Pointers. They hooted the Three Pointers. They urged them to go home and tuck themselves up in bed. The spectators were mostly Irishmen, and it offended them to see what should have been a spirited fight so grossly bungled.

"G'wan away home, ye quitters!" roared one.

A second member of the audience alluded to them as "stiffs."

It was evident that the besieging army was beginning to grow a little unpopular. More action was needed if they were to retain the esteem of Broster Street.

Suddenly there came another and a longer explosion from below, and more bullets wasted themselves on air. John sighed.

"You make me tired," he said.

The Irish neighbors expressed the same sentiment in different and more forcible words. There was no doubt about it—as warriors, the Three Pointers were failing to give satisfaction.

A voice from the passage called to John.

"Say!"

"Well?" said John.

"Are youse comin' down off out of dat roof?"

"Would you mind repeating that remark?"

"Are youse goin' to quit off out of dat roof?"

"Go away and learn some grammar," said John severely.

"Hey!"

"Well?"

"Are youse—?"

"No, my son," said John, "since you ask it, I am not. I like being up here. How is Sam?"

There was silence below. The time began to pass slowly. The Irishmen on the other roof, now definitely abandoning hope of further entertainment, proceeded with hoots of derision to climb down one by one into the recesses of their own house.

And then from the street far below there came a fusillade of shots and a babel of shouts and counter-shouts. The roof of the house next door filled again with a magical swiftness, and the low wall facing the street became black with the backs of those craning over. There appeared to be great doings in the street.

John smiled comfortably.

In the army of the corridor confusion had arisen. A scout, clattering upstairs, had brought the news of the Table Hillites' advent, and there was doubt as to the proper course to pursue. Certain voices urged going down to help the main body. Others pointed out that this would mean abandoning the siege of the roof. The scout who had brought the news was eloquent in favor of the first course.

"Gee!" he cried, "don't I keep tellin' youse dat de Table Hills is here? Sure, dere's a whole bunch of dem, and unless youse come on down dey'll bite de hull head off of us lot. Leave dat stiff on de roof. Let Sam wait here wit' his canister, and den he can't get down, 'cos Sam'll pump him full of lead while he's beatin' it t'roo de trapdoor. Sure!"

John nodded reflectively.

"There is certainly something in that," he murmured. "I guess the grand rescue scene in the third act has sprung a leak. This will want thinking over."

In the street the disturbance had now become terrible. Both sides were hard at it, and the Irishmen on the roof, rewarded at last for their long vigil, were yelling encouragement promiscuously and whooping with the unfettered ecstasy of men who are getting the treat of their lives without having paid a penny for it.

The behavior of the New York policeman in affairs of this kind is based on principles of the soundest practical wisdom. The unthinking man would rush in and attempt to crush the combat in its earliest and fiercest stages. The New York policeman, knowing the importance of his safety, and the insignificance of the gangsman's, permits the opposing forces to hammer each other into a certain distaste for battle, and then, when both sides have begun to have enough of it, rushes in himself and clubs everything in sight. It is an admirable process in its results, but it is sure rather than swift.

Proceedings in the affair below had not yet reached the police-interference stage. The noise, what with the shots and yells from the street and the ear-piercing approval of the roof audience, was just working up to a climax.

John rose. He was tired of kneeling by the trap, and there was no likelihood of Sam making another attempt to climb through. He got up and stretched himself.

And then he saw that Betty was standing beside him, holding with each hand a small and—by Broster Street standards—uncannily clean child. The children were scared and whimpering, and she stooped to soothe them. Then she turned to John, her eyes wide with anxiety.

"Are you hurt?" she cried. "What has been happening? Are you hurt?"

John's heart leaped at the anxious break in her voice.

"It's all right," he said soothingly. "It's absolutely all right._Everything's over."

As if to give him the lie, the noise in the street swelled to a crescendo of yells and shots.

"What's that?" cried Betty, starting.

"I fancy," said John, "the police must be taking a hand. It's all right. There's a little trouble down below there between two of the gangs. It won't last long now."

"Who were those men?"

"My friends in the passage?" he said lightly. "Those were some of the Three Points gang. We were holding the concluding exercise of a rather lively campaign that's been—"

Betty leaned weakly against the chimney. There was silence now in the street. Only the distant rumble of an elevated train broke the stillness. She drew her hands from the children's grasp, and covered her face. As she lowered them again, John saw that the blood had left her cheeks. She was white and shaking. He moved forward impulsively.

"Betty!"

She tottered, reaching blindly for the chimney for support, and without further words he gathered her into his arms as if she had been the child she looked, and held her there, clutching her to him fiercely, kissing the brown hair that brushed against his face, and soothing her with vague murmurings.

Her breath came in broken gasps. She laughed hysterically.

"I thought they were killing you—killing you—and I couldn't leave my babies—they were so frightened, poor little mites—I thought they were killing you."

"Betty!"

Her arms about his neck tightened their grip convulsively, forcing his head down until his face rested against hers. And so they stood, rigid, while the two children stared with round eyes and whimpered unheeded.

Her grip relaxed. Her hands dropped slowly to her side. She leaned back against the circle of his arms, and looked up at him—a strange look, full of a sweet humility.

"I thought I was strong," she said quietly. "I'm weak—but I don't care."

He looked at her with glowing eyes, not understanding, but content that the journey was ended, that she was there, in his arms, speaking to him.

"I always loved you, dear," she went on. "You knew that, didn't you? But I thought I was strong enough to give you up for—for a principle—but I was wrong. I can't do without you—I knew it just now when I saw—" She stopped, and shuddered. "I can't do without you," she repented.

She felt the muscles of his arms quiver, and pressed more closely against them. They were strong arms, protecting arms, restful to lean against at the journey's end.

CHAPTER XXVII
A LEMON

That bulwark of *Peaceful Moments*, Pugsy Maloney, was rather the man of action than the man of tact. Otherwise, when, a moment later, he thrust his head up through the trap, he would have withdrawn delicately, and not split the silence with a raucous "Hey!" which acted on John and Betty like an electric shock.

John glowered at him. Betty was pink, but composed. Pugsy climbed leisurely on to the roof, and surveyed the group.

"Why, hello!" he said, as he saw Betty more closely.

"Well, Pugsy," said Betty. "How are you?"

John turned in surprise.

"Do you know Pugsy?"

Betty looked at him, puzzled.

"Why, of course I do."

"Sure," said Pugsy. "Miss Brown was stenographer on de poiper till she beat it."

"Miss Brown!"

There was utter bewilderment in John's face.

"I changed my name when I went to *Peaceful Moments*."

"Then are you—did you—?"

"Yes, I wrote those articles. That's how I happen to be here now. I come down every day and help look after the babies. Poor little souls, there seems to be nobody else here who has time to do it. It's dreadful. Some of them—you wouldn't believe—I don't think they could ever have had a real bath in their lives."

"Baths is foolishness," commented Master Maloney austerely, eying the scoured infants with a touch of disfavor.

John was reminded of a second mystery that needed solution.

"How on earth did you get up here, Pugsy?" he asked. "How did you get past Sam?"

"Sam? I didn't see no Sam. Who's Sam?"

"One of those fellows. A coon. They left him on guard with a gun, so that I shouldn't get down."

"Ah, I met a coon beating it down de stairs. I guess dat was him. I guess he got cold feet."

"Then there's nothing to stop us from getting down."

"Nope. Dat's right. Dere ain't a T'ree Pointer wit'in a mile. De cops have been loadin' dem into de patrol-wagon by de dozen."

John turned to Betty.

"We'll go and have dinner somewhere. You haven't begun to explain things yet."

Betty shook her head with a smile.

"I haven't got time to go out to dinners," she said. "I'm a working-girl. I'm cashier at Fontelli's Italian Restaurant. I shall be on duty in another half-hour."

John was aghast.

"You!"

"It's a very good situation," said Betty demurely. "Six dollars a week and what I steal. I haven't stolen anything yet, and I think Mr. Jarvis is a little disappointed in me. But of course I haven't settled down properly."

"Jarvis? Bat Jarvis?"

"Yes. He has been very good to me. He got me this place, and has looked after me all the time."

"I'll buy him a thousand cats," said John fervently. "But, Betty, you mustn't go there any more. You must quit. You—"

"If *Peaceful Moments* would reengage me?" said Betty.

She spoke lightly, but her face was serious.

"Dear," she said quickly, "I can't be away from you now, while there's danger. I couldn't bear it. Will you let me come?"

He hesitated.

"You will. You must." Her manner changed again. "That's settled, then._Pugsy, I'm coming back to the paper. Are you glad?"

"Sure t'ing," said Pugsy. "You're to de good."

"And now," she went on, "I must give these babies back to their mothers, and then I'll come with you."

She lowered herself through the trap, and John handed the children down to her. Pugsy looked on, smoking a thoughtful cigarette.

John drew a deep breath. Pugsy, removing the cigarette from his mouth, delivered himself of a stately word of praise.

"She's a boid," he said.

"Pugsy," said John, feeling in his pocket, and producing a roll of bills, "a dollar a word is our rate for contributions like that."

* * * * *

John pushed back his chair slightly, stretched out his legs, and lighted a cigarette, watching Betty fondly through the smoke. The resources of the Knickerbocker Hotel had proved equal to supplying the staff of *Peaceful Moments* with an excellent dinner, and John had stoutly declined to give or listen to any explanations until the coffee arrived.

"Thousands of promising careers," he said, "have been ruined by the fatal practise of talking seriously at dinner. But now we might begin."

Betty looked at him across the table with shining eyes. It was good to be together again.

"My explanations won't take long," she said. "I ran away from you. And, when you found me, I ran away again."

"But I didn't find you," objected John. "That was my trouble."

"But my aunt told you I was at *Peaceful Moments*!"

"On the contrary, I didn't even know you had an aunt."

"Well, she's not exactly that. She's my stepfather's aunt—Mrs. Oakley. I was certain you had gone straight to her, and that she had told you where I was."

"The Mrs. Oakley? The—er—philanthropist?"

"Don't laugh at her," said Betty quickly. "She was so good to me!"

"She passes," said John decidedly.

"And now," said Betty, "it's your turn."

John lighted another cigarette.

"My story," he said, "is rather longer. When they threw me out of_Mervo—"

"What!"

"I'm afraid you don't keep abreast of European history," he said. "Haven't you heard of the great revolution in Mervo and the overthrow of the dynasty? Bloodless, but invigorating. The populace rose against me as one man—except good old General Poineau. He was for me, and Crump was neutral, but apart from them my subjects were unanimous. There's a republic again in Mervo now."

"But why? What had you done?"

"Well, I abolished the gaming-tables. But, more probably," he went on quickly, "they saw what a perfect dub I was in every—"

She interrupted him.

"Do you mean to say that, just because of me—?"

"Well," he said awkwardly, "as a matter of fact what you said did make me think over my position, and, of course, directly I thought over it—oh, well, anyway, I closed down gambling in Mervo, and then—"

"John!"

He was aware of a small hand creeping round the table under cover of the cloth. He pressed it swiftly, and, looking round, caught the eye of a hovering waiter, who swooped like a respectful hawk.

"Did you want anything, sir?"

"I've got it, thanks," said John.

The waiter moved away.

"Well, directly they had fired me, I came over here. I don't know what I expected to do. I suppose I thought I might find you by chance. I pretty soon saw how hopeless it was, and it struck me that, if I didn't get some work to do mighty quick, I shouldn't be much good to anyone except the alienists."

"Dear!"

The waiter stared, but John's eyes stopped him in mid-swoop.

"Then I found Smith—"

"Where is Mr. Smith?"

"In prison," said John with a chuckle.

"In prison!"

"He resisted and assaulted the police. I'll tell you about it later. Well, Smith told me of the alterations in *Peaceful Moments*, and I saw that it was just the thing for me. And it has occupied my mind quite some. To think of you being the writer of those Broster Street articles! You certainly have started something, Betty! Goodness knows where it will end. I hoped to have brought off a coup this afternoon, but the arrival of Sam and his friends just spoiled it."

"This afternoon? Yes, why were you there? What were you doing?"

"I was interviewing the collector of rents and trying to dig his employer's name out of him. It was Smith's idea. Smith's theory was that the owner of the tenements must have some special private reason for lying low, and that he would employ some special fellow, whom he could trust, as a rent-collector. And I'm pretty certain he was right. I cornered the collector, a little, rabbit-faced man named Gooch, and I believe he was on the point of—What's the matter?"

Betty's forehead was wrinkled. Her eyes wore a far-away expression.

"I'm trying to remember something. I seem to know the name, Gooch. And I seem to associate it with a little, rabbit-faced man. And—quick, tell me some more about him. He's just hovering about on the edge of my memory. Quick! Push him in!"

John threw his mind back to the interview in the dark passage, trying to reconstruct it.

"He's small," he said slowly. "His eyes protrude—so do his teeth—He—he—yes, I remember now—he has a curious red mark—"

"On his right cheek," said Betty triumphantly.

"By Jove!" cried John. "You've got him?"

"I remember him perfectly. He was—" She stopped with a little gasp.

"Yes?"

"John, he was one of my stepfather's secretaries," she said.

They looked at each other in silence.

"It can't be," said John at length.

"It can. It is. He must be. He has scores of interests everywhere. He prides himself on it. It's the most natural thing."

John shook his head doubtfully.

"But why all the fuss? Your stepfather isn't the man to mind public opinion—"

"But don't you see? It's as Mr. Smith said. The private reason. It's as clear as daylight. Naturally he would do anything rather than be found out. Don't you see? Because of Mrs. Oakley."

"Because of Mrs. Oakley?"

"You don't know her as I do. She is a curious mixture. She's double-natured. You called her the philanthropist just now. Well, she would be one, if—if she could bear to part with money. Yes, I know it sounds ridiculous. But it's so. She is mean about money, but she honestly hates to hear of anybody treating poor people badly. If my stepfather were really the owner of those tenements, and she should find it out, she would have nothing more to do with him. It's true. I know her."

The smile passed away from John's face.

"By George!" he said. "It certainly begins to hang together."

"I know I'm right."

"I think you are."

He sat meditating for a moment.

"Well?" he said at last.

"What do you mean?"

"I mean, what are we to do? Do we go on with this?"

"Go on with it? I don't understand."

"I mean—well, it has become rather a family matter, you see. Do you feel as—warlike against Mr. Scobell as you did against an unknown lessee?"

Betty's eyes sparkled.

"I don't think I should feel any different if—if it was you," she said. "I've been spending days and days in those houses, John dear, and I've seen such utter squalor and misery, where there needn't be any at all if only the owner would do his duty, and—and—"

She stopped. Her eyes were misty.

"Thumbs down, in fact," said John, nodding. "I'm with you."

As he spoke, two men came down the broad staircase into the grill-room._Betty's back was towards them, but John saw them, and stared.

"What are you looking at?" asked Betty.

"Will you count ten before looking round?"

"What is it?"

"Your stepfather has just come in."

"What!"

"He's sitting at the other side of the room, directly behind you. Count ten!"

But Betty had twisted round in her chair.

"Where? Where?"

"Just where you're looking. Don't let him see you."

"I don't— Oh!"

"Got him?"

He leaned back in his chair.

"The plot thickens, eh?" he said. "What is Mr. Scobell doing in New_York, I wonder, if he has not come to keep an eye on his interests?"

Betty had whipped round again. Her face was white with excitement.

"It's true," she whispered. "I was right. Do you see who that is with him? The man?"

"Do you know him? He's a stranger to me."

"It's Mr. Parker," said Betty.

John drew in his breath sharply.

"Are you sure?"

"Positive."

John laughed quietly. He thought for a moment, then beckoned to the hovering waiter.

"What are you going to do?" asked Betty.

"Bring me a small lemon," said John.

"Lemon squash, sir?"

"Not a lemon squash. A plain lemon. The fruit of that name. The common or garden citron, which is sharp to the taste and not pleasant to have handed to one. Also a piece of note paper, a little tissue paper, and an envelope.

"What are you going to do?" asked Betty again.

John beamed.

"Did you ever read the Sherlock Holmes story entitled 'The Five Orange Pips'? Well, when a man in that story received a mysterious envelope containing five orange pips, it was a sign that he was due to get his. It was all over, as far as he was concerned, except 'phoning for the undertaker. I propose to treat Mr. Scobell better than that. He shall have a whole lemon."

The waiter returned. John wrapped up the lemon carefully, wrote on the note paper the words, "To B. Scobell, Esq., Property Owner, Broster Street, from Prince John of *Peaceful Moments*, this gift," and enclosed it in the envelope.

"Do you see that gentleman at the table by the pillar?" he said. "Give him these. Just say a gentleman sent them."

The waiter smiled doubtfully. John added a two-dollar bill to the collection in his hand.

"You needn't give him that," he said.

The waiter smiled again, but this time not doubtfully.

"And now," said John as the messenger ambled off, "perhaps it would be just as well if we retired."

CHAPTER XXVIII
THE FINAL ATTEMPT

Proof that his shot had not missed its mark was supplied to John immediately upon his arrival at the office on the following morning, when he was met by Pugsy Maloney with the information that a gentleman had called to see him.

"With or without a black-jack?" enquired John. "Did he give any name?"

"Sure. Parker's his name. He blew in oncst before when Mr. Smith was here. I loosed him into de odder room."

John walked through. The man he had seen with Mr. Scobell at the Knickerbocker was standing at the window.

"Mr. Parker?"

The other turned, as the door opened, and looked at him keenly.

"Are you Mr. Maude?"

"I am," said John.

"I guess you don't need to be told what I've come about?"

"No."

"See here," said Mr. Parker. "I don't know how you've found things out, but you've done it, and we're through. We quit."

"I'm glad of that," said John. "Would you mind informing Spider Reilly of that fact? It will make life pleasanter for all of us."

"Mr. Scobell sent me along here to ask you to come and talk over this thing with him. He's at the Knickerbocker. I've a cab waiting outside. Can you come along?"

"I'd rather he came here."

"And I bet he'd rather come here than be where he is. That little surprise packet of yours last night put him down and out. Gave him a stroke of some sort. He's in bed now, with half-a-dozen doctors working on him."

John thought for a moment.

"Oh," he said slowly, "if it's that—very well."

He could not help feeling a touch of remorse. He had no reason to be fond of Mr. Scobell, but he was sorry that this should have happened.

They went out on the street. A taximeter cab was standing by the sidewalk. They got in. Neither spoke. John was thoughtful and preoccupied. Mr. Parker, too, appeared to be absorbed in his own thoughts. He sat with folded arms and lowered head.

The cab buzzed up Fifth Avenue. Suddenly something, half-seen through the window, brought John to himself with a jerk. It was the great white mass of the Plaza Hotel. The next moment he saw that they were abreast of the park, and for the first time an icy wave of suspicion swept over him.

"Here, what's this?" he cried. "Where are you taking me?"

Mr. Parker's right hand came swiftly out of ambush, and something gleamed in the sun.

"Don't move," said Mr. Parker. The hard nozzle of a pistol pressed against John's chest. "Keep that hand still."

John dropped his hand. Mr. Parker leaned back, with the pistol resting easily on his knee. The cab began to move more quickly.

John's mind was in a whirl. His chief emotion was not fear, but disgust that he should have allowed himself to be trapped, with such absurd ease. He blushed for himself. Mr. Parker's face was expressionless, but who could say what tumults of silent laughter were not going on inside him? John bit his lip.

"Well?" he said at last.

Mr. Parker did not reply.

"Well?" said John again. "What's the next move?"

It flashed across his mind that, unless driven to it by an attack, his captor would do nothing for the moment without running grave risks himself. To shoot now would be to attract attention. The cab would be overtaken at once by bicycle police, and stopped. There would be no escape. No, nothing could happen till they reached open country. At least he would have time to think this matter over in all its bearings.

Mr. Parker ignored the question. He was sitting in the same attitude of watchfulness, the revolver resting on his knee. He seemed mistrustful of John's right hand, which was hanging limply at his side. It was from this quarter that he appeared to expect attack. The cab was bowling easily up the broad street, past rows and rows of high houses each looking exactly the same as the last. Occasionally, to the right, through a break in the line of buildings, a glimpse of the river could be seen.

A faint hope occurred to John that, by talking, he might put the other off his guard for just that instant which was all he asked. He exerted himself to find material for conversation.

"Tell me," he said, "what you said about Mr. Scobell, was that true?_About his being ill in bed?"

Mr. Parker did not answer, but a wintry smile flittered across his face.

"It was not?" said John. "Well, I'm glad of that. I don't wish Mr._Scobell any harm."

Mr. Parker looked at him doubtfully.

"Say, why are you in this game at all?" he said. "What made you butt in?"

"One must do something," said John. "It's interesting work."

"If you'll quit—"

John shook his head.

"I own it's a tempting proposition, things being as they are, but I won't give up yet. You never know what may happen."

"Well, you can make a mighty near guess this trip."

"You can't do a thing yet, that's sure," said John confidently. "If you shot me now, the cab would be stopped, and you would be lynched by the populace. I seem to see them tearing you limb from limb. 'She loves me!' Off comes an arm. 'She loves me not!' A leg joins the little heap on the ground. That is what would happen, Mr. Parker."

The other shrugged his shoulders, and relapsed into silence once more.

"What are you going to do with me, Mr. Parker?" asked John.

Mr. Parker did not reply.

* * * * *

The cab moved swiftly on. Now they had reached the open country. An occasional wooden shack was passed, but that was all. At any moment, John felt, the climax of the drama might be reached, and he got ready. His muscles stiffened for a spring. There was little chance of its being effective, but at least it would be good to put up some kind of a fight. And he had a faint hope that the suddenness of his movement might upset the other's aim. He was bound to be hit somewhere. That was certain. But quickness might save him to some extent. He braced his leg against the back of the cab. And, as he did so, its smooth speed changed to a series of jarring jumps, each more emphatic than the last. It slowed down, then came to a halt. There was a thud, as the chauffeur jumped down. John heard him fumbling in the tool box. Presently the body of the machine was raised slightly as he got to work with the jack. John's muscles relaxed. He leaned back. Surely something could be made of this new development. But the hand that held the revolver never wavered. He paused, irresolute. And at the moment somebody spoke in the road outside.

"Had a breakdown?" enquired the voice.

John recognized it. It was the voice of Kid Brady.

* * * * *

The Kid, as he had stated that he intended to do, had begun his training for his match with Eddie Wood at White Plains. It was his practise to open a course of training with a little gentle road-work, and it was while jogging along the highway a couple of miles from his training camp, in company with the two thick-necked gentlemen who acted as his sparring partners, that he had come upon the broken-down taxicab.

If this had happened after his training had begun in real earnest, he would have averted his eyes from the spectacle, however alluring, and continued on his way without a pause. But now, as he had not yet settled down to genuine hard work, he felt justified in turning aside and looking into the matter. The fact that the chauffeur, who seemed to be a taciturn man, lacking the conversational graces, manifestly objected to an audience, deterred him not at all. One cannot have everything in this world, and the Kid and his attendant thick-necks were content to watch the process of mending the tire, without demanding the additional joy of sparkling small talk from the man in charge of the operations.

"Guy's had a breakdown, sure," said the first of the thick-necks.

"Surest thing you know," agreed his colleague.

"Seems to me the tire's punctured," said the Kid.

All three concentrated their gaze on the machine.

"Kid's right," said thick-neck number one. "Guy's been an' bust a tire."

"Surest thing you know," said thick-neck number two.

They observed the perspiring chauffeur in silence for a while.

"Wonder how he did that, now?" speculated the Kid.

"Ran over a nail, I guess," said thick-neck number one.

"Surest thing you know," said the other, who, while perhaps somewhat deficient in the matter of original thought, was a most useful fellow to have by one—a sort of Boswell.

"Did you run over a nail?" the Kid enquired of the chauffeur.

The chauffeur worked on, unheeding.

"This is his busy day," said the first thick-neck, with satire. "Guy's too full of work to talk to us."

"Deaf, shouldn't wonder," surmised the Kid. "Say, wonder what's he doing with a taxi so far out of the city."

"Some guy tells him to drive him out here, I guess. Say, it'll cost him something, too. He'll have to strip off a few from his roll to pay for this."

John glanced at Mr. Parker, quivering with excitement. It was his last chance. Would the Kid think to look inside the cab, or would he move on? Could he risk a shout?

Mr. Parker leaned forward, and thrust the muzzle of the pistol against his body. The possibilities of the situation had evidently not been lost upon him.

"Keep quiet," he whispered.

Outside, the conversation had begun again, and the Kid had made his decision.

"Pretty rich guy inside," he said, following up his companion's train of thought. "I'm going to rubber through the window."

John met Mr. Parker's eye, and smiled.

There came the sound of the Kid's feet grating on the road, as he turned, and, as he heard it, Mr. Parker for the first time lost his head. With a vague idea of screening John, he half-rose. The pistol wavered. It was the chance John had prayed for. His left hand shot out, grasped the other's wrist, and gave it a sharp wrench. The pistol went off with a deafening report, the bullet passing through the back of the cab, then fell to the floor, as the fingers lost their hold. And the next moment John's right fist, darting upward, crashed home.

The effect was instantaneous. John had risen from his seat as he delivered the blow, and it got the full benefit of his weight. Mr. Parker literally crumpled up. His head jerked, then fell limply forward. John pushed him on to the seat as he slid toward the floor.

The interested face of the Kid appeared at the window. Behind him could be seen portions of the faces of the two thick-necks.

"Hello, Kid," said John. "I heard your voice. I hoped you might look in for a chat."

The Kid stared, amazed.

"What's doin'?" he queried.

"A good deal. I'll explain later. First, will you kindly knock that chauffeur down and sit on his head?"

"De guy's beat it," volunteered the first thick-neck.

"Surest thing you know," said the other.

"What's been doin'?" asked the Kid. "What are you going to do with this guy?"

John inspected the prostrate Mr. Parker, who had begun to stir slightly.

"I guess we'll leave him here," he said. "I've had all of his company that I need for to-day. Show me the nearest station, Kid. I must be getting back to New York. I'll tell you all about it as we go. A walk will do me good. Riding in a taxi is pleasant, but, believe me, you can have too much of it."

CHAPTER XXIX

A REPRESENTATIVE GATHERING

When John returned to the office, he found that his absence had been causing Betty an anxious hour's waiting. She had been informed by Pugsy that he had gone out in the company of Mr. Parker, and she felt uneasy. She turned white at his story of the ride, but he minimized the dangers.

"I don't think he ever meant to shoot. I think he was going to shut me up somewhere out there, and keep me till I promised to be good."

"Do you think my stepfather told him to do it?"

"I doubt it. I fancy Parker is a man who acts a good deal on his own inspirations. But we'll ask him, when he calls to-day."

"Is he going to call?"

"I have an idea he will," said John. "I sent him a note just now, asking if he could manage a visit."

It was unfortunate, in the light of subsequent events, that Mr. Jarvis should have seen fit to bring with him to the office that afternoon two of his collection of cats, and that Long Otto, who, as before, accompanied him, should have been fired by his example to the extent of introducing a large yellow dog. For before the afternoon was ended, space in the office was destined to be at premium.

Mr. Jarvis, when he had recovered from the surprise of seeing Betty and learning that she had returned to her old situation, explained:

"T'ought I'd bring de kits along," he said. "Dey starts fuss'n' wit' each odder yesterday, so I brings dem along."

John inspected the menagerie without resentment.

"Sure!" he said. "They add a kind of peaceful touch to the scene."

The atmosphere was, indeed, one of peace. The dog, after an inquisitive journey round the room, lay down and went to sleep. The cats settled themselves comfortably, one on each of Mr. Jarvis' knees. Long Otto, surveying the ceiling with his customary glassy stare, smoked a long cigar. And Bat, scratching one of the cats under the ear, began to entertain John with some reminiscences of fits and kittens.

But the peace did not last. Ten minutes had barely elapsed when the dog, sitting up with a start, uttered a whine. The door burst open and a little man dashed in. He was brown in the face, and had evidently been living recently in the open air. Behind him was a crowd of uncertain numbers. They were all strangers to John.

"Yes?" he said.

The little man glared speechlessly at the occupants of the room. The two Bowery boys rose awkwardly. The cats fell to the floor.

The rest of the party had entered. Betty recognized the Reverend Edwin T. Philpotts and Mr. B. Henderson Asher.

"My name is Renshaw," said the little man, having found speech.

"What can I do for you?" asked John.

The question appeared to astound the other.

"What can you—! Of all—!"

"Mr. Renshaw is the editor of *Peaceful Moments*," she said. "Mr. Smith was only acting for him."

Mr. Renshaw caught the name.

"Yes. Mr. Smith. I want to see Mr. Smith. Where is he?"

"In prison," said John.

"In prison!"

John nodded.

"A good many things have happened since you left for your vacation. Smith assaulted a policeman, and is now on Blackwell's Island."

Mr. Renshaw gasped. Mr. B. Henderson Asher stared, and stumbled over the cat.

"And who are you?" asked the editor.

"My name is Maude. I—"

He broke off, to turn his attention to Mr. Jarvis and Mr. Asher, between whom unpleasantness seemed to have arisen. Mr. Jarvis, holding a cat in his arms, was scowling at Mr. Asher, who had backed away and appeared apprehensive.

"What is the trouble?" asked John.

"Dis guy here wit' two left feet," said Bat querulously, "treads on de kit."

Mr. Renshaw, eying Bat and the silent Otto with disgust, intervened.

"Who are these persons?" he enquired.

"Poison yourself," rejoined Bat, justly incensed. "Who's de little squirt, Mr. Maude?"

John waved his hands.

"Gentlemen, gentlemen," he said, "why descend to mere personalities? I ought to have introduced you. This is Mr. Renshaw, our editor. These, Mr. Renshaw, are Bat Jarvis and Long Otto, our acting fighting editors, vice Kid Brady, absent on unavoidable business."

The name stung Mr. Renshaw to indignation, as Smith's had done.

"Brady!" he shrilled. "I insist that you give me a full explanation. I go away by my doctor's orders for a vacation, leaving Mr. Smith to conduct the paper on certain clearly defined lines. By mere chance, while on my vacation, I saw a copy of the paper. It had been ruined."

"Ruined?" said John. "On the contrary. The circulation has been going up every week."

"Who is this person, Brady? With Mr. Philpotts I have been going carefully over the numbers which have been issued since my departure—"

"An intellectual treat," murmured John.

"—and in each there is a picture of this young man in a costume which I will not particularize—"

"There is hardly enough of it to particularize."

"—together with a page of disgusting autobiographical matter."

John held up his hand.

"I protest," he said. "We court criticism, but this is mere abuse. I appeal to these gentlemen to say whether this, for instance, is not bright and interesting."

He picked up the current number of *Peaceful Moments*, and turned to the Kid's page.

"This," he said, "describes a certain ten-round unpleasantness with one Mexican Joe. 'Joe comes up for the second round and he gives me a nasty look, but I thinks of my mother and swats him one in the lower ribs. He gives me another nasty look. "All right, Kid," he says; "now I'll knock you up into the gallery." And with that he cuts loose with a right swing, but I falls into the clinch, and then—'"

"Pah!" exclaimed Mr. Renshaw.

"Go on, boss," urged Mr. Jarvis approvingly. "It's to de good, dat stuff."

"There!" said John triumphantly. "You heard? Mr. Jarvis, one of the most firmly established critics east of Fifth Avenue stamps Kid Brady's reminiscences with the hall-mark of his approval."

"I falls fer de Kid every time," assented Mr. Jarvis.

"Sure! You know a good thing when you see one. Why," he went on warmly, "there is stuff in these reminiscences which would stir the blood of a jellyfish. Let me quote you another passage, to show that they are not only enthralling, but helpful as well. Let me see, where is it? Ah, I have it. 'A bully good way of putting a guy out of business is this. You don't want to use it in the ring, because rightly speaking it's a foul, but you will find it mighty useful if any thick-neck comes up to you in the street and tries to start anything. It's this way. While he's setting himself for a punch, just place the tips of the fingers of your left hand on the right side of the chest. Then bring down the heel of your left hand. There isn't a guy living that could stand up against that. The fingers give you a leverage to beat the band. The guy doubles up, and you upper-cut him with your right, and out he goes.' Now, I bet you never knew that before, Mr. Philpotts. Try it on your parishioners."

"*Peaceful Moments*," said Mr. Renshaw irately, "is no medium for exploiting low prize-fighters."

"Low prize-fighters! No, no! The Kid is as decent a little chap as you'd meet anywhere. And right up in the championship class, too! He's matched against Eddie Wood at this very moment. And Mr. Waterman will support me in my statement that a victory over Eddie Wood means that he gets a cast-iron claim to meet Jimmy Garvin for the championship."

"It is abominable," burst forth Mr. Renshaw. "It is disgraceful. The paper is ruined."

"You keep saying that. It really isn't so. The returns are excellent. Prosperity beams on us like a sun. The proprietor is more than satisfied."

"Indeed!" said Mr. Renshaw sardonically.

"Sure," said John.

Mr. Renshaw laughed an acid laugh.

"You may not know it," he said, "but Mr. Scobell is in New York at this very moment. We arrived together yesterday on the *Mauretania*. I was spending my vacation in England when I happened to see the copy of the paper. I instantly communicated with Mr. Scobell, who was at Mervo, an island in the Mediterranean—"

"I seem to know the name—"

"—and received in reply a long cable desiring me to return to New York immediately. I sailed on the *Mauretania*, and found that he was one of the passengers. He was extremely agitated, let me tell you. So that your impudent assertion that the proprietor is pleased—"

John raised his eyebrows.

"I don't quite understand," he said. "From what you say, one would almost imagine that you thought Mr. Scobell was the proprietor of this paper."

Mr. Renshaw stared. Everyone stared, except Mr. Jarvis, who, since the readings from the Kid's reminiscences had ceased, had lost interest in the proceedings, and was now entertaining the cats with a ball of paper tied to a string.

"Thought that Mr. Scobell—?" repeated Mr. Renshaw. "Who is, if he is not?"

"I am," said John.

There was a moment's absolute silence.

"You!" cried Mr. Renshaw.

"You!" exclaimed Mr. Waterman, Mr. Asher, and the Reverend Edwin T._Philpotts.

"Sure thing," said John.

Mr. Renshaw groped for a chair, and sat down.

"Am I going mad?" he demanded feebly. "Do I understand you to say that you own this paper?"

"I do."

"Since when?"

"Roughly speaking, about three days."

Among his audience (still excepting Mr. Jarvis, who was tickling one of the cats and whistling a plaintive melody) there was a tendency toward awkward silence. To start assailing a seeming nonentity and then to discover he is the proprietor of the paper to which you wish to contribute is like kicking an apparently empty hat and finding your rich uncle inside it. Mr. Renshaw in particular was disturbed. Editorships of the kind to which he aspired are not easy to get. If he were to be removed from *Peaceful Moments* he would find it hard to place himself anywhere else. Editors, like manuscripts, are rejected from want of space.

"I had a little money to invest," continued John. "And it seemed to me that I couldn't do better than put it into *Peaceful Moments*. If it did nothing else, it would give me a free hand in pursuing a policy in which I was interested. Smith told me that Mr. Scobell's representatives had instructions to accept any offer, so I made an offer, and they jumped at it."

Pugsy Maloney entered, bearing a card.

"Ask him to wait just one moment," said John, reading it.

He turned to Mr. Renshaw.

"Mr. Renshaw," he said, "if you took hold of the paper again, helped by these other gentlemen, do you think you could gather in our old subscribers and generally make the thing a live proposition on the old lines? Because, if so, I should be glad if you would start in with the next number. I am through with the present policy. At least, I hope to be in a few minutes. Do you think you can undertake that?"

Mr. Renshaw, with a sigh of relief, intimated that he could.

"Good," said John. "And now I'm afraid I must ask you to go. A rather private and delicate interview is in the offing. Bat, I'm very much obliged to you and Otto for your help. I don't know what we should have done without it."

"Aw, Chee!" said Mr. Jarvis.

"Then good-by for the present."

"Good-by, boss. Good-by, loidy."

Long Otto pulled his forelock, and, accompanied by the cats and the dog, they left the room.

When Mr. Renshaw and the others had followed them, John rang the bell for Pugsy.

"Ask Mr. Scobell to step in," he said.

The man of many enterprises entered. His appearance had deteriorated since John had last met him. He had the air of one who has been caught in the machinery. His face was even sallower than of yore, and there was no gleam in his dull green eyes.

He started at the sight of Betty, but he was evidently too absorbed in the business in hand to be surprised at seeing her. He sank into a chair, and stared gloomily at John.

"Well?" he said.

"Well?" said John.

"This," observed Mr. Scobell simply, "is hell." He drew a cigar stump mechanically from his vest pocket and lighted it.

"What are you going to do about it?" he asked.

"What are you?" said John. "It's up to you."

Mr. Scobell gazed heavily into vacancy.

"Ever since I started in to monkey with that darned Mervo," he said sadly, "there ain't a thing gone right. I haven't been able to turn around without bumping into myself. Everything I touch turns to mud. I guess I can still breathe, but I'm not betting on that lasting long. Of all the darned hoodoos that island was the worst. Say, I gotta close down that Casino. What do you know about that! Sure thing. The old lady won't stand for it. I had a letter from her." He turned to Betty. "You got her all worked up, Betty. I'm not blaming you. It's just my jinx. She took it into her head I'd been treating you mean, and she kicked at the Casino. I gotta close it down or nix on the heir thing. That was enough for me. I'm going to turn it into a hotel."

He relighted his cigar.

"And now, just as I got her smoothed down, along comes this darned tenement business. Say, Prince, for the love of Mike cut it out. If those houses are as bad as you say they are, and the old lady finds out that I own them, it'll be Katie bar the door for me. She wouldn't stand for it for a moment. I guess I didn't treat you good, Prince, but let's forget it. Ease up on this rough stuff. I'll do anything you want."

Betty spoke.

"We only want you to make the houses fit to live in," she said. "I don't believe you know what they're like."

"Why, no. I left Parker in charge. It was up to him to do what was wanted. Say, Prince, I want to talk to you about that guy, Parker. I understand he's been rather rough with you and your crowd. That wasn't my doing. I didn't know anything about it till he told me. It's the darned Wild West strain in him coming out. He used to do those sort of things out there, and he's forgotten his manners. I pay him well, and I guess he thinks that's the way it's up to him to earn it. You mustn't mind Parker."

"Oh, well! So long as he means well—!" said John. "I've no grudge against Parker. I've settled with him."

"Well, then, what about this Broster Street thing? You want me to fix some improvements, is that it?"

"That's it."

"Why, say, I'll do that. Sure. And then you'll quit handing out the newspaper stories? That goes. I'll start right in."

He rose.

"That's taken a heap off my mind," he said.

"There's just one other thing," said John. "Have you by any chance such a thing as a stepfather's blessing on you?"

"Eh?"

John took Betty's hand.

"We've come round to your views, Mr. Scobell," he said. "That scheme of yours for our future looks good to us."

Mr. Scobell bit through his cigar in his emotion.

"Now, why the Heck," he moaned, "couldn't you have had the sense to do that before, and save all this trouble?"

CHAPTER XXX

CONCLUSION

Smith drew thoughtfully at his cigar, and shifted himself more comfortably into his chair. It was long since he had visited the West, and he had found all the old magic in the still, scented darkness of the prairie night. He gave a little sigh of content. When John, a year before, had announced his intention of buying this ranch, and, as it seemed to Smith, burying himself alive a thousand miles from anywhere, he had disapproved. He had pointed out that John was not doing what Fate expected of him. A miracle, in the shape of a six-figure wedding present from Mrs. Oakley, who had never been known before, in the memory of man, to give away a millionth of that sum, had happened to him. Fate, argued Smith, plainly intended him to stay in New York and spend his money in a civilized way.

John had had only one reply, but it was clinching.

"Betty likes the idea," he said, and Smith ceased to argue.

Now, as he sat smoking on the porch on the first night of his inaugural visit to the ranch, a conviction was creeping over him that John had chosen wisely.

A door opened behind him. Betty came out on to the porch, and dropped into a chair close to where John's cigar glowed redly in the darkness. They sat there without speaking. The stirring of unseen cattle in the corral made a soothing accompaniment to thought.

"It is very pleasant for an old jail bird like myself," said Smith at last, "to sit here at my ease. I wish all our absent friends could be with us to-night. Or perhaps not quite all. Let us say, Comrade Parker here, Comrades Brady and Maloney over there by you, and our old friend Renshaw sharing the floor with B. Henderson Asher, Bat Jarvis, and the cats. By the way, I was round at Broster Street before I left New York. There is certainly an improvement. Millionaires now stop there instead of going on to the Plaza. Are you asleep, John?"

"No."

"Excellent. I also saw Comrade Brady before I left. He has definitely got on his match with Jimmy Garvin."

"Good. He'll win."

"The papers seem to think so. *Peaceful Moments*, however, I am sorry to say, is silent on the subject. It was not like this in the good old days. How is the paper going now, John? Are the receipts satisfactory?"

"Pretty fair. Renshaw is rather a marvel in his way. He seems to have roped in nearly all the old subscribers. They eat out of his hand."

Smith stretched himself.

"These," he said, "are the moments in life to which we look back with that wistful pleasure. This peaceful scene, John, will remain with me when I have forgotten that such a man as Spider Reilly ever existed. These are the real Peaceful Moments."

He closed his eyes. The cigar dropped from his fingers. There was a long silence.

"Mr. Smith," said Betty.

There was no answer.

"He's asleep," said John. "He had a long journey to-day."

Betty drew her chair closer. From somewhere out in the darkness, from the direction of the men's quarters, came the soft tinkle of a guitar and a voice droning a Mexican love-song.

Her hand stole out and found his. They began to talk in whispers.

THE END

Printed in Dunstable, United Kingdom